BEYOND
the
THRESHOLD

A NOVEL

By Mark Ristau

A Hero Dreams
Beyond the Threshold

BEYOND
the
THRESHOLD

A NOVEL

MARK RISTAU

— Beaver's Pond Press —
Saint Paul, MN

Winter
Words and Music by Tori Amos
Copyright © 1989 Sword and Stone Publishing, Inc. (ASCAP)
International Copyright Secured All Rights Reserved
Reprinted by Permission of Hal Leonard LLC

Cover photograph by Konstanttin/Shutterstock.com
Book design and typesetting by Dan Pitts
Adobe Garamond Pro

ISBN 13: 978-1-64343-794-1
Library of Congress Catalog Number: 2021913846
Printed in the United States of America
First Printing: 2022
26 25 24 23 22   5 4 3 2 1

Beaver's Pond Press
939 Seventh Street West
Saint Paul, MN 55102
(952) 829-8818
www.BeaversPondPress.com

To order, visit www.ItascaBooks.com.
Reseller discounts available.

Visit www.MarkRistau.com for information regarding speaking engagements and interviews with the author.

For Mom

TRUTH

When you gonna make up your mind
When you gonna love you as much as I do
When you gonna make up your mind
'Cause things are gonna change so fast

—Tori Amos

CHAPTER ONE

Tuesday, August 28, 2001

*I*T'S AFTER MIDNIGHT. I'M RUNNING HALF-BLIND *through a stifling, hot forest. Salty drops of perspiration sting my eyes. An amalgamation of dry leaves and brittle twigs crunches and snaps under my feet . . . betraying me . . . There's something out there . . . something . . . something faceless and sinister . . . A bloodthirsty tribe of savages catches a whiff of the fear I'm exuding. They're hunting me . . . pursuing me like a rabid dog in the night. Their drums of war pound—pound relentlessly in my head with an ancient, primal beat.*

Da-doom, da-doom, da-doom . . .

The rhythm grows faster and louder. It passes through my outer defenses and sinks into my core, mixing my insides into a toxic froth.

Da-doom, da-doom, da-doom . . .

It's hopeless. Escape is impossible. My fate inevitable. The end is near . . . They're closing in on me . . . I keep running . . . The path is uneven . . . the footing treacherous . . . a minefield of pebbles and rocks lies hidden in the underbrush . . . a tangle of serpentine roots slithers through the sandy soil—

What's that?

A heavy curtain of trees parts, revealing a sliver of flickering light. A log cabin materializes . . . and a window . . . A thin, dimly lit candle sits on the sill and beckons to me. Its flame flutters helplessly in the wind. If only I can get there before it goes out . . .

Da-doom, da-doom, da-doom . . .

My heart beats wildly. My lungs gasp for air. A fiery dose of lactic acid attacks the muscles in my legs and cramps them in a vise grip of agony. I will myself to ignore the pain and continue toward the light . . . I'm getting closer . . . almost there, but I make a fatal error—foolishly, I risk a glance over my shoulder. Expecting to see the war-painted faces of fierce cannibals, I see nothing; yet I can feel them breathing down the nape of my neck, setting the tiny hairs there ablaze . . . A root leaps up from the forest floor and catches my foot, sending me into a free fall . . .

Buzzzzz!

I raised my arm and—*thwack*—my fist came down hard and hit the snooze bar squarely on the nose.

4:30 a.m.

Got to . . .

My befogged brain scrambled for the words.

Got to . . . got to get up . . .

Now!

But I'm so tired, so very tired. Please, God, let me sleep . . . just a little longer . . .

Right now!

"Ooooohhh!" *My jaw, my neck, my aching back—*

I said, right now!

I rolled out of bed and landed with a dull thud on a worn and unforgiving shag carpet.

Get moving, Ricky.

Ricky? Oh yeah, that's right. I'm Ricky . . . Tried going by Richard once; it didn't stick, though. I'm Ricky . . . Ricky Williamson, thirty-five-year-old male, single (never married), no children, horny as hell, profession: in-house corporate lawyer, current employer: Caste Enterprises.

Where am I?

A trace of must tainted the air.

I was in the mostly finished attic of a postwar bungalow, anonymously situated in a quiet urban neighborhood tucked just within the southern border of Heartland City. A moderately large flyover community, Heartland City was nestled deep within the bosom of our beloved country's midwestern region. Next stop: a seemingly endless sprawl of undifferentiated suburbia. The cruel and heartless winters were long and ruthlessly cold; the summers short and oppressively hot. It was late August, and I'd been sleeping with the windows open. A cool breeze blew into the room, portending an early fall.

What the hell am I doing here?

Time to go running and then get your ass to work.

With no less than a heroic effort, I lifted myself off the floor. A palpably thick gloom descended upon me as I felt my way toward the landing and down the stairs to the ground floor. I fumbled for the light and flicked it on.

Same dream every night. Am I ever gonna reach that goddamned cabin? Will I ever discover what lies within?

I took a quick detour into the house's only bathroom before staggering into my makeshift yoga studio. From a lotus-flower perch, a statuette of the Buddha contemplated me with a bemused smile as I commenced my stretching routine. After a strenuous hour of reaching, grasping, squeezing, holding (breathing), turning, twisting, pushing, pulling (breathing), exerting, striving, and straining (*gasping*), my muscles began to release me from their tyrannical hold. Only then was I ready to change into my running gear, lace up my Asics, and stumble outside.

Sunrise was still an hour away, yet a huge ensemble of birds had gathered to begin their daily ritual. They were everywhere—on the fence bordering the backyard of my city lot, on rooftops, treetops, lilac bushes, telephone poles, and on the power line stretched overhead along the alleyway. They had me surrounded.

Suddenly, the ensemble burst into song.

Strange. There's no sign of daylight, and they don't have alarm clocks, but somehow, these winged creatures know when it's time to wake and start their day . . . and they seem to do so with little or no effort. Certainly, they have no need to put themselves through the rigors of a daily stretching routine.

Before beginning my run, I checked and double-checked the spring bolt and recently installed dead bolt on the door leading into the back of the garage.

Good. That'll keep the neighborhood kids from sticking their fucking noses where they don't belong.

Satisfied the garage was secure, I made my way to the alley, turned north, and started running toward Lake Weston, which lay a mile from my house. Gradually, I built up speed, ignoring objections raised by my poor, overworked, leaden legs. Within half a mile, I was breathing hard. The air was refreshingly cool.

It wouldn't stay that way for long, though. The week's forecast was for above-average temperatures and uncomfortable dew points—a final blast of summer before autumn arrived.

I ran every morning, no matter how exhausted I was when that damned alarm clock buzzed me out of bed, and regardless of the weather. Why was I so obsessive about running? What choice did I have? I ran to escape . . . escape from the steady stream of jitters that pulsed through my body from the instant I woke up each morning until that elusive moment when I finally succumbed to sleep at night . . . and even then, the jitters followed me doggedly into my dreams . . . I ran to escape feeling sad, lonely, worthless, hopeless . . . I ran to escape from the memory of my father . . . and of that night at the pond . . .

I ran to escape from my monkey mind, that chattering brain of mine, those incessant thoughts. Of course, they always caught up with me. This morning was no exception.

Everything's in place and ready to go. The plan's ready to execute. All I need to do is pull the trigger, but . . . but . . . but . . . But nothing! Bringing those assholes at Caste to justice is the right thing to do. Mine is a noble cause in the war against tyranny! When the smoke settles, I'm gonna savor my victory. It'll taste so sweet, sooooo very sweet . . .

Yes, but you'll be throwing away your life.

My life. What life?

Your life, Ricky. Your precious life.

My precious life . . . Am I willing . . . Am I . . . Am I? Yes! Yes, goddamn it! Yes, of course I'm willing. They've disrespected me time and time and time again, and they deserve what's coming. Fucking bastards. I've suffered one injustice after another, and now the time has come to make things right, no matter what the cost.

A procession of armor-clad sentinels lit my way through the city streets. In the park system, they became increasingly sporadic. Still, there was just enough illumination to lead me along a pedestrian path that wound its way through a wooded area—sanctuary from the hustle and bustle of daily urban life. After a few minutes, the path merged with another—a three-mile loop around the lake. Turning left, I began to circumnavigate the water in a clockwise direction.

A god-awful racket arose from the lake's southwest corner. Ducks! Hidden in the shadows of the predawn morning, a paddle of mallards quacked and splashed helter-skelter, sending a splattering of the lake across the path. It sounded as if a dispute over mating rights had erupted between two males, a conflict that was escalating into tribal war involving the paddle's entire social hierarchy.

I turned north. The disturbance receded behind me. Focusing my eyes on the path, I settled into a decent pace and made good time along the backstretch of the lake. As I approached the north end (and halfway point of my journey), the first few hints of a new day's light crept over the trees lining the eastern shore.

They don't take me seriously. They ask for my advice, and when they don't like what they hear, they dismiss it. Fucking unprincipled hypocrites! They talk about doing business with integrity, but if they really meant it, they would listen to what I have to say.

You need to be a team player and get on board, Williamson.

What? And sell my soul to the devil just to strike a lousy deal?

No. Do what you're paid to do. Support your clients by providing world-class service and facilitating the business.

How eloquent. How very eloquent. You can dress it up however you want—

It's your choice, Williamson. After all, lawyers like you are a dime a dozen.

Are you threatening me?

I'll be straight with you, Ricky. You've become a liability. You're good for one thing and one thing only. Covering your ass.

Covering my ass? Covering my ass? Can you hear yourself?

I'm talking about teamwork—

You need to listen to me. You need to value my opinion. You need to respect the process. You need to respect—

Maybe if you respected yourself.

—me!

It's my own damn fault. I let them get away with it. I've been letting those bastards at Caste take advantage of me ever since . . . well, ever since the acquisition . . . the acquisition—that's when it all started. But it's gonna stop now. They'll be sorry. They'll be so sorry. They won't even see it coming. They think I'm a feckless wimp. I'll show them. I'll show them the real Ricky Williamson.

Having worked myself into a frenzy, I increased my pace to a full sprint. Pushed beyond the point of exhaustion, my brain clouded up with fatigue. Coherent thought became impossible. Wavering from one side of the path to the other, I started to lose consciousness.

Out of the corner of my eye, I caught a glimpse of something lying in the water. Partially hidden under a shroud of shadows, an object resembling a human body had washed ashore. I slowed and came to a stop. By this time, I'd reached the lake's southeast corner, and the sun's crown was blooming over the trees. Breathing hard, I tried to focus my eyes and confirm whether the object was indeed a body or merely an image conjured up by a brain suffering from acute oxygen debt. Leaving the path, I trotted down to the grassy shore to investigate.

It was a boy! Nine or maybe ten years old, lying faceup among the cattails and reeds. Crouching, I grasped his shoulders and carefully pulled him from the water. His supple body slid easily over the shore's edge and onto the soft grass. His skin was cold. I scanned his face for signs of life. Finding none, I placed a hand on his chest. Slowly and almost imperceptibly, yet rhythmically, his rib cage rose and fell. He was breathing.

A pair of waterlogged jeans and a soaked blue-and-white T-shirt clung to the boy's slender frame. Upon the T-shirt, the words "Camp Abenaki Valley Honor" were printed over his breastbone.

Camp Abenaki Valley?

The blood in my veins turned to ice water.

"It's not possible!" The words escaped from my lips in a shrill whisper that carried across the lake before fading into the morning mist.

Leaning forward, I examined the boy more closely. His hair was dark brown, almost black. Like mine. His face . . . his face was . . . curiously familiar . . .

I know this boy.

I reached for his hand. His lids fluttered open, revealing a pair of eyes that dazzled me with a burst of pure azure radiance. Dancing in the whites of those eyes were the iridescent hues of daybreak.

He's okay. Thank God!

Suddenly, his face contorted into a tangled maze of ridges and valleys. His body tensed, and he started to tremble and quake all over. It appeared he was trying to sit up. But he couldn't. Some invisible force was holding him down. I feared he was having a seizure, so I cried out for help.

As if in response, the tremors ceased, and his body relaxed. He sat up, took a breath, and let it go. Our eyes met. He reached for me and fell into my arms, his heart opening in a flowing river of tears.

Caught off guard by the boy's unbridled show of emotion and overcome with compassion, I held him close.

"It's okay," I said. "You're safe now. Everything'll be all right. I promise."

I gently rocked him back and forth as my lips formed the words to a song that had been lost, buried in my memories. I hadn't sung a note in years. Yet there I was, kneeling on the grassy shore of Lake Weston and singing the refrain from Bob Marley's "Three Little Birds."

Ricky . . . Ricky, my love . . .

I quit singing and listened. From somewhere in my past, a faint yet distinct voice was calling my name. The voice of an angel.

Together, we're going to make it right.

The boy's tears stopped flowing. An expression of calm surrender unfurled across his face. He gazed up at me with a trusting smile. Returning his gaze, I lost myself in his eyes—a deep azure-blue sea of serenity and peace—and my childhood, which was anything but either serene or peaceful, came flooding into conscious memory . . .

My Childhood: 1976–1984

Attacked. Assaulted. Raped. Life as I'd known it came to an end in those bone-chilling waters of Parson's Pond in Abenaki Valley, Maine. It was the night of the dance. *Stupid.* I trusted those older boys—*I wanted them to like me!*—and I let my guard down. It was all my fault. I should have listened to Sam. He was right. Spencer was a bad guy—a *really* bad guy.

I never told anyone about that night . . . until now . . .

Somehow, I made it to the end of summer. When your life no longer means anything to you, it gets easier, I guess. I went back to school that fall and entered the fifth grade. Nothing was the same. The other kids looked at me funny. Children have a remarkable ability to know things, and I think my classmates knew something had changed in me. Except for maybe my closest friend, Joey, they kept their distance, as if to avoid catching whatever disease I'd contracted.

Soon, the nightmares began. Nightmares of being trapped deep underwater, my ankle wedged under the toppled mast of a sunken pirate ship. Each night, I struggled frantically to free myself from the murky bottom, my lungs on fire for a sip of cool air.

A drumbeat commences, counting the remaining seconds in my life . . .

Da-doom, da-doom, da-doom . . .

After an exhausting effort, my ankle comes loose, and I begin an agonizingly slow ascent to the surface . . . Above, a white light glows with otherworldly incandescence. Below, there's only darkness . . . darkness and death . . . All around me, that dreadful beating of the drum, vibrating through the water, penetrating my skin, and sinking into the depths of my soul . . . The incessant tempo of this death march steadily increases. With each beat, the sound reverberates more loudly in my head.

Da-doom, da-doom, da-doom . . .

Soon, the drum is beating so fast, the individual beats seem to blur together.

Da-da-da-da-da-dooooom—

The beating stops. A pair of translucent hands appears, grasps my outstretched wrists, and slowly pulls me toward the surface . . . I'm almost there when a pair of bony claws emerges from the murky darkness below, clutches my ankles, and pulls me downward with a sharp jerk. I have become the rope in a classic game of tug-of-war.

The death march resumes.

Da-doom, da-doom, da-doom . . .

The following summer, my mother moved our beleaguered family of three away from South Orange—from the familiar and all we held dear—to the northernmost province of our beloved country's midwestern region, where she'd grown up, where my grandparents still lived. She told Danny and me she couldn't do it alone anymore. She needed help. She needed to be close to her mom and dad.

Danny and I protested and whined and cried and carried on and on and on. But in the end, we said our goodbyes, packed our things, and watched the moving truck lumber down Grove Road and out of sight. Mom ushered us into a taxicab. From the back seat, I stole a final glance at the redbrick house, which had bred so many memories of our childhood and of our dear father.

On that muggy, dreary afternoon in the waning days of August 1977, made otherwise remarkable only by the death of Elvis Presley, we obediently followed our mother onto a jet airplane. Three hours later, the plane touched down at the Heartland City regional airport. Our grandparents—Nana and Papa—met us at the gate.

Danny and I moved in with Nana and Papa on a temporary basis only, we were assured. Mom checked into a substance abuse treatment center. When I asked why, Nana explained that our mother needed time—thirty days—to learn how to take care of herself. After that, the three of us would move into a house just down the street. Nana meant well, of course, but her words did little to help me understand the situation and even less to comfort me.

I was scared. Lonely and lost somewhere in a world that hardly seemed real. Everything in Heartland City was shallow and flat, like a two-dimensional model of reality. The streets, sidewalks, trees, houses, people . . . even the sky lacked depth. It was like living in a dream surrounded only by cardboard cut-outs . . . and without the possibility of waking . . .

That fall, I turned twelve and enrolled in the sixth grade at a school with boys and girls who spoke a language only vaguely familiar to me. I learned the proper answer to just about any question was: "Ooooohhh, yaaah shuuurer, yah betcha." Since he was a fifth grader and one year shy of middle school, Danny pursued his education in a building located halfway across town. Soon, he would claim the midwestern dialect as his own.

I did my best to fit in with these seemingly well-meaning midwesterners yet couldn't get comfortable in my new surroundings. I felt like an alien on a strange planet. My new classmates were polite, but I saw that look in their eyes. I knew that look. I'd seen it in the eyes of my fifth-grade classmates back in South Orange. *Caution! Maintain a safe distance.* It was as if these well-mannered, clean-cut midwestern boys and girls knew all about my tainted past and wanted nothing to do with it.

Even the adults had a look. Theirs was one of pity mixed with revulsion. Every once in a while, a well-intentioned teacher would reach out to me and try to establish a connection. But they didn't know how. Neither did I.

Making friends wasn't going to be easy. At the end of my first week, however, I did meet one boy—named Eugene—who enjoyed a mad passion for a mysterious game called Dungeons & Dragons. We struck up a conversation while waiting in line for lunch in the West Lake Middle School cafeteria.

"You're not from around here, are ya?"

The voice startled me out of one of my increasingly frequent trances. I'd been standing there with my hands in my front pockets, leaning slightly forward and focusing intently on a small crack in the linoleum at my feet. *The aperture of a wormhole that leads to another place . . . another time . . .* Sometimes I could see things other people couldn't.

"Who? Me?"

A scrawny boy with grimy, fingerprint-smudged eyeglasses nodded and smiled reassuringly. His curly drab-brown hair was cut short and tight over Dumbo-size ears. He carried a *Star Wars* lunch box.

"I'm Eugene. You can call me Gene, if you like. Some people call me Euge. I'm not so sure it fits, though. Whaddya think?" He didn't wait for an answer. "I have food allergies. I can't eat most of the food they serve here." He pointed to his lunch box.

"I'm Ricky."

"I know. I've seen you around and figured you weren't from here. Most of these kids went to elementary together. Everyone seems to know each other. It's only the first week, and the cliques have already formed."

"Where you from?" I asked, trying to identify his decidedly non-midwestern accent.

"I'm from New Yawk," he said.

Yes, of course! Brooklyn, maybe?

"My family moved here last winter, for my dad's work."

"I'm from New Jersey."

"A Joisey boy!" he said with a chuckle.

Eugene and I had lunch together that day and every day for the remainder of the school year. We usually sat in the back corner, away from the cliques and bustling chaos of that below-ground, windowless room. Speaking with passion and a great deal of authority on the subject of Dungeons & Dragons, he recruited me to play. At first, I resisted his entreaties but eventually relented and joined him and his friends—a couple of first-generation outcasts named Arun and Chen—for a game. Soon, the four of us settled into a routine of playing D&D at Eugene's house every Saturday afternoon. More often than not, we'd stay for dinner and continue our marathon sessions well into the evening.

As adolescence approached, Eugene and I saw less and less of each other. At some point, we must have arrived at the same conclusion: We had very little in common. Gradually, our weekly D&D games petered out. Remaining amicable, we'd exchange a nod or an occasional "hey" between classes, but that was it. Toward the end of eighth grade, Eugene's father was transferred, and the family moved back to New York.

In the fall of 1980, I began my freshman year at Heartland City High. It was painfully clear I would never fit in. Eugene was long gone. Arun and Chen had both been sent to an exclusive private school located in an affluent western suburb. Walking the crowded, claustrophobic hallways of my new school, I felt like an outsider. I would always be an outsider, I decided. I would always have difficulty making friends. I would always feel self-conscious and awkward in social situations.

When the freshman mixer came along, my mother encouraged me to go. I stubbornly refused. Instead, I locked myself in my room and did homework. After my experience at Camp Abenaki Valley, I'd made a solemn vow: I would never attend another dance. Of course, my mother, who was terribly worried about me, had no way of knowing this. She simply wanted me to get involved and make friends.

"Leave me alone," I snapped at her from behind my door. "Let me make my own decisions!"

The year went on, and I became more and more isolated. As a fatherless child and rape victim, I believed there was something terribly wrong with me, that I deserved to be alone. I deserved my fate. Something was missing . . . something essential . . .

Somewhere along the way, I discovered an outlet for my teenage angst. Schoolwork. I developed a passion for my studies. And with this newfound passion, I became an excellent student. Unfortunately, this gained me no favor with my classmates. In fact, they ridiculed me for my academic accomplishments, calling me *nerd, geek*, and *computer*.

Computer?

I reluctantly accepted the *nerd* and *geek* monikers, but *computer* felt unearned and unjust. Our school had just opened its first computer lab, equipped with two dozen Apple II Plus machines, yet I was intimidated by the new technology and avoided the lab at all costs. Adjacent to the math and science center, it lay well outside my comfort zone.

I felt much more at home in the humanities wing, where ideas, words, and language were conceived in the human mind and born on the page. My favorite subjects were literature, composition, history, and civics. I did well enough in math and science, but success in those subjects required no less than a heroic effort on my part.

One autumn day in my ninth-grade world history and comp class, Mr. Blanchard returned our essays on the causes and events leading to World War I.

"Well done, Ricky," he said, placing the paper faceup on my desk. "Excellent work!"

I got an A. I was pleased yet wondered what I could have done to earn an A-plus. Mr. Blanchard, disappointed with most of the class for their inability to write an effective and cogent essay, asked me to stand and explain my writing process.

No! Please, Mr. Blanchard, anything but that. I just want to be left alone. Don't you get it?

Feeling the weight of a classroom full of resentful eyes upon me, I somehow rose to my feet without toppling over.

"I d-d-don't know. I just write."

The ensuing chorus of moans and groans made it clear my explanation wasn't being well received, so I sat as quickly as I could.

"Thanks for the advice," said the boy next to me. "That was a big help . . . Not!"

The boy sitting behind me leaned forward. "Next time, keep it to yourself, geek."

A voice I recognized as belonging to the prettiest girl in class—Juliet was her name—reached my tender ears.

"What a nerd," she said as if referring to a noxious pool of pond scum, one hardly worthy of her notice.

Instead of coming to my aid, Mr. Blanchard ignored the comments and continued class as if nothing had happened.

After that experience, I stopped giving schoolwork my best efforts, and of course, my grades suffered. I figured if I didn't do quite so well, the name-calling would stop. Perhaps, I would even become popular. And if I became popular, maybe, just maybe, Juliet would change her mind about me . . . and if she did—*boy, if she did*—maybe, just maybe, I could find the courage to ask her out.

On a date?

Well . . . yes, on a date. We might even become boyfriend and girlfriend. That's not too crazy, is it? I could be your Romeo . . .

Alas, in my pathetic attempt to become well liked, I accomplished nothing—nothing other than to betray my father's memory and forsake his advice to be true to myself regardless of the opinions of others.

I hadn't picked up a baseball glove since we'd moved to Heartland City. Why? I dunno. I guess I was afraid of the inevitable comparisons to Danny, whose game continued to improve. As an eighth grader, he'd been invited to participate in winter drills with the varsity team. When the coach clocked his fastball at eighty miles an hour, Danny Williamson was immediately pegged for that spring's starting rotation.

As Danny excelled in sports, I faltered. In gym class, I was the skinny kid always targeted for an easy out in dodgeball. Those rubber four-square balls packed quite a punch. I learned the hard way just how much damage they could inflict.

In the heat of a particularly intense game, I caught a ball with my face, fell like a sack of potatoes, and hit my head on the hard maple parquet.

When I came to, church bells chimed hallelujah in my ears. The gym teacher peered down at me with a grave expression etched into his face. *Why so serious? Can't you hear the pretty bells?* These questions arose from the foggy bottom of my semiconscious mind and evaporated, unexpressed. His lips began to form words. Using an index finger, I traced them in the space between us. *A concussion*, he mouthed. Apparently, I'd suffered a concussion.

The school administrator called my mom, who picked me up in the parking lot and rushed me to the hospital. The emergency room was a fury of sound and a whirling blur of motion. It smelled of antiseptic. And it was cold. Very cold.

Sitting next to Mom, I watched my hands turn blue as we waited two and a half hours to see a doctor. After apologizing for the delay—there'd been a horrific multi-vehicle accident on an icy stretch of freeway—the doctor shined a light in my eyes and confirmed the gym teacher's diagnosis. With rest, he assured me, I'd be back to normal within a few days.

"Was anyone killed?" I asked.

The doctor regarded me with a long, penetrating gaze.

"Three DOAs and eight others in surgery."

Gym class presented another challenge—one more serious than a ball in the face. I was embarrassed by my body. To my deep chagrin, it was developing more slowly than those of other boys my age. In particular, I was ashamed of my girlishly skinny arms and lack of body hair. Other boys in the locker room had hair covering their forearms, legs, chests, bellies, and pubic areas. I had none. I hated my body! I hated being different from everyone else.

Worst of all were the grotesque scars I bore on my back as a reminder of the whipping I'd received four years earlier at Parson's Pond. That hickory branch had left its mark. A permanent one. No matter the cost, I had to keep my scars and their dark secret hidden.

To this end, I developed sophisticated strategies for maintaining a low profile. I changed into my athletic gear only when no one was watching. If I couldn't find a window of opportunity, I'd skip gym and spend the hour dodging hall monitors and hiding in the library stacks. When I changed, I did so quickly. I never showered afterward. Rather, I simply towel-dried myself and got dressed while the other boys were showering or otherwise distracted. For the most part, they ignored me, even the jocks and bullies.

Falling victim to some moronic prank or other, however, was inevitable.

The gloom of winter lifted and made way for spring. It was a bright, shiny day late in the second semester of my freshman year. I was walking with a skip in my step—and much too quickly—toward the locker room. Gym class would be held outside for the first time in months, and I needed to beat the rush so I could change before anyone else arrived. Thus preoccupied, I was about to have an encounter with a football player, a six-foot-four senior named Chet with a full beard and cannons for arms.

Just as I reached for the door handle, Chet and one of his teammates burst from the locker room and sent me flying backward. I landed square on my tailbone, dazed and bewildered. The two young men towered over me like a pair of redwoods. My brain scrambled to take stock of the situation.

It was a poorly kept secret that Chet was on steroids and prone to bouts of sudden and violent fits of anger. On this occasion, he was in an especially foul mood. This wasn't going to end well. Taking immediate offense, he decided to teach me a lesson on the spot.

"What th' fuck!" A volley of spit exploded from his mouth. "Watch where you're goin', kid." He eyed me suspiciously. "Do I know you? Whatcha name?"

I told him.

"You know what a swirly is, Williamson?"

I responded that I didn't.

"Well, dork, you're about to find out."

Grabbing my collar, Chet dragged me through the doors with no more difficulty than if he'd been dragging a rag doll. And like a rag doll, I rolled and twisted and turned, gathering dust and grime along the way. I considered shouting for help but thought it best not to do anything that might add fuel to Chet's fire. His companion followed us inside.

The locker room had low, asbestos-infected ceilings. Caged lightbulbs cast an ominous glow onto the hard concrete floor. Cobwebs adorned each corner. It felt as if we'd entered a condemned coal mine, one that might collapse at any moment.

The two gridiron giants picked me up—each taking an arm—and escorted me toward the bathroom. My legs dangled, useless. In an attempt to free myself, I broke into a ridiculous dance, furiously shimmying my shoulders and gyrating my hips. It was futile, of course. They were impressive physical specimens, these two, each weighing well over two hundred pounds and each having recently signed a national letter of intent to play Division I football. I weighed no more than a buck twenty, soaking wet.

The bathroom's interior, made up of gray cement, ceramic tile, and an overhead labyrinth of pipes, was empty. There'd be plenty of activity when the third-period bell rang. For now, though, it was just the three of us. A faucet dripped. A radiator valve gasped and hissed a final farewell to winter. A colony of beads dampened my brow. Thick with the odor of human waste, the air stung my eyes and seeped into my pores. Along the top edge of the back wall, a textured glass-block window permitted a few streams of diffused light to pass into an otherwise gloomy sepulcher.

They carried me past a row of sinks and a urinal long enough to accommodate ten users at a time. We stopped at the first of five stalls, all with the doors removed. The stench was overpowering.

Chet took control of the operation, grabbing my ankles and hanging me upside down over the toilet. Blood rushed into my cranium, inducing a woozy, disoriented state. A hand that must have belonged to Chet's accomplice flipped up the lid and directed my head into the bowl. I thrashed about wildly, succeeding only in banging my crown against the rim. Stars appeared. Breakfast surged into the back of my throat. Willing myself not to throw up, I closed my eyes, took a deep breath, and held it.

Take your medicine, you worthless little shit.

Within seconds, my scalp was submerged. *It's cold!* The toilet flushed. A deafening roar surrounded me as my skull bounced and clattered helplessly against the unforgiving porcelain.

When it was over, Chet backed out of the stall and deposited me in front of a mirror.

"He makes a pretty girl, don't cha think?"

The other boy howled.

My hair, which had taken no less than twenty minutes to style with Dippity-do that morning, was now done into a toilet-bowl swirly. After a good laugh, they left me standing there in front of the mirror, head bruised, cold, foul water dripping down the sides of my face, and hot, salty tears welling up in my eyes.

But I didn't cry.

The following day, I struck back. It was stupid. I know. But . . .

Unable to focus on trigonometry, I'd spent the entire evening stewing. Behind a locked door and hunched over my desk, I wallowed for hours in a sea of self-pity and humiliation, replaying my encounter with Chet over and over again. *What could I have done differently?* Finally, I grew tired of this pointless exercise and fell into an abyss of resignation and profound sadness.

My mind grew still.

The clock on my desk slipped past midnight.

The sine and cosine functions swirled randomly across the page, flew out of the textbook, and danced, flickering like tiny stars before my weary eyes.

Take your medicine, you worthless little shit.

My sadness mutated into anger—an anger that simmered in the pit of my stomach . . . all night long . . .

I was a pretty good shot at camp. If only I could get my hands on a gun . . .

By morning, my anger had boiled into rage. I needed to act quickly—strike while the iron was hot.

When Chet appeared at the far end of the hallway that ran alongside the library's glass wall, my opportunity had come. Instantly, I was transported back to Camp Abenaki Valley. It was no longer a clean-cut, 225-pound football player stomping toward me but rather a lanky, pimply, long-haired boy, slouching and lumbering forward, thumbs hanging from the belt loops of his tattered blue jeans. *Spencer* . . . It was Spencer Black! Smirking, he winked at me.

Winked at me! The bastard winked at me!

Like an inferno, my rage flared up, consuming me from the inside out. My face burned. My vision turned red. My heart pounded. My breath came in short, hot bursts. I was no longer a helpless victim lying in the silty waters of Parson's Pond but rather a powerful warrior ready to engage in mortal combat.

I reached into my book bag and grabbed a pencil. Taking aim, I threw it.

With once-in-a-lifetime accuracy, the sharp end plunged into the corner of Chet's left eye, coming within a millimeter of piercing his cornea. Stunned, he stood motionless before extracting the foreign object with a frantic yank, falling to his knees, and letting loose a barbaric wail that reverberated off the glass wall and echoed down the hallway. There were many witnesses, including a hall monitor, who immediately identified me as the perpetrator and marshaled me to the principal's office.

When asked to explain my actions, I refused to do so, leaving the principal and disciplinary committee with no choice other than to lower the boom. Due primarily to my uncooperative attitude and the heinous nature of my crime, they seriously considered expelling me from school. In the end, I was given a stern reprimand, a week's suspension, and a full year's probation.

My mother was more shocked by my behavior than angry.

"Ricky, this is so unlike you," she said, still in a state of disbelief a week later when the principal handed down my sentence. "What on earth has gotten into you?"

Little did she know this behavior was exactly like me.

As a coping mechanism, I learned to suppress my rage. Summoning all my strength, I pushed it down—into the remotest depths of my gut—and held it there . . . all day, every day, day in and day out. This required all my energy, and the effort left me exhausted. Chronic abdominal pain set in. It was so severe, it prevented me from falling to sleep at night. During waking hours, I was almost unable to function. Yet I persevered. In time, I became numb and felt nothing.

After serving my suspension, I returned to school and resumed classes. Chet left me alone. The administration must have instructed him to stay clear of me for the remaining two months of the academic year, perhaps warning him that any attempt to seek retribution would jeopardize his Division I scholarship. In any event, I had no further run-ins with Chet or anyone else. School ended without incident. A long, hot summer of mowing lawns ensued.

In my sophomore year, things changed for the better. Life became easier, less exhausting, and less stressful—at least on the surface—and on the surface is where I kept things . . . for a while . . .

I got my grades back on track and even made a few friends. From that point forward, I had a fairly normal high school experience. Yet I couldn't shake the feeling that deep down there was something fundamentally wrong with me.

Yes, my love. Something's wrong . . .

By the time I became a senior, I was ready to move on to the next phase of my life. So, I started counting. When Christmas break arrived, 172 calendar days remained until graduation. All my college applications were complete, and I was looking forward to two and a half weeks free from the daily grind before revving up for the homestretch. There'd be no senior slide for me that spring. Sliding was for slackers. I was a serious student.

Of course, even serious students deserve a holiday, and I took full advantage of my time off, sleeping late and spending virtually every waking moment lounging around the house. I read a little. Albert Camus's *The Stranger* was next on my list. Mostly, however, I watched television. When I got hungry, I'd raid the refrigerator and return with an armful of provisions to my lair in the basement, where the couch would invite me to plop myself down and resume watching a mind-numbing marathon of daytime drivel.

Darkness descended upon the afternoon of the winter solstice, which fell that year on the twenty-second. We'd been on break for almost a week. I was on the couch, curled up under an old, moth-eaten blanket. A canister of Pringles rested in my lap. An empty bowl, a spoon, an open can of Sprite, and a plate covered with bread crumbs and a smear of mayonnaise lay scattered around my feet. *The People's Court* was in session, the Honorable Joseph A. Wapner presiding.

About halfway through the episode, my mother hollered at me from the kitchen. "Ricky! What are you doing down there?"

"Goin' blind."

"What?"

"Watching TV."

"You've been down there all afternoon!"

"I know."

"The sink is full of dirty dishes. Come up here, rinse them off, and put them in the dishwasher!"

"They're not mine."

I was always the responsible one. Danny, on the other hand—

"Honestly, Ricky, I can't believe how lazy you've become. What did you say?"

"They're not mine. They're Danny's!"

"Oh, for chrissakes, Ricky. Danny isn't even home. Come upstairs right now and clean up this mess!"

"But my dishes are down here."

"Ricky, are you listening to me?"

"Yes, Mom," I said, staring catatonically at the screen. "I'll be right there."

Judge Wapner was lecturing the litigants on the importance of observing the rules of decorum in his courtroom.

"Ricky . . . Ricky! I'm warning you. Get your butt up here!"

Transfixed by Wapner's steely presence, I remained perfectly still.

"Now!"

Snapping out of my stupor, I abandoned the Pringles, collected my dirty dishes, and ambled upstairs. Mom was waiting for me in the kitchen with arms crossed and eyes shooting daggers.

"What's the matter with you, Ricky?"

"Nothing," I said.

"Nothing? Ever since Christmas break began, you've either been moping around the house or holed up in the basement watching TV. I swear to you, Ricky, I can't wait for you kids to go back to school. In the meantime, why don't you do something with yourself, something worthwhile?"

"Mom, there's absolutely nothing to do."

"Danny's out with his friends. They went down to the lake to go ice-skating. Why don't you go—"

"Mom, it's cold outside. It's freezing!"

"Why don't you—"

"Mom, I told you—there's *nothing* to do!"

"Nothing to do? Nothing to do? Do something. Anything! Make yourself useful."

"How?"

"For starters, clean up this mess." She motioned to the sink.

"They're not my dishes. I told you, they're—"

"Don't talk back to me, Ricky. I'm not in the mood."

"But they're—"

"Ricky, stop testing my patience. Just do it!"

She was on the verge of losing it, so I decided to comply. Reluctantly.

The sink was filled with stacks of dirty dishes. Setting mine on the counter, I got to work. The first dish was smudged with a swirl of a peanut butter and jelly. PB&J on white bread was Danny's favorite. I removed the sticky residue with a sponge and rinsed it clean. Meanwhile, with her arms still crossed, Mom watched my every move. I deposited the dish into the dishwasher's bottom rack, picked up another, and repeated the process. A plate, a bowl, a spoon, a knife, a glass . . .

"It's garbage night," she said. "When you're done, take out the trash."

"I will."

I rinsed the last dish, placed it in the dishwasher, and headed toward the basement.

"Hey, buster! Where do you think you're going?"

"To watch the end of *The People's Court.*"

"I told you to take out the trash!"

Now, she *was* losing it. She clenched her trembling hands

into fists. Her knuckles turned white, then purple. Her lips quivered. Her eyes grew cartoonishly wide.

"But Mom—"

"Richard Atticus Williamson!" Her voice rose to a screech. "When I tell you to do something, I expect it to be done immediately!"

Losing control of the rage I'd been suppressing for so long, I let out a scream. "Why are you being so goddamned unfair? I did just like you asked and cleaned the dirty dishes. They weren't my dirty dishes. It wasn't my mess. It was Danny's. Now, you want me to take out the trash. Okay, fine! I'll take out the trash. But does it need to be done right away?"

"I want it done now."

"For God's sake, Mom! The garbagemen don't come until morning."

She took a step forward and shook a finger at my nose. "Ricky, I'm warning you . . ."

Her face was as red as a beet. White puffs of smoke surged from her ears.

"Warning me?" I said. "How come you're being so hateful? You would never treat Danny this way. Never! You know what this is? I'll tell you what this is. It's . . . it's . . . it's a double standard."

These words stopped her dead in her tracks. All color drained from her face. Deflated, she stood before me with her mouth hanging open. Speechless. She knew it was true. Danny was the golden boy and could do no wrong. I was the problem child—the family fuckup.

"That's it, isn't it? A double standard. Am I right? Am I? Am I?"

I knew I was right, but I wanted to hear her say it. I needed to hear her say it.

A painfully long silence followed, and then a single drop of water fell from the faucet and pinged the stainless steel interior of the kitchen sink.

"Yes," she said meekly.

Sensing I was onto something, I went in for the kill.

"Why? Tell me why!"

Avoiding my fierce gaze, she fixed her eyes on the floor and said nothing.

"Is it because I'm not really your son?" I demanded, putting voice to an idea I'd been harboring for some time now.

Without looking up, she said, "Of course you're my son—"

"Tell me the truth, goddamn it! Was I adopted?"

"Ricky, please stop—"

"Was I?"

"Don't make me—"

"Tell me the truth! I deserve to know. Was I adopted? Was I?"

"Yes."

"*What?*"

I thought I was prepared, but the truth hit me harder than I'd expected. Instinctively, I'd always known I was different. Having this confirmed, however, was like being hit square in the chest by a train—*a runaway locomotive*—like the one that killed those boys so many years ago on the tracks just outside the South Orange station . . . I imagined severed body parts flying across my field of vision, painting the night red . . .

"Yes. Yes, Ricky. Yes, you were adopted."

"I knew it!"

"We brought you home when you were only six weeks old—"

"I knew it!"

"You were the sweetest baby. God, you were beautiful."

She was crying now.

"I knew it! I knew it! I knew it!"

"We were going to tell you when you were old enough to understand, and then your father died."

My father . . .

This time, it hit me like a slingshot between the eyes.

Daddy was not my real father!

"No!" I bolted out of the kitchen. "Nooooo!"

I scrambled upstairs, locked my bedroom door behind me, and threw myself facedown on the bed.

My father was forever lost to me. *Again.*

Adopted!

Everything made sense now—all of it—my lonely childhood, my angst-ridden teenage years, my entire life.

Adopted!

It made perfect sense. It explained why I'd always felt like an outsider. I'd never been part of the family. Not really. I didn't resemble any of them. Not Danny. Not Mom. Not Daddy. Well, I looked a little like Daddy, just enough to pass for his son. Our features weren't dissimilar, I'd always told myself, and we both had brown hair. Yet his eyes were amber, and mine were as blue as the sky.

There was a special relationship between Mom and Danny. Exclusive. Members only. They belonged to a club from which I was forever banned. Only the worthy ones, the privileged, those who shared a common bloodline, could join.

And don't get any cute ideas, Ricky. There's no hope of ever learning the password or secret handshake.

Mom and Danny shared a bond, a love that could never, would never, be mine.

I don't belong . . . anywhere . . . I'm all alone . . .

Lying flat on my stomach with eyes squeezed shut, I breathed in the freshly laundered scent of the sheets. A sudden tremor ran through the mattress. *What the hell was that?* More tremors followed, and soon the mattress vibrated with such ferocity I feared it would explode.

Hold on, Ricky . . . this is it . . .

With a thump, the vibrations ceased, and the entire bed dematerialized, leaving me suspended in midair and dangling from a thread attached to the ceiling on one end and a point between my shoulder blades on the other. Below me, a dark passageway extended downward like a black hole into another world. The thread strained from gravity's pull. My senses were inexplicably enhanced, and I could hear the individual fibers unraveling and beginning to tear at the subatomic level. It would be only a matter of seconds before the thread snapped.

A blast of organ music—like that of some faraway carousel—rose from the darkness and beckoned for me to follow. The passageway started to spin and draw me into its vortex. Passing the event horizon, I entered the black hole. The thread stretched yet didn't break.

As the vortex's velocity increased, so did the tempo and volume of the music, which took me on a journey into the past. My head became filled with images of flashing, bright golden lights and multicolored ponies bobbing up and down and flying through a night of my childhood at the Essex County Fair. Amber stars as large as melons speckled a purple sky. Hot, buttered popcorn infused the air with its intoxicating aroma. A wave of laughter surged above the music. The merry-go-round came to rest. A throng of eager children mounted painted palominos whose names were etched into their basswood manes in an elaborate cursive script. Diego, Johannes, Raphael, Rembrandt, Michelangelo, and Leonardo floated by as I watched in awe of their beauty—

A tap at my door, and the organ stopped playing. The ponies vanished.

"Please let me in, Ricky."

Just leave me alone.

After a lengthy silence, she attempted to console me from the hallway.

"Ricky, you were my very first. You will always be my very first. Don't you see? You're special. You're special because we chose you."

We?

In a flash of clarity, I knew it hadn't been Mom's idea to adopt me. I knew it just as surely as if she'd told me herself. It had been Daddy's idea. When they thought they couldn't have children of their own, he must have talked her into adopting. Believing she was unable to conceive, she'd agreed—reluctantly—to the plan.

From the very beginning, being my mother had been not a choice but an obligation, a duty imposed on her. Upon my arrival, I was a burden, and as I grew into adolescence, I became an even greater burden. I would never be Mom's pride and joy. That honor was reserved for Danny, the child whose conception and birth defied all odds. The miracle child.

A red-hot fire flared up from deep within and jolted me forward. A disembodied image of Danny's face appeared above the

headboard. He gazed down at me and smiled with the fresh inno-
cence of a child not yet touched by the meanness of this world.
I was overcome with envy. He had everything I'd always wanted.
Happiness, confidence, and an unshakable sense of belonging.

You can't imagine what it's like to be unwanted, can you?

His smile broadened.

I hate you! I hate you! I hate you!

Unperturbed by my outburst and as placid as a north-
ern-woods lake at dawn, he continued gazing at me with nothing but pure love shining in his eyes.

Now I understood why my father's death had hit me so
much harder than Danny. My brother was fortified by a deeply
rooted feeling of security I'd never known. A belief that all
would be well. He was able to weather the storm. I was not.

"I love you, Ricky." Mom's words trickled into my room.
"I've always loved you and always will. I love you . . . I love you
with all my heart . . ."

It didn't matter how many times she repeated these decla-
rations. I did not, could not, feel her love. I was incapable of
feeling her love. I was inconsolable. She and I were adversaries
in a long, drawn-out war. We were both fighting for love . . .
and losing one battle after another . . .

Now it appeared the war was finally over.

With a sigh I could hear quite clearly, she backed away,
plodded down the hallway's hardwood floor . . .

Please don't go.

. . . and closed her door.

Then I thought I heard . . . weeping . . . yes, weeping . . .

My mother was in her bedroom, crying, and I was the
cause. It hadn't occurred to me she had feelings. I'd been too

preoccupied with my own woes to notice. I chastised myself yet took no action to remedy the situation.

Ungrateful, unworthy, spiteful son . . .

I wanted to reach out to her, but the wall I'd built was too high. Hopelessness set in. Loneliness bled into the cells of my body and formed stagnant clots of physical pain in each one. Even the slightest movement provoked a whimper.

If only this pain would go away. I'd do anything not to feel this way anymore . . . anything . . . If only I could put an end to it somehow. If only . . . if only I could stop . . . if only there were no more me, there'd be no more pain.

That's it!

A solution had come. A very simple, practical, and reasonable solution. Mom kept a bottle of Valium in her medicine cabinet.

I wonder how many of those little yellow pills it would take . . .

In the coming days, I fantasized obsessively about my death and the relief it would surely provide. At least now I knew there was a way out.

My depression lasted through the holidays and well into the new year. Mom was so worried, she sent me to see a psychiatrist at the university hospital. After only a thirty-minute session, the doctor prescribed a tricyclic antidepressant—sold under the brand name Elavil—and sent me on my way.

Years later, when use of the internet had become commonplace, I did some research and discovered the identity of my biological mother—a Nancy Jones, originally from Brighton Beach. I contacted her immediately. She denied ever having a son and hung up the phone. A few days later, she called me back and indicated she would need time to get used to the idea.

After a year of corresponding by regular mail (her preferred method of communication), we agreed to meet, and I booked a flight to New York.

During our meeting, which lasted just over an hour in a Lower Manhattan café, I scanned her face for some trace of similarity in our appearances but found none other than the deep azure-blue color of our eyes. Just the color of our eyes, not the shape. From this, I concluded I must have borne at least a modest resemblance to my biological father, whoever and wherever he might be.

Toward the end of the meeting, I happened to glance down, and there it was. Nancy and I had the same hands. Same knuckles, same long, bony fingers, and same protruding veins (arranged in identical meandering patterns). When I shared these observations with her, she withdrew her hands from the table and informed me she didn't wish to discuss the matter. Apparently, she had no interest in speaking about anything that might establish a tangible connection between us.

Not wanting the conversation to end, I expressed my desire to learn as much as possible about my origins. She had very little to say, though, about the events leading up to my birth, and she flatly refused to reveal the identity of my father. When I pressed her on this point, her face turned crimson, and she insisted I leave her alone. I tried to apologize, but it was too late. In an unceremonious huff, she got up, knocked over her tea, and stomped out of the café. The check was soaked through and illegible. Translucent beads of tawny liquid rolled off the table and formed a puddle at my feet. Not the type of reunion I'd hoped for. Even after so many years, she seemed to be holding on to the shame of giving birth to a child out of wedlock. A bastard child.

After our little tête-à-tête, I resumed my research, this time focusing my efforts on determining my paternal parentage. I even visited the agency that had arranged for my adoption, without success.

Finally—and not without first having to clear some major bureaucratic hurdles—I discovered my biological father was an Egyptian immigrant named Hassan al-Wahhabi. Shortly after arriving in America with his wife and three children, Hassan met Nancy in a New York City nightclub. Working there as an underage cocktail waitress, Nancy harbored pretensions of becoming a famous actress and mistook the handsome and charismatic Egyptian for Omar Sharif, who'd been known to frequent the establishment—a well-known hot spot of Manhattan high society. Thinking he might be willing to help advance her career, she swallowed a mouthful of bourbon and approached him. That night, the couple dived precipitously into an impetuous affair that lasted until sometime in the spring of 1965 when Nancy informed Hassan she was pregnant. Receiving the news with an impassive stare, Hassan put an immediate end to the relationship and severed all connections with her. Having just turned eighteen, and with no means to support both herself and a child, Nancy saw no other choice but to put me up for adoption.

Six weeks after my birth in early December, the adoption agency delivered me to my new mom and dad with a note safety-pinned to my chest:

"Hello! My name is Richard Atticus Williamson."

As for Hassan, he continued living in New York with his wife and their three boys. Two years later, his wife gave birth to a fourth boy, whom they named Jihad. A Muslim, although not devoutly so, Hassan thought Jihad was a good, strong Islamic name for a boy.

"Jihad means 'striving in the path of God,'" he explained to his wife, Aamera, who'd grown up in a secular family.

Aamera was perplexed by the idea, but in the end, she deferred to her husband.

Tuesday, August 28, 2001

"Are you okay, mister?"

The boy with dazzling azure-blue eyes was no longer smiling but instead staring up at me with his brow furrowed and face awash with worry.

"Mister . . ."

Coming out of my trance, I returned to Heartland City and the grassy shore along the southeast corner of Lake Weston. I was still holding the boy in my arms. His clothes were soaking wet. Goose bumps speckled his skin. Yet he didn't shiver. Behind us, the sun crept into the sky and cast its nascent light through the treetops and across the shoreline in long, wavy filaments. I could see his face more clearly now.

Does he ever seem familiar! How do I know this boy?

"Mister, are you okay?"

"Me? Yes . . . yes, I'm fine. Except I should be asking you that question. How are you? How did you get here?"

"I feel much better now, but . . . I can't remember how I got here."

"Where do you live?"

"South Orange, New Jersey." He turned his head toward the lake. "This doesn't look like South Orange, though."

"It's not," I confirmed.

This was getting weird. The boy was from South Orange *and* he was wearing a Camp Abenaki Valley T-shirt *and* he looked so damned familiar.

Thinking I might already know the answer, I took a deep breath and swallowed hard before asking my next question.

"Where are your parents?"

The boy's face darkened. "My father . . . well . . . he died. He's still with me, though. As for my mother, I'm not sure where she is. She must be in South Orange."

Your father died . . .

Feeling light-headed and a bit queasy, I moved on to what was surely the next most obvious question.

"What's your name?"

He hesitated. "I can't remember."

"You can't remember?"

"No . . . I . . . I can't."

Wishing to set his mind at ease, I did my best to maintain composure despite the eerie coincidences that were piling up.

"It's okay," I assured him. "Really, it's okay. It'll come to you. Until it does, we'll just call you . . . um . . . David. How about David?"

His face brightened. "Sure!"

"That was my father's name."

"Mine too," he said.

Mine too? Our fathers were both named David?

"What's your name?"

"My name?" I said. "I'm, I'm Richard, but you can call me Ricky."

"Ricky . . . I like that name."

Staring into his eyes, which now radiated an auric glow from within, I attempted to wrap my mind around this unsettling situation, but it was hopeless. Try as I might, I could find no logical explanation to account for the fact I was face-to-face with a boy who looked just like me when I was nine or ten years old.

It was like having some kind of bizarre out-of-body experience . . . or being visited by a ghost come to haunt me for my past sins . . . or finding myself in the middle of an elaborate illusion, designed for some unknown, possibly devious purpose. If so, who could be the orchestrator of such an illusion? What master magician was pulling at my strings?

Maybe I'm simply dreaming. That's it! I'm dreaming. I'm back home in bed dreaming all of this—running around Lake Weston to the point of exhaustion, finding this strange boy floating among the cattails and reeds, pulling him out of the water, having this perplexing conversation, and encountering all these implausible synchronicities. Of course it's a dream. It has to be a dream. On the other hand, if it's a dream, why am I covered from head to toe in sweat? Do people perspire in their dreams?

There was no getting around it. This boy was me!

According to Sherlock Holmes, "When you have eliminated the impossible, whatever remains, *however improbable*, must be the truth." Following Holmes's logic, I had reached the utterly insane conclusion that this boy was me at the age of either nine or ten.

I gazed upon his hair, his face. Yes, he was me, all right. The more closely I scrutinized him, the more certain I became.

His hair, so dark it was almost black, was wet and slicked back, retaining a subtle curl around the ears and along the neck. A prominent forehead presided over his long, oval-shaped face. There could be no doubt he was Caucasian. To the discerning eye, however, his skin bore a copper tinge that revealed the Arab ancestry of his biological father, likely descended from a lost tribe of bedouin nomads who'd roamed the sun-scorched deserts of northern Africa for centuries. His eyes, courtesy of his biological mother, were as blue as the sky on a bright summer afternoon—like mine, except with twenty-five years' less worry in them. His lashes were much too long and—to his great embarrassment—the envy of all the ladies in his mother's Junior League group. The boy's nose was pronounced. Flat cheekbones sloped downward into a sturdy chin that held its own among his peers yet did little to balance out his beak. His well-appointed ears were dignified and featured attached earlobes—evidence perhaps, not of bedouins but of a royal bloodline dating back to the days of ancient Egypt and the reign of Cleopatra.

Ample lips curved into an ironic, good-natured smile. To one side of that smile lay a mole that graced his face with all the charm and sex appeal of a Hollywood beauty mark—the type many famous actors and models fabricated and wore with pride. I hated mine. Growing up, I wished to be rid of it. So, I picked at it, tenaciously, sometimes drawing blood. When I was fourteen, I asked my mom to take me to a surgeon to have the damned thing removed. She refused my request, assuring me my beauty mark was "darling."

Darling. The last thing a fourteen-year-old boy wants to hear in relation to his face.

Whether he liked it or not, his features suited him. He was a good-looking boy. In fact, he was perfect.

If only I could trade places with him and be that age once again, I would do everything differently . . . everything . . .

I probably should have taken him straight to the emergency room or police station. Yet something was telling me this was no chance encounter. After all, how often do you meet yourself?

If this boy really is me—and by now, I'd convinced myself he was—*there must be some cosmic reason for our meeting, and I want to find out what it is.*

So, I made an impulsive decision.

"Well, um, David, you must be cold in those wet clothes. It's about a mile to my house. Do you think you can walk?"

"No problem, Ricky. Let's go!"

I helped him to his feet, and together, we made our way toward home.

CHAPTER TWO

Tuesday, August 28, 2001

L EAVING THE LAKE BEHIND, WE FELL INTO a leisurely
pace and proceeded along a creek that weaved aimlessly
through the city's park system. I felt positively buoyant.
In fact, I was walking on air, suspended gracefully above the
earth and gliding forward without my feet ever touching the
path below. A strange yet welcome sensation arose from some
hidden place within and filled my chest cavity like helium
inflating a balloon. *Joy?* We spoke hardly at all but rather listened to a symphony of songbirds infusing the morning with
their glorious music. In the background, I could just make out
the distant hum of the day's first commuters motoring toward
the freeway. In that blessed moment, though, it was a sound
that belonged to another world—an order of reality separate
from the one David and I were creating together.

Up ahead, a very determined dachshund was leading an
elderly man in our direction. The man sported a shaggy beard

and uncombed wisps of silver hair that billowed in the breeze. Doing his best to keep up with the pooch, he hung on to the leash with a white-knuckled grip and his arm extended to its full length.

"Whoa!" he said, chiding the dog. "What's the hurry, Max? Give your old man a break!"

David and I giggled in unison.

As they approached us, the man, not seeming to notice David at all, locked eyes with me.

"Good morning, young man!"

"Good morning!" I said.

Max was on a beeline along the path, with no intention of slowing down. As he passed us, however, he turned his muzzle toward David, made a friendly yipping sound, and licked David's outstretched hand. This exchange, which apparently escaped the old man's attention, lasted long enough only to allow the tiniest bit of slack in the leash before Max resumed his relentless trek forward.

A few minutes later, a young woman with a ponytail, a low-cut tank top, skintight shorts, long, slender legs, and a pair of white-and-red Nikes jogged toward us. My heart fluttered. The sweetest, demurest of smiles graced her face. Her flawless skin glistened in the morning light. Her radiant eyes met mine—for no more than an instant—and she was gone.

"Good morning!" I cried out before her Nikes had a chance to carry her out of earshot.

"Good morning!" she replied over her shoulder as she continued toward the lake.

David winked at me approvingly. I winked back.

I was happy—happier than I'd felt in a long while, perhaps

since I was a little boy in South Orange, going for walks with Daddy along the thickly wooded paths of South Mountain Reservation and visiting the monkeys at Turtle Back Zoo. Being with David was like spending time with the son I never had. All thoughts of my difficulties at work vanished.

When we got home, David informed me he was tired and wished to sleep. Eager to accommodate my guest, I led him upstairs and fetched him a T-shirt and a pair of boxer shorts from my dresser. Then I called work with a hastily concocted excuse. Severe gastrointestinal pain. I'd be fine, I told my secretary. It was probably something I ate.

In the meantime, David had removed his wet things and slipped into the comically oversize change of clothes I'd provided. He was a good sport and didn't complain. Instead, he thanked me and crawled into bed. Pulling my great-grandmother's embroidered rocking chair to the bedside, I watched him fall immediately into a deep sleep. A contented smile spread across his face. His chest rose and descended in long, steady movements. Entranced, I drifted back to my senior year of high school . . . and what lay beyond . . .

My Early Adult Years: 1984–1992

With the help of a daily dose of Elavil and weekly psychiatric appointments, I survived my bout of depression, or "midwinter malaise," as the doctor so euphemistically described my condition. After eight weeks, he announced he was satisfied by my progress. I was no longer a threat to attempt suicide. "Our time together has come to an end, Ricky," he said in a bland tone that oozed with clinical indifference, before referring me to a therapist at the university's mental health clinic. At the clinic, he assured me, I would learn to accept my adopted-child status.

In June, I graduated from high school as a member of the class of 1984. There were no obvious signs of George Orwell's Big Brother prophecy, yet I stayed alert and watched the news religiously, just in case. In particular, I kept my eyes peeled for any subtle changes in our country's political landscape. The policies of the Reagan administration didn't appear to pose a threat to our civil liberties. I listened carefully, though, as the president made his case for assisting the Contras in Nicaragua. He called the Contras *freedom fighters*. I was skeptical. After all, in the world created by Orwell in his *1984*, the state redefined words like *freedom* and used language to enslave the minds of its citizens. Expressing one's views was punishable by torture or even death. So, keeping the Orwellian prophecy in mind, I remained vigilant.

That spring, I'd received a handful of acceptance letters, including one from my long shot, Princeton University.

Princeton—one of the most elite undergraduate institutions in the nation, and only an hour's drive from South Orange! I wonder what I should do . . .

Despite Princeton's offer of admission, which surely must have been the result of a clerical error, I decided to remain in Heartland City and attend a small, unremarkable liberal arts school located just across town.

My college counselor advised me against selling myself short. Mom and Danny urged me to go to Princeton—*Are they trying to get rid of me?*—but I dug my heels in and refused. When asked for my reasons, I was at a loss. Not only was I unable to explain my decision to them, I was unable to explain it to myself. I knew Princeton was an amazing opportunity—*The chance of a lifetime!*—yet something held me back . . . something powerful . . . perhaps a fear of not being good enough—*Now lie still and take your medicine, you worthless little shit!*—of not having what it would take to measure up to Ivy League standards.

Whi-kisssh! Whi-kisssh! Whi-kisssh!

Ever since moving from South Orange, I felt lost . . . lost in a dark and hostile wasteland . . . snatched from home, the last tangible connection to my father severed forever . . . imprisoned . . . yes, *imprisoned* somewhere in the northernmost province of our beloved country's midwestern region, desperately wanting to escape and start a new life . . .

Princeton was my ticket out. Princeton! The perfect opportunity—an offer of admission and generous financial aid package to boot. Yet I declined. Turned down Princeton! What was the matter with me? Was I crazy? Yes, I most certainly must have been crazy. It was a once-in-a-lifetime opportunity, and I let it slip through my fingers, opting instead to lead a life of quiet desperation. Henry David Thoreau would have been disappointed but not surprised. Rather than taking the required leap of faith, I played it safe and stayed within my comfort zone, close to what had become all too familiar.

Pushing all thoughts of Princeton out of my mind, I decided to make the best of my self-imposed exile. The solstice marked the beginning of another summer in Heartland City. Each morning,

I rose with the sun and earned money for school on the back of a John Deere. Time passed in its usual mulish way. Then, on a Wednesday in late August, we moved my things across town and into a ten-by-fifteen box of a dorm room. Misty-eyed, Mom wrapped me in her arms and held me tight. Danny leaned in as if to kiss me before pounding me on the back with a fist . . . and they were gone . . .

The following day, my roommate, Allen, arrived from Waterloo, Iowa. Without warning, he appeared in the doorway. Tall, thin, and fair-skinned, his insubstantial form seemed to hover there, inches above the floor. He made no sound until he was almost upon me. Speaking in a tremulous whisper, he introduced himself. His hand was cold and clammy, a dead fish. Pale gray irises emerged from behind milky eyes. A clump of hair sat on his head like a powdered wig. His lips puckered into a colorless grin. *He's a ghost*, I thought, *a benevolent ghost.* I liked him immediately.

The academic year officially commenced on the Tuesday before Labor Day weekend. Classes were okay. My professors seemed competent. All was going well. It felt good to be out of the house and on my own. I found it impossible, though, to cut the cord completely, returning home with laundry every Sunday and almost always staying for dinner.

As the weeks tumbled by, I adjusted to college life, made a few friends, and studied hard. Before I knew it, the leaves of summer had transformed themselves into brilliant yellows, golds, oranges, and reds. In contrast to these colors, which adorned the cluster of maples outside our third-floor window, the campus's meticulously manicured and well-irrigated lawns retained a lustrous emerald hue well into mid-October. Soon, however, the turf lost its luster as, one by one, each blade of grass turned brown and slipped into dormancy. The autumn colors faded. The trees thinned. Midterms arrived.

Four days before my first exam, I was in the dorm, attempting to study. A bad idea. A very bad idea, as it turned out. It was seven o'clock in the evening. I had the room to myself. Allen wasn't around. As usual, he was with his girlfriend, Mary Sue—also from Iowa and of the same ghostly pallor. They'd met during the first week of school, and I hadn't seen much of him since.

A built-in desk spanned the room's length. Hunched over it, I stared at a page in chapter 1 of my Intro to Philosophy textbook. An example of a categorical syllogism stared back. It was hopeless. I couldn't concentrate. There were too many distractions.

The guys three doors down had part-time jobs at a nearby electronics store and easy access to the latest, state-of-the-art sound equipment. If you believed the local dorm gossip, the two accounting majors had outfitted their room by lifting the store's most expensive components from inventory and fixing the company's books to cover their tracks. Currently, a pair of allegedly hot Harman Kardon speakers spewed the Genesis song "Abacab" through their open door, into the hallway, and from one end of the dormitory to the other. My window buzzed in time to the music's bass-laden beat.

Four doors down, our resident assistant had been locked into his room by a trio of sophomores—the three amigos—who'd strategically inserted pennies into the doorframe. This had become, by far, the dorm's most popular prank. The amigos howled with glee. The pennied-in RA pounded his fists on the door and screamed over Phil Collins's digitally amplified tenor.

"You assholes better let me out of here, or . . . or . . . or—"

"Or what?"

"There will be hell to pay. That's what!"

This threat was met by a chorus of derisive laughter and mockery.

"Loser!" "Dickweed!" "Faggot!"

Faggot?

A couple of freshmen darted out of the showers and chased each other up and down the hallway, their voices echoing off the ceiling and feet thumping the linoleum floor. I caught a glimpse as they ran by. They were stark naked. One of them whipped the other with a wet towel that had been rolled into a lethal rattail.

"Fucker! You got me right in the nuts!"

Seriously? Are these morons for real? Am I back in the high school locker room? Is this Camp Abenaki Valley all over again?

Annoyed at their antics, I got up from my desk and closed the door.

I sat back down. The door swung open. Brad, our next-door neighbor, marched in. He'd just returned from dinner and was looking for a good time. He was always looking for a good time. Brad was a nice guy with a heart of gold and the most loyal friend you could ever ask for. He wasn't terribly interested in his studies, though, and he wasn't at all interested in respecting the rights of those who wished to study. Stopping in the center of the room, he struck a pose à la Michael Jackson and pointed a finger at me.

"Hey, Ricky-mania! Whassup, buddy? How ya doin'?"

"Hey, Brad," I growled through clenched teeth.

"Oooooo! What's wrong, bud? Why so serious?"

"I'm studying, Brad."

"Studying? Oh, come on now. Whaddya talkin' 'bout? It's Thursday night. The weekend's almost here. Come on, dude, let's party! Party! Party! Party!"

Breaking into a moonwalk, he glided effortlessly across the floor.

"No, really, Brad—"

"'No, really, Brad,' nothin'!" Abandoning the moonwalk, he strutted over to the desk. "Come on, bud, loosen up. Let's have some fun. Whaddya say? Let's you and me go find some chicks and get laid!"

"Brad—"

"How 'bout a smile? Just a little one? Come on, Ricky-mania, you can do better than that. I know you got one in you."

He was very close now. Too close. I leaned forward, planted my forearms on the desk, and peered back over my shoulder. His nose was no more than a hand's length from mine.

"Just a little smile?" he said, raising his voice into a ridiculous falsetto and contorting his features into an expression that reminded me of Felix the Cat. "C'mon. Who's your buddy? Who's your pal?"

Ordinarily, I would have cracked a smile at this point, but midterms were just around the corner, and I was in no mood for games.

He leaned in closer. "What's the matter, chumpy? Life gotcha down?" He puckered up and leaned in closer still. "Give us a kiss."

Thwack!

Before I could stop myself, I'd slapped him across the cheek. Hard. Much too hard. His face turned to stone. Glaring at me in disbelief, he stood straight up. Crimson shaded his skin at the point of impact. Fury burned in his eyes. But there was something else. Shock? Confusion? Pain? Yes. Pain. Pain and deep sadness. He was hurt, heartbroken that his chumpy had responded to his harmless clowning around with an absurd act of violence. It was clear he wanted to retaliate. He should have retaliated. I deserved it. Instead, he left without a word.

I felt immediate remorse. Brad was just being Brad and having fun like he always did. *And I hit him!* I wanted to apologize yet didn't trust myself to find words that would make things right between us. So, I did what I should have done in the first place. I gathered my books and went to the library.

The library was no better than the dormitory. The school's nerve center for socializing and gossip, the fourth-floor stacks pulsed and buzzed with raw energy. The area designated for quiet study was besieged by a flurry of activity. Folded into paper airplanes, notes soared across the room. Unnoticed, one of them bounced off the shoulders of a couple engaged in a passionate kiss. Only partially hidden in the shadows of a towering bookcase, a hand groped feverishly for a breast. Careless whispers echoed off vaulted ceilings. A group of coeds congregated around a long, rectangular table and recruited each other for an excursion to a neighborhood tavern.

Another bad idea.

My search for solitude and uninterrupted silence continued. Finally, I found what I was seeking two floors below ground level in the library's rarely frequented subbasement, otherwise known as the Tombs. Most of the building closed at midnight. The Tombs were kept open late to accommodate night owls. I wasn't a night owl by nature, but I was willing to do whatever it took to ace my midterms, even at the expense of a good night's sleep—and my health.

There were a few other hard-core students scattered about. The cobweb-infested fluorescent lights crackled and hummed. An occasional page fluttered, flipped, and came to rest. An unoccupied carrel beckoned to me from a secluded corner. I unloaded my backpack and went to work. Opening my philosophy textbook, I began by reviewing a summary of Immanuel Kant's categorical imperative, sure to be on the midterm.

At some point after midnight, my head grew heavy and my eyelids flickered. If I could just rest for a few minutes, everything would be all right . . . My weary noggin floated gently onto the carrel's Formica desktop, and I fell fast asleep . . .

I'm underwater. My lungs are aching for air. I'm playing the part of the rope in a hotly contested game of tug-of-war. A pair of warm, translucent hands pulls me up toward a distant ball of light. A pair of cold, bony claws yanks me downward into the abyss . . . A drum keeps the beat of a death march. Its hypnotic sound is both repulsive and irresistible. It's consuming me . . .

Da-doom, da-doom, da-doom . . .

With a resolute kick of my legs, I escape the grip of the bony claws and rise to the surface, guided by the translucent hands each agonizingly slow fathom of the way . . . Breaking through, I gasp for air and refill my depleted lungs. Treading water, I survey the horizon. There's no sign of the hands or their owner. I swim ashore and collapse at the water's edge. I'm exhausted, but I'm alive. I lie here relishing my good fortune and taking long, slow breaths of nectar-laced air . . .

A distant rumble . . . and another, closer this time. I raise my head and scan the vast body of water from which I just emerged. Blotting out the sky like an enormous bruise on the backside of creation, a purple cloud streaked with dark bands of split-pea green and sulfuric yellow expands over the water and advances toward me . . . Suddenly, there's a tremendous gust of wind, and the branch of a nearby tree pokes me . . . once, twice, three times . . .

Tapping me on the shoulder, a night watchman informed me it was time to go home. I fumbled for my watch. It was two thirty in the morning.

Three more late nights in the Tombs, and Monday arrived. Waking up late, I skipped breakfast and went directly to philosophy. A blue book was waiting for me at an assigned desk. In it, I regurgitated, in form and style appropriate to the questions posed, the laundry list of facts and concepts I'd stored in short-term memory. Earning an A, I promptly forgot all about Immanuel Kant and his categorical imperative.

And so it went for the remainder of my freshman year. Forgoing an active and fulfilling social life, I studied late, fell asleep in my private corner of the Tombs, and dutifully attended class each morning. I finished the year with a near-perfect academic record, an A-minus in differential calculus representing the only blemish on my transcript.

After a summer of living at home with Mom and Danny and working outdoors for an urban tree service, where I earned a buck or two, a few muscles, and a decent tan, I moved into an apartment with Allen and two other guys from the dorm. Less than a mile from campus, the cramped two-bedroom unit was on the top floor of a three-story building that stood on the bluffs overlooking the Mississippi. In autumn, when the trees lost their leaves, we'd have an unobstructed view of the great river.

Classes began, and we were officially sophomores. I was anxious to choose a major, yet undecided. Part of me wanted to follow my father's footsteps into a teaching career. Another part was considering law school. We weren't required to declare until the end of the year, but I disliked the ambiguity and wanted to resolve the matter as soon as possible. So, I agonized . . . and took a strange pleasure in my agonizing . . . In the meantime, I enrolled in courses that would satisfy both paths, including English, history, political science, and economics.

Economics. Ah yes, economics. That fall, I took Principles of Microeconomics with Professor Hartley. Class met at nine o'clock each morning, and I wouldn't have missed it for the world. Why? Well, it wasn't because I loved microeconomics, although the ideas were fairly interesting. And it wasn't because I loved Professor Robert Hartley, although he was a fine teacher, one of the finest. What I loved about that class was a girl . . . a girl named Kimberly . . . Kimberly Turner . . .

No less than ten minutes late on the first day of class, Kimberly Turner sashayed into the lecture hall, her hips swaying with a relaxed, almost careless grace. Announcing her arrival with a triumphant sigh that reverberated in the upper register of her voice (key of D major, I guessed), she plopped her perfect proportions onto the only remaining seat—the one to my immediate right. Her book bag hit the floor and produced a syncopated *da-da-doom* that drew a scowl from Professor Hartley.

Turning casually in my direction, she cast me an unapologetic and irresistibly guileless smile.

"Hey, sailor," she said.

Who, me?

The subtly sweet, intoxicating scent of her perfume permeated my senses and left me feeling woozy and disoriented.

"My car wouldn't start," she said with a shrug, not so much to explain her lateness but merely to fill the space her greeting had opened.

Temporarily losing the power of speech, I managed to squeak out a "Hi" just before the socially acceptable window of opportunity closed.

What a knockout!

She wore skintight denim-and-white-leather Guess jeans that accentuated her athletic thighs and left her exquisitely slender ankles exposed for all the world to see. Her relaxed-fit, off-the-shoulder top revealed a tantalizing hint of cleavage and flawlessly smooth skin that glowed with youthful vitality. A few loose strands fell from a heap of curly chestnut hair. Absent-mindedly, she twirled one of them with a finger as she half listened to Professor Hartley's lecture. Her mocha eyes, big and round as saucers, lit up whenever she spoke. When she finished speaking, her rosy lips curved themselves into a self-assured smile that melted my heart and transported me to another world.

Am I dreaming?

For the first time in a very long while, I felt a surge of passion crackling beneath the surface of my skin and shooting from one extremity to another. A healthy dose of air filled my lungs. I was coming to life . . .

After class, we made our way out of the lecture hall and into a bustling hallway, where I learned she was a transfer student from the university. In her opinion, the "U" was too cold, too impersonal, and way too big. In fact, there were over three hundred students in her freshman comp class alone. Besides, there was an ex-boyfriend she wished to avoid. All in all, she was sure she'd be more comfortable in her new surroundings. Then, without another word, she flashed her smile, waved goodbye, and pranced toward a nearby stairwell, leaving me dumbstruck in the middle of a growing swarm of undergrads, my jaw hanging open, head spinning, and heart churning.

I must admit the hot-blooded nineteen-year-old boy in me fell head over heels, crazy in *lust* with Kimberly Turner as soon as he laid eyes on her. By the time she disappeared down those stairs, though, it had become much more than mere desire. I was in love. The desire remained, but it had faded into the background, transcended by love's pure luminosity. It was an innocent love—the kind that shines only through the eyes of a gloriously happy little boy . . . until tragedy strikes and chases it into exile. I'd just learned that such love never dies. Rather, it bides its time waiting, waiting patiently for the right moment to return home.

Once again ten minutes late, Kimberly sat next to me the following day. And the day after that. And much to my delight, she continued to do so for the balance of the semester. *Is this really happening?* Not only was Kimberly Turner the most beautiful girl in a school of two thousand undergraduates, she was relaxed, unpretentious, outgoing, fun . . . oh, and one other small detail—she liked to talk . . . *a lot* . . .

Speaking in low whispers to avoid detection, she talked straight through class, commenting on everything from world events to the outrageous colors of Professor Hartley's floral neckties. Her constant chatter prevented me from focusing on the lectures. But I didn't mind. I would simply learn the principles of microeconomics directly from the textbook. No problem.

Whenever she flashed that self-assured smile of hers, which seemed to come so naturally, my knees became weak, my mouth turned dry, my heart thundered. Deep within me, butterflies would awaken, spread their wings, and take flight. By the end of class each day, I was putty in her hands. If only she'd asked, I'd have traveled to the end of the world and back for her—barefoot . . . with blisters . . . with blisters on top of my blisters . . . and a song of undying devotion in my heart. All she wanted, however, was for me to listen. I was more than happy to oblige.

In heaven. That's where I was. I knew it couldn't last, though. She was out of my league. *Way out of my league.* I didn't dare dream of asking her out. A girl like Kimberly Turner could date whomever she chose—captain of the football team, student council president, a graduate student . . . Why would she go out with a nervous, insecure, skinny little dweeb like me?

Still, we continued sitting next to each other, and she jabbered on and on about school, friends, family, you name it. Oblivious, Professor Hartley cheerfully sketched supply-and-demand curves across the chalkboard. Of course, Kimberly's curves were much more interesting than his. Nevertheless, I managed to get an A on the midterm. Kim earned an A-plus. As I'd suspected, she was more than just a pretty face. Much more. A member of Mensa since early childhood, she had genius-level intelligence. Talking her way through class was a coping mechanism that had grown out of sheer boredom. The material was simply beneath her. She secured her A-plus without breaking a sweat. Possessing a very average IQ, I paid for my A with blood, sweat, and tears . . . and nightly visits to the Tombs . . .

With each passing day, I fell more deeply in love with this amazing young woman. Fantasies of asking her out invaded my every thought and occupied each waking hour. With midterms in the rearview mirror, finals loomed. Time was slipping, slipping, slipping away . . . If it were going to happen, I knew I'd better act quickly. Yet I kept putting it off . . . and putting it off . . . and putting it off . . .

The fantasies persisted. In my head, I came up with every possible scenario for the encounter. Only one made any sense. As casually as my nerves would allow, I'd be direct and simply ask her out.

When?

When? Well . . . after class one day.

One day?

One day soon . . . one day soon . . . one day soon . . .

K-K-Kimberly, w-would you like to go out some time?

Yes, Ricky. I'd love to!

Snap out of it, Ricky! What are you thinking? She'll never say yes. She'll laugh at you, that's what she'll do. She'll laugh at the very absurdity of the idea! Come on, Rick. Get real. She's out of your league.

    Yeah, I know . . . but . . . but still . . . I have to try . . . If I don't try, I'll always wonder . . . Yes. Yes, goddamn it! I've got to ask her out, even if it kills me . . .

I woke on the Friday morning before Thanksgiving. Something was wrong. Very wrong. *Trapped!* I struggled to free myself, but—like an Egyptian mummy—my body was bound up in sheets clinging tenaciously to my skin. My linen shroud was moist with sweat . . . and cold . . . very cold. A shiver ran up and down my spine. I tried to move my hands, but they were swollen and too heavy to lift. My stomach gurgled, and my intestines produced a cloud of gas that formed a bubble—an invisible sarcophagus—around my mummified corpse.

"Oh, God," I wailed. "Help me!"

A light tap at the bedroom door, and my wrappings loosened. The shroud fell away. Allen's disembodied head appeared. He asked if I was okay. Without replying, I rolled to my side and stared at the dingy, off-white plaster wall, only inches from my face. It stared back, offering no relief, no words of comfort, no advice. What did I expect? It was just a wall. The door closed, and Allen left for class.

The Kimberly dilemma had gone on too long. In my mind's eye, I could see the last grain of sand on the verge of slipping into the neck of an hourglass. I reached for the glass, but my hand passed right through and struck the plaster. It was now or never. There'd be no time for dating between Thanksgiving and finals. And after the econ final, there was no telling when I might see Kimberly again.

It's got to be this morning. I'll ask her out right after class. No more procrastinating. No beating around the bush. I'll just ask her . . . and maybe, just maybe, she'll be free this weekend . . .

Extracting myself from bed, I prepared for school, and without eating breakfast—*far too nervous to eat*—I braced against the morning chill and embarked on the mile-long trek to the Economics and Business Sciences Building.

By the time I reached the twin-doored threshold that led into the lecture hall, I'd become an absolute basket case. My guts churned themselves into a boiling cauldron. A bitter concoction rose to the back of my throat. Dry and tacky as sandpaper, my tongue fastened itself to the roof of my mouth. With difficulty, I swallowed, and the concoction receded. My free hand—the one not white-knuckling the strap of my book bag—trembled visibly. And my heart . . . my poor, desperate heart was attempting to jackhammer its way out of my chest.

There's no turning back now.

Taking a deep breath, I entered the room and secured my accustomed seat. Class began. True to form, Kimberly's chair was empty. A single bead of sweat rolled down the back of my neck. A few minutes later, she strutted in and sat down.

The entire hour was pure agony. Except for a brief glance, a forced, tight-lipped smile, and perfunctory nod when she first sat down, I didn't look at her. I couldn't. Instead, I kept my eyes pointed toward the front of the room and tried listening to Professor Hartley's lecture on the cross-price elasticity of demand in international commodities markets. *Hopeless.* It was hopeless! I couldn't focus to save my life. My thoughts came like a wild stampede of ten thousand head of cattle, spooked by a pack of ravenous wolves.

Where should I do it? Here or in the hallway?

The hallway, Ricky. The hallway's much better.

What if there are too many people around? I'd feel—

Fuck your feelings. Just ask her out, for chrissakes!

What if she says no?

Of course she'll say no.

Isn't there even the slightest possibility?

No. Don't kid yourself.

Okay, fine, but just for the sake of argument, what if she says yes? What then?

Kimberly must have sensed something was wrong because she was less gabby than normal. Much less gabby. Professor Hartley, on the other hand, droned on . . . and on . . .

After an excruciating eternity, the bell rang. Leaping from their seats and forming a herd, my fellow classmates bolted for the doors, spurred forward, no doubt, by thoughts of what the weekend might bring. I tried to get up but couldn't move. Although I hadn't yet had a thing to eat, my stomach felt like a lead balloon that weighed me down and made it impossible to stand.

She's getting away!

Summoning all my strength and fueled by a sudden jolt of adrenaline, I gathered my things and hoisted myself out of the chair. The herd encircled me and dragged me after Kimberly and into the hallway. With intensely alert eyes, I searched for an opening, any opening. I found none. There were just too many bodies.

I'll just have to spit it out right here and now, and to hell with what other people think!

"K-K-Kimberly . . ." I stammered.

Then, as if by magic, the herd thinned out, and we found ourselves standing alone at the top of a poorly lit stairwell. *Hey! This is where I fell in love with her!* Above us, a light fixture discharged a weak crackle and fizzled out. A dry cough escaped my throat.

Deep grooves appeared in her brow as she peered sideways at me.

"Well . . . Ricky . . . have a nice weekend . . ."

An awkward silence followed.

My heart raced.

Got to maintain control. No matter what.

I slid my quivering hands into my front pockets and inclined my head in a deferential bow toward the floor. She was wearing open-toed shoes. In November! Even her feet were lovely . . .

"So . . . um . . . would you . . . would you like to . . . to go out sometime? Maybe this weekend?"

No response.

With a sliver of hope, I raised my gaze.

Like a slasher film heroine cornered by the bogeyman, she gasped and took a dramatic step backward. Her eyes grew impossibly large. Her once-carefree face contorted into an unrecognizably hideous mask. Her mouth opened into a silent scream. A string of saliva dangled from her upper lip. She seemed to be searching, searching for a response. *Any* response.

"You mean on a date? With *you?*"

In the physical world with which we're all so well acquainted, my face flushed, and I became so light-headed I feared I would lose consciousness. Instead, I somehow found the strength to hold my ground. I took a breath . . . and another . . .

In the world of my all-too-vivid imagination, however, I staggered backward from the sheer force of her blow and fell to the floor, landing hard on my behind. Dazed, I watched in disbelief as the ceiling tile directly over my head cracked and crumbled before giving way and raining down on me in a torrent of asbestos and dust. Then, just as the storm was letting up, the entire ceiling gave way and collapsed, burying me alive. The rubble produced a hole just large enough for me to peek through and catch a glimpse of Kimberly's expression of utter horror.

Back in the physical world, I continued breathing while struggling to maintain my composure, to hold back the tears. My eyes stung. My cheeks burned. My ears blazed hot.

Finally, I managed to respond. "Well . . . no . . . no, not really . . . It wouldn't have to be an actual date . . . I mean, yeah . . . I guess . . ."

"I didn't think . . . I mean, Ricky . . . gimme a break. I *never* thought . . ."

"No, no, of course not . . . I just thought maybe—"

"Well, I can't this weekend. I made plans with a friend . . . and, and, well . . . next week is Thanksgiving. You know that, don't you? It's just not a good time. I'm much too busy right now . . ."

At a loss for any more words, she turned from me and disappeared down the shadowy stairwell.

I'm such an idiot!

I scanned the ceiling. It was still intact. Cautiously backing away, I found myself once again in the middle of a massive herd of humanity. Feeling their eyes upon me like needles penetrating my flesh, I was convinced that each of them had witnessed every detail of the humiliation I'd just suffered. Some snickered. Others cast pitying glances in my direction. A bug under a microscope, I attempted to navigate the crowded hallway yet made little progress.

Time had come to a crawl. I was moving in slow motion.

Got . . . to . . . get . . . out . . . of . . . here . . . now!

I tried forcing my legs to go faster, to break into a run. But it was no use. It was like trudging through quicksand with a fifty-pound load strapped to my back . . . one agonizing step after another . . .

After what seemed like a life sentence in purgatory, I finally reached the stairwell at the opposite end of the hallway.

Time returned to normal.

I'm free!

I sprinted down to the first floor and out of the building.

That night, I joined Allen and our fellow tenants, Jacob and Nate, in the living room for *Miami Vice*. The opening sequence commenced with a sudden salvo of drums. Palm trees, flamingos, jai alai, fast cars, scantily clad women, sandy beaches, whitecaps, and speedboats splashed across the screen. The others cried out in delight. I remained unmoved.

Hanging out in our apartment and drinking fire-brewed Stroh's while watching undercover detectives Crockett and Tubbs put their lives on the line was for us a sacred Friday-night ritual. According to house rules—strictly enforced, though no one had ever bothered putting them into writing—my physical presence was mandatory. So there I lay, sprawled across our tattered, secondhand sofa and staring mindlessly at the TV, my thoughts a million miles away.

After *Vice*, there was always an off-campus party in the neighborhood. This Friday night was no exception. In fact, the infamous Margolis house would be hosting its annual preholiday kegger. Anyone who was anyone would be there.

As soon as the last of the closing credits rolled off the screen, Allen, Jacob, and Nate jumped up, grabbed their autumn-weight jackets, and headed for the door. I begged off, claiming an illness of unknown origin. Truth be told, I was too depressed to go to a kegger, and being around people would only worsen my condition. Besides, I didn't want to risk running into Kimberly.

"Come on, Rick!" said Nate. "You can't miss the Margolis house kegger. It's the biggest blowout of the year. Every hot chick in school will be there!"

"I'm feeling really sick, guys. Think I'm coming down with something nasty."

"Loser! Put your rally cap on!"

"You guys go ahead. I'll catch up with you later if I'm feeling better."

After a few more unsuccessful attempts to light a fire under me, they threw on their jackets and left for the party. The old sofa cradled me in its soft embrace. *Alone now . . .* Everything turned black . . .

I'm at the water's edge. A dark, formidable cloud approaches. I turn away from the impending storm and crawl onto dry land. A sinister forest stands before me. It's immense. As far as I can see in either direction, its monstrous trunks reach upward and fade into the charcoal sky . . . Rivers of Spanish moss flow hideously from crooked branches, which beckon with gnarled hands and twisted, arthritic fingers. Unable to resist, I advance toward the evil that awaits within.

A tree, acting as sentry, stops me. Its bark is covered with rotting green lichen. The stench is overpowering. Behind me, a purple flash lights up the sky. A clap of thunder rattles my bones and leaves the hairs on the back of my neck standing on end. Satisfied with my credentials, the tree instructs me to enter. I hesitate. A sudden explosion of hail falls from above and pelts my skin with merciless fury. I hurl myself into the forest . . .

Blind, I stumble into the darkness with hands outstretched. A bolt of lightning strikes a nearby oak, which lands across my path. The hail turns to rain. The forest closes in . . . cold, bloodless fingers clutch my throat . . . I can't breathe . . . I try crying out for help, but I'm unable . . .

Gasping for air, I sat straight up. The sofa lurched and came to rest. It was dark. Very dark. Except for the wheeze of my lungs replenishing themselves, it was quiet. Very quiet.

Silence swallows the sound of each breath . . . leaving nothing but pure silence in its wake . . . portending something . . . something beyond sound, beyond sight, beyond touch . . .

A chill crept into my bones.

It's snowing, Ricky.

Snowing? Who's there? Am I still dreaming?

Recovering my breath, yet groggy and disoriented, I staggered over to the living room window and peered into the courtyard.

A pair of antique fixtures, mounted on each side of the building's front portal, cast a globe of pale yellow light into the surrounding gloom. Within the sphere's hazy perimeter, swirling wisps of autumn snowflakes coalesced into dancing figure eights. Mesmerized, I stood before the window—motionless as a stone statue—and watched the performance.

After only a few precious moments, the dance was interrupted by a stiff gust of wind and the rumble of a distant thunder—unusual for that time of year. Very unusual. The rumble receded . . . and then returned, a little louder this time and getting closer . . . A flash of lightning lit up the sky. The snow turned to rain. More thunder and more lightning. Within seconds, the rain was pouring out of the sky in a ferocious deluge.

I could no longer see the courtyard. Raindrops as large as marbles struck the window with such force, I feared the glass would shatter. I stepped back and tripped over the coffee table. Cursing my clumsiness, I climbed to my feet and found myself in the middle of a shadowy cave. *What the hell?* Covered with stalactites, the ceiling began to descend, and the walls closed in. The air was so stale and thick that I choked on each breath. My chest grew heavy, and a furious stream of palpitations rippled through my heart.

I've got to get out of here!

Without pausing to grab a coat or even my keys, I darted through a crack in one of the approaching walls and into the hallway. It was dark and smelled of mold. A flicker of lightning illuminated the 302 on our neighbors' door. From there, I attacked the stairs—two at a time—and burst out of the front portal and into the storm.

I'm free!

Exhilarated, I ran through sheets of unrelenting rain, across River Road, and down a treacherously steep slope of rocks, dirt, and scattered shrubbery. Losing my footing, I rolled head over heels the last ten yards of the way and landed with a bruising crash on the muddy banks of the Mississippi. Ignoring the pain, I sprang to my feet and shouted into the raging night.

"Is this all you got? You call this a storm? This ain't no storm! I'll show you a storm. You think I need a girlfriend to make me happy? I don't need no fuckin' girlfriend. I don't need anybody. I've got my whole life in front of me. I can do whatever I want. You think I'm afraid of you? I'm not afraid of you. Come on, you bastard! Take your best shot. You're not taking me down. Not this time. I'm gonna work my fucking ass off and strive, strive to be the very best, and there's nothing you can do to stop me!"

That night, I made myself a promise. Come hell or high water, I would go to law school and study to become a world-class trial lawyer.

A trial lawyer?

I'm going to make something of my life. No matter what it costs me, I'm going to become the greatest lawyer ever. Better than Clarence Darrow. Better than Atticus Finch.

Atticus Finch?

I'm going to make my father proud. Can you hear me, Daddy? Are you watching?

The following week, I met with my academic adviser, who exercised infinite patience in the face of a full hour of my probing questions. Afterward, I visited the registrar's office and officially declared an economics major with minors in political science and philosophy. From that point forward, I focused all my energies on my studies and committed every waking moment of my remaining college experience to getting into law school.

In the spring of 1988, I graduated from college Phi Beta Kappa—a nice accomplishment, but still . . . there was a deep, underlying feeling of being unworthy of the honor . . .

"Mr. Williamson!"

The moment I'd been dreading finally arrived. I'd been in law school for over a month and hadn't yet been called upon to stand up in class and face what all first-year law students must face sooner or later. The infamous Socratic method. It was now my turn to endure the rack.

"Is there a Mr. Richard Williamson here?"

Mr. Williamson! Mr. Richard Williamson . . .

In law school, I did everything within my power to conceal the existence of my middle initial *A*, wishing to avoid altogether the question of what it stood for. It might just as well have been a scarlet letter *A* for all the trouble I went through to avoid sharing it with anyone, including the registrar's office, which knew me simply as Richard Williamson. I was well aware of how high a bar my father had set for me, and I lacked the confidence to deal with the inevitable comparisons to the iconic Atticus Finch, even if he was only a fictional character.

"Mr. Williamson?"

Not at all certain my legs would support me, I rose from my assigned seat. A hush fell across the cavernous amphitheater-style classroom. Two hundred fifty pairs of eyes turned toward me. Behind their penetrating stares lay the sharpest minds I'd ever encountered. This was the class of 1991.

Who am I kidding? I don't belong here. I'm not one of them. I'm nothing but a fraud. A fraud! In a few seconds, everybody here will see—

"Ah! There you are, Mr. Williamson. I hear there's a bug going around. I was beginning to think you'd taken ill."

If you only knew . . .

My knees knocked together in a desperate rhythm. My left hand shook. My right hand didn't. Tightly bandaged, it was immobile and aching from what had happened the night before. *The night before . . .* My heart thumped, my head spun, my vision blurred, my throat gagged on something bitter . . .

"Mr. Williamson, will you please recite for us the facts in the case of *Hadley v. Baxendale?*"

I tried to clear my throat but couldn't. A whimper arose.

Is there a chill in the room?

"Mr. Williamson?"

My mind was blank. Nothing there. I'd been up until three in the morning, reading *Hadley* and seven other cases as well, and I had nothing to draw upon. My resources were completely depleted. In fact, they'd been depleted for some time, as I'd been up late every night since classes began in the final week of August—just three months after graduating from college, now a distant memory . . . an insubstantial fleck flittering and fading over the horizon . . .

In a chronic state of sleep deprivation, I was in no condition to recite my name, address, or phone number, let alone the facts of *Hadley v. Baxendale*. Could a person die from lack of sleep? If so, I had one foot planted firmly in the grave. *At least death would put me out of my misery*, I thought grimly.

A single drop of steaming-hot perspiration broke through my icy skin and crawled down the back of my neck.

"Mr. Williamson?"

"Um—"

"Mr. Williamson, we're waiting."

"I . . . uh—"

"Mr. Williamson, did you read this case or not?"

"Uh . . . yes, sir . . . I, I did."

"Then please provide us with the basic facts."

It had been only five hours since I'd read *Hadley*. By then, though, my brain had long since turned to mush.

Sitting at a long, narrow desk in my studio apartment—not much larger than my college dorm room—I tried to wrap my fully saturated brain around the meanings of all those words—*so many of them!*—glaring defiantly at me from page 237 of my contract law casebook. I read the first paragraph of the *Hadley* opinion—my eighth of the night—over and over and over again. Not a single word slipped through.

We're very sorry, sir, but we are filled to capacity, and we cannot accept any more orders until after Christmas, the voice of an insolent clerk informed me.

For at least ten minutes, I stared blankly at that first paragraph—no more than an unintelligible block of randomly distributed letters and symbols—before attempting to read it again. This time, I got through the first two sentences before my mind drifted off . . .

What time is it? Oh God, it's almost two o'clock in the morning! How much longer do I have to suffer before I can put this shit aside and get some sleep? Sleep . . . oh, how good it would feel to just—

I wonder if my classmates are still up . . . Don't be an idiot! They wouldn't be awake at this insane hour. They're legal geniuses. It's easy for them . . . so very easy! Then why does it have to be so hard for me? Because . . . because . . . because . . . well . . . the harder it is now, the sweeter my reward when I reach the pot of gold at the end of the rainbow . . .

Right?

Wrong! The reason it's so hard for me is simple—I don't deserve to be here. I'm in over my head, drowning, drowning, drowning . . .

Pale blue water . . . all around me, swirling bubbles . . . above me, a distant sun . . .

Becoming aware of the fact my mind had wandered away, I clenched my jaw, drilled my eyes more deeply into the page, and tried again and again and again . . .

How will I ever finish reading this goddamned case if I can't even get through the first paragraph?

Clasping my hands together in my lap, I rocked back and forth in my chair, seeking solace in the movement . . .

What's wrong with me? Why can't I do this? Maybe I should just quit and do something else, anything else . . . Quit? Never! I've never quit anything in my life. I'll get through this night and three years of law school if it kills me!

It might.

Leaning forward, I drew *Contract Law* to within inches of my face and tried once again to decode that elusive first block of text. The words blurred, came into focus, and blurred again. I tried again and again and again . . .

No fuckin' way! It's im-fucking-possible. I can't do this. No matter how many times I read this fucking paragraph, it doesn't sink in. It's never gonna sink in. Oh God, what if I get called on in class? I'm fucked. Fucked!

With that thought, my head came dangerously close to exploding. An image appeared. It was one of broken pieces of skull and gray matter strewn across the wall. I threw my hands into the air and cried out in utter frustration.

"I'm fucked!"

My mechanical pencil smacked the ceiling and landed behind me, splintering into multiple pieces that rolled around for a few seconds before coming to rest.

"Fuck! This is fucking bullshit! I can't do this! I can't do this! I can't do this!"

My face hot with fury and eyes stinging with sharp, needle-like tears, I leaped up and swiped a forearm across the full length of the desk. Everything went flying into the air—books, notebooks, pencils, pens, highlighters, paper clips, Post-it Notes, a green-shaded banker's lamp, a coffee mug filled with loose change, and a photograph of the family, taken the Christmas before Daddy died. The frame hit the floor with a *thwack* that cracked the glass into an intricate web of jagged lines, which obscured our smiling faces and distorted the picture into a bizarre cubist rendition, reminiscent of Picasso's early-twentieth-century work. My father's jaw had shifted to the right and become part of my mother's face. My nose appeared to take the place of one of Danny's ears. The dog's tail protruded from Danny's other ear.

The dog.

Our dog, Charlie.

Hit by a car the very next day . . .

My fury intensifying with each breath, I stomped over to the dresser, pulled out a drawer, emptied its contents, and tossed the drawer aside. On top of the dresser stood a rack with my CD collection alphabetized from *A* to *Z*. In one fell swoop, I sent the entire collection crashing to the floor. My next target, the couch, sat beside the dresser, just asking for it. Reaching over, I snatched a cushion and launched it into space. The projectile soared across the room and struck the opposite wall, taking out my high school and college diplomas. Following its diagonal flight path, I made for the bed and began a ruthless assault, stripping away the sheets before separating the mattress from the box spring and heaving it into the middle of the tiny apartment.

My rage wasn't yet satisfied. Breathing hard and with sweat dripping down both sides of my face, I flung myself into the bathroom, glared at the mirror, and growled. Staring back at me was a madman with veiny, bloodshot eyes and wild hair.

"Bastard! You're nothing but a worthless piece of shit. I hate you!"

I hammered my fist into the glass . . .

After cleansing the wound and bandaging my hand, I dug through the rubble in search of *Contract Law*. Finding the book buried under a swirling pile of bedsheets and a slew of notebooks, I returned to my desk and resumed working. Forcing myself to read to *Hadley's* bitter end, I retained almost nothing, except that a broken crankshaft was somehow involved.

When I'd read the very last word, I got up from the desk, staggered over to my stripped-down mattress, and collapsed, falling asleep before making contact.

"Mr. Williamson . . . Mr. Williamson! You're trying my patience. Can you tell us anything, *anything at all*, about this case?"

"Well . . . uh . . . it's . . . it's a case . . . an important legal case . . . involving a broken crankshaft . . . and, um—"

Someone behind me snickered. Wishing I could disappear, I shifted anxiously from one foot to the other. Another drop of perspiration rolled down the back of my neck.

"Please continue."

I racked my brain trying to come up with something more. It was over. I sat down.

"Mr. Williamson, please stand up and continue."

"For God's sake, give the poor kid a break," someone in my row whispered under her breath.

I don't want your pity.

"I can't, sir."

"And why not?"

"I think I've taken ill, after all."

"Well, then, instead of wasting any more of our precious time, why don't you go home and get some rest?"

Believe me, I wish I could go home.

Feeling the weight of those 250 pairs of eyes bearing down on me, I descended the steeply sloping stairs and passed the professor's lectern before exiting the hall and returning to my decimated studio apartment.

The commitment I'd made on the muddy banks of the Mississippi dwindled as law school continued to douse me with stiff doses of a cold, harsh reality I hadn't anticipated. *Clarence Darrow, indeed!* I'd be lucky to graduate. I was more than smart enough—I'd proven that in college—yet I lacked the confidence to succeed.

I'd been suffering from this crisis of confidence ever since the first day of classes. The other 1Ls were bright, capable, and self-assured—much more so than I could have possibly imagined. When called upon to face the Socratic method, each of them, in turn, had remained cool and composed, answering the professor's questions with both poise and eloquence. They were bound for greatness. And they knew it. When my turn finally came, I was a nervous wreck and left the room in disgrace. Clearly, I didn't measure up. Did I even belong in law school? If not, where did I belong?

When first-semester grades came out, I was placed on academic probation. Somehow, though, I made it through spring semester and completed my first year of law school with passing marks. In my second and third years, I loosened my ironclad grip and relaxed—just a little—into the flow of things. Remarkably, my performance improved. I never became the next Clarence Darrow, but I did manage to graduate in the middle third of the class. Through sheer determination and persistence, I survived the experience. More often than not, it felt like pushing a reluctant elephant up a flight of stairs, yet I endured and graduated in May of 1991.

After the pomp and circumstance of a rather tedious graduation ceremony, I returned to Heartland City, where my mother still lived. But not Danny. He'd moved on. After four years of college ball, Danny Williamson was making progress as a gifted southpaw and top prospect in the New York Mets' farm system. In fact, he'd just been promoted to the team's AAA affiliate in Norfolk, Virginia, a breath away from the big leagues. I was envious, *very* envious. After all, what could be better than getting paid to play baseball? I was also proud of my brother, *very* proud.

Finding an apartment within a few miles of Mom's house, I got settled and landed a job almost immediately as an associate attorney for a boutique law firm that specialized in defending wealthy individuals and corporate clients against, among other things, claims of malfeasance, corruption, fraud, and misrepresentation. Under the supervision of the firm's most senior partner, one James Arthur Kidwell III, I began a daily routine of performing such mundane tasks as wading through bankers' boxes and reviewing clients' financial statements. Meanwhile, I spent my evening hours and weekends preparing for the bar exam.

At first, I felt fortunate the firm's most senior partner had taken me under his wing. Later, I learned how ill fated my situation truly was.

During the job interview for my position with the law firm of Kidwell, Hammond & Joyce, Mr. Kidwell had been pleasant enough. On my first day of work, however, his persona changed dramatically. The unquestioned autocrat of the firm—even his partners cringed in his presence and kowtowed to his every whim—he summoned me that morning for a brief orientation and overview of the firm's ground rules.

Leaping from my chair, I threw on my blazer and made for his office. My brand-new wing tips sent a series of dull clicks echoing down the long and unusually narrow hallway. His door was closed. I gave it a light tap.

"Come!" he barked.

I braced and entered.

From behind his imposing mahogany desk, Jim Kidwell peered at me over a pair of reading glasses perched on the end of a stubby, rounded snout. His condescending eyes clearly communicated I was of no more importance to him than an insect. He motioned for me to sit. I took my place on the front edge of the proffered hardwood chair and fidgeted until I was reasonably comfortable.

He returned to his work—marking up some unfortunate associate's draft motion with a red pen, using a scorched-earth technique made infamous by an English professor of mine in college. Muttering to himself in a steady stream of expletives, he slashed and burned his way through the draft with such intense focus I began to suspect he'd forgotten about me. A clock with gilded roman numerals hung on the wall behind him. I followed the second hand's journey as it traveled in steady increments around the clock's drawn and weary face. A minute passed . . . and then two . . .

Jim Kidwell was about forty-five, maybe fifty years of age. His graying hair was thinning on top and cut cleanly over the ears. He had a round head and bulldog-like jowls that hung over the classically spread collar of a well-starched and immaculately pressed white dress shirt. A paisley tie was strapped around his thick neck and bound into a full Windsor knot, so tight it acted as a tourniquet that prevented the flow of blood from his head and turned his plump face bright red. A heaving barrel chest filled out his British-cut three-piece suit, charcoal gray with subtle chalk pinstripes. His brow furrowed and his mouth set into a permanent scowl, he leaned forward over his desk and assaulted the draft with vengeful swipes of his pen.

After five minutes—it seemed more like twenty—Mr. Kidwell put down the pen and stared hard at me as if trying to remember my name.

"Now, then, Mr. Williamson, there are a few items we need to cover before you begin your first day of work for the firm . . ."

The firm. He gave voice to these words in a way that made it clear he was referring not to *the* firm but *his* firm. His voice sharp and petulant, he blew through my orientation with an impatient air that suggested he ought not to be bothered with the chore of training a recent law school graduate. When finished with his monologue, he asked if I had any questions.

"No, sir."

"No, sir, what?" he shot back.

One of the ground rules was that he insisted on the formality of being addressed as "Mr. Kidwell" by the firm's associate attorneys, although he did allow his partners the privilege of referring to him as "Jim."

"No, sir, Mr. Kidwell."

"Good. Now get to work and don't disappoint me."

A motivational speaker Mr. Kidwell was not.

My first week on the job went by like the dizzying blur of the Erie Lackawanna passing the South Orange station of my youth . . .

Ya know, Ricky, we could make a killing sellin' lemonade to the suits when they return from work in the city. All we'd have to do is set up a stand right here on the platform—say, about five o'clock— and the money would roll in . . .

Yeah! We could make a killing. Let's do it!

Here comes another train, Ricky . . .

That Friday morning, I was at my desk early, preparing for a busy day, when Mr. Kidwell barged in to brief me on the facts of a case. The case involved a claim against a highly valued client, a successful serial entrepreneur named Charles McBridge. Throughout the briefing, Mr. Kidwell referred to the client as "Chaz," while sporting a wicked smile suggesting he was privy to a secret that would cause Mr. McBridge considerable embarrassment if it ever became public knowledge. According to the complaint, Mr. McBridge misrepresented the value of an industrial cleaning services business he'd built from the ground up before running it into the ground and selling off its assets to a soon-to-be disgruntled group of investors.

My task was to review every piece of paper in the war room— nothing more than a closet filled with bankers' boxes—and find something exculpatory. The boxes contained copies of all financial documents related to Mr. McBridge's business affairs, including the transaction transferring ownership of the cleaning business to the disgruntled investors. I knew what *exculpatory* meant, of course, but Mr. Kidwell hadn't given me much else to go on. So, without a well-defined mission and hardly any strategy at all, I accepted my marching orders and set about the task of methodically eyeballing each of thousands of documents in search of that one piece of evidence—the silver bullet that would stop the plaintiffs' lawsuit cold in its tracks, save the day for our client, and win me favor in the condescending eyes of James Arthur Kidwell III.

I entered the war room at eight thirty that morning and worked straight through the day, without breaking for either lunch or dinner. By eight o'clock that evening, I'd gone through each box and reviewed every document yet found nothing exculpatory. Discouraged, hungry, and exhausted, I fell to the floor and rubbed the sting out of my eyes with fingers hopelessly lacerated by paper cuts.

Now what? Do I start all over again?

It had been almost twelve hours since I'd seen the light of day. During that time, I'd been breathing the same old stale air, recycled over and over again through the office's outdated HVAC system. A tickle crawled up the back of my throat. I coughed. My vision blurred, and tiny, rotating stars appeared on the ceiling. A sharp flash of pain bolted up and down the back of my neck. Rolling to my side, I wiped my nose. It had been running incessantly, due, no doubt, to the clouds of dust that had risen from the bankers' boxes I'd opened throughout the day.

Reflecting on the goose egg my work had produced, it occurred to me I easily could have come across what I was seeking without even knowing it, for by midafternoon, all documents had begun to look the same. Getting up off the floor, I exited the war room and went to the bathroom. I splashed cool water on my face and vigorously blew my nose. It was still running, though, when I entered Mr. Kidwell's office to report my lack of success. Furtively wiping it on the sleeve of my wrinkled shirt, I braced myself to face the music.

"Unacceptable!"

His voice echoed down the empty corridors of the venerable law offices of Kidwell, Hammond & Joyce.

Everyone had gone home for the evening. Mr. Kidwell and I were the last men standing.

"Tomorrow morning, you will return to that war room and—leaving no stone unturned—you will go through each and every box and review each and every scrap of paper until you find me documentation that will put an end to this goddamned, frivolous, piece-of-shit lawsuit!"

"But it's Saturday, and I—"

"I don't care if it's Christmas Day! You will come in tomorrow morning, and you will not report back to me until your search has produced results. Understand?"

"Yes, sir, Mr. Kidwell," I said, resigning myself to my fate.

"Good. Now get out of my sight."

As I turned to go, I heard him muttering something like, "How the fuck can I bill the client for the time of an attorney who's not producing results? Unacceptable . . ."

My God . . . what have I gotten myself into?

Returning to the war room the following morning armed with eye drops, a box of Kleenex, and a bottle of Advil extra-strength caplets, I resumed my task with renewed vigor. My sleeves rolled up to my elbows, I dived in and spent the entire weekend scouring those dusty bankers' boxes for something, *anything* that might be of some use in defending against the investors' lawsuit. My search yielded nothing.

Perhaps the investors' lawsuit isn't so frivolous, after all.

On Monday morning when I reported back to Mr. Kidwell, he slammed down his pen, took a deep breath, and rolled his eyes toward the ceiling. His face turned fire-engine red. I braced for the inevitable lambasting. Instead, he simply frowned and handed me my next assignment. He said nothing—not a word of either criticism for my failure or thanks for the effort—but motioned me out of his office with a dismissive wave of his hand. Obediently, I left him stewing in his silent rage and plodded down the long, narrow hallway to my office, my head hung low.

Things settled down between Mr. Kidwell and me, and I was graced with a honeymoon period that lasted until the bar exam results were announced in early October. Opening the envelope from the Board of Law Examiners, I cautiously peered inside and then pumped my fist in an ecstatic burst of celebration when I saw that I'd passed. The celebration didn't last long, however. Soon after, Mr. Kidwell resumed his crusade to make my life a living hell.

"Now that you're an attorney, I'll pay you more, but in return, I expect a higher level of performance—a *much* higher level of performance."

He shot me his characteristic scowl, daring me to disappoint him.

At first, his tirades were sporadic—I never knew when he might strike—then, after the first of the new year, they became almost a daily occurrence.

It was a Monday in early January. As usual, I was filled with dread from head to quivering toe. Because Mr. Kidwell insisted on reviewing all my work before it went out the door, I was making one of my regular treks down the hallway with a motion to compel production of documents clutched tightly in my hand. I'd been working on the motion for hours, and it was almost seven o'clock in the evening when I entered his office.

"Unacceptable!" he erupted after reading for only a few seconds. "This is a simple motion to compel, and your argument is so convoluted that no judge could possibly follow it. Even I can't follow it, and I'm familiar with the case. Start over and bring me a revised draft by the end of the day."

"But the end of the day was two hours ago, and I—"

He shot me a fierce glance that stopped me midsentence. I turned away and left his office, my tail tucked between my legs.

On Tuesday, I stepped timidly into Mr. Kidwell's office with a memorandum summarizing the elements of a cause of action for fraud in federal court.

"Sit."

I handed him the memo and sat down.

Brandishing his favorite pen, he spent the next ten minutes slashing and burning his way through my memo, leaving a long trail of red behind. Meanwhile, I sat there clenching my fists in a futile attempt to stop my hands from trembling. The tremors had grown steadily worse. Now, they followed me home and into bed each night.

Before reaching the end of the memo, he stopped and smashed the desk with his fist. The clock fell from the wall and shattered.

"This is a waste of my time. Goddamn it, Williamson, you've totally butchered the English language. Again! This memorandum is a personal insult to me and a disservice to the client."

His face turned as red as the ink in his pen, which rolled lazily back and forth on his leather desk pad.

"Unacceptable! Totally unacceptable. Get out of my sight, Williamson."

In need of no further prodding, I got up and scurried out.

"Gross incompetence . . . makes me want to puke," he muttered as I started down the hallway.

On Wednesday, I hid in my office with the door closed, hoping to avoid another such encounter. He didn't summon me. Not wishing to tempt fate, I went home promptly at five o'clock.

On Thursday, he called me into his office and demanded a verbal summary of all case law in our jurisdiction in which the court addressed the availability of consequential damages in the event of a breach of contract for the sale of a business.

"I haven't finished my research. I need some more time."

"Let's hear what you have so far."

"Well . . . uh—"

"Speak up!"

Nervously, I stood before him—once again a lowly law student being subjected to the terrors of the Socratic method—and began my summary of the few on-point cases I'd found, stumbling badly over my words.

"Gibberish!" he interrupted. "Absolute gibberish. You haven't the slightest idea what you're talking about. Do you?"

He knew the answer but wanted me to say it.

I opened my mouth. No words came out.

"Oh, for God's sake. This is ridiculous. I might as well be talking to a deaf-mute. Richard *Atticus* Williamson, attorney-at-law extraordinaire," he said with a mocking laugh.

Atticus! How does he know?

"Your very presence in this office is an affront, a personal insult to me. Unacceptable! Your performance is unacceptable."

"But—"

"Leave!" He pointed to the door with his pen.

And so it went. I lived my life forever bouncing back and forth between states of absolute terror on the one hand and utter boredom on the other. The boredom engulfed me during endless hours in front of the computer doing legal research and writing countless memoranda of law either in support of this proposition or in opposition to that one. The terror set in whenever I was summoned to walk the long and narrow hallway to face the unrelenting wrath of Mr. James Arthur Kidwell III.

It would have been quite impossible during those days to articulate just why I stayed with the firm. But stay I did. Month after month, I endured Mr. Kidwell's escalating verbal assaults, too timid to fight back.

Whi-kisssh! Whi-kisssh! Whi-kisssh!

Swallowing my emotions, I buried them in the pit of my stomach, where they festered like a virulent cancer. Deep down, I must have believed I deserved to be the object of his outbursts. After all, he was right. I wasn't performing well. In fact, I was a miserable excuse for an attorney.

One afternoon in early May, I was drafting a response to a motion for production of documents when one of Kidwell's partners, a soft-spoken shadow of a man by the name of Lanny Hammond, came into my office and closed the door. Lanny was in his fifties yet appeared older. Age spots speckled his gray complexion. His hair was ghost white. Veiny hands dangled life-lessly at the sides of his navy trousers. Bent forward in a posture of heavy resignation, he seemed to be biding his time, waiting for a retirement of inevitable boredom and confusion.

"Jim treats all new attorneys like . . . well, you know . . . like this . . ."

Not so new anymore.

"For whatever it's worth, my advice is to ride out the storm."

His sunken, baggy eyes scanned the ceiling for something more to say.

"Well, anyway, I'll let you get back to it."

Without any further ado, he left me to contemplate his words.

Ride out the storm. Thanks for the sage advice, Lanny, but this is a storm without end . . .

The phone rang. It was Kidwell. He wanted me in his office right away.

Soon after Lanny Hammond's visit, the lilacs behind my apartment building sprang to life and released their intoxicating fragrance into the neighborhood. That scent—the *essence* of that scent—was of the kind that infuses one's entire being with joy and makes it possible to fall in love—if not with a person, then with life itself. And yet, it was at this very time when spring was reaching out to summer with a hopeful embrace that I fell into a deep depression. It was also at this time that I began to frequent the singles bars with a college acquaintance named Ethan Crane.

Although we had friends in common, Ethan and I were never especially close in school. In the spring of 1992, however, we reconnected and soon became "best friends," really just a euphemism for "drinking buddies." At first, we met only on the weekends. Then we discovered the Urban Experience, located only four blocks from my office. Soon, the Experience became our habitual after-work sanctuary. We started each night with a burger, a shot, and a beer chaser. After dinner, we drank . . . and drank . . . and then drank some more. Ethan drank because he liked to party and get laid. I drank to escape from the living nightmare of my unendurable situation at work.

After getting warmed up at the Experience, Ethan and I would meet up with our posse and go barhopping into the wee hours of the night. On those nights when I was too impaired to drive home—a circumstance that was becoming more the rule than the exception—I would simply crash at Ethan's place on the seventeenth floor of a downtown high-rise located less than a mile from my office. In the morning, I'd peel my dehydrated and aching body from Ethan's couch, get dressed, and stumble to work, picking up coffee and something for breakfast along the way.

After receiving yet another blistering rebuke from Kidwell—I was, of course, still butchering the English language—I left work on a brilliant Friday afternoon in early June and met Ethan for happy hour on the recently opened rooftop deck of the Experience.

Unacceptable!

Basking in the glorious sun with rush hour traffic buzzing below us like a swarm of bees returning to the hive, we kicked off the weekend. A plate of stupid-hot wings and blue cheese sauce arrived, followed by a pitcher of icy-cold Miller Genuine Draft and a couple of shots of 101 proof Wild Turkey. The first few notes of "Under the Bridge"—a Red Hot Chili Peppers anthem to loneliness and longing—trickled from the bar's rooftop speakers. An image of Kidwell's chubby face turning crimson as he berated me for my latest failure appeared and then evaporated into the bright sunlight . . .

"Here's to the weekend!" Ethan raised his shot glass. "*C'mooooon!*"

"To the weekend—"

Interrupting our toast, a bevy of the most beautiful young women I'd ever seen pranced past our table, their summer fashions on full display—fashions that left little to the imagination. Feeling a familiar sensation rising from deep within my loins, I watched longingly as they commandeered two tables directly across from us. One girl in particular caught my eye—a girl with golden hair. Floating in the breeze, her locks reflected the sun's rays into a translucent spiral that encircled her head like a halo.

A friend whispered in her ear. Her eyes grew wide. Clapping her hands together, she threw back her head and let out a laugh of unrestrained exuberance, one that made it abundantly clear she loved life, loved it with all her soul . . .

What's your secret?

Huh?

Realizing her laughter could be heard across the rooftop, she blushed and covered her cherry lips with a graceful sweep of her hand. Then, forgetting all about her embarrassment, she returned her friend's whisper. Soon, they were both laughing.

The final chord of "Under the Bridge" lingered in the space between us before finally yielding to the opening salvo of U2's "Mysterious Ways."

The girl with golden hair reminded me of someone from my past. I desperately wanted to reach out and connect with her, to speak with her, to know her. But I couldn't move. I was frozen to my seat. A cold sweat covered my body. My heart pounded. My vision blurred. She receded into a thick screen of mist. Her face, her golden hair, the halo . . . all gone . . .

A girl no more than ten years of age appeared from behind the screen. An angel . . . *My* angel! She was in a state of utter bliss, smiling and laughing and dancing to the beat of a music that had stopped playing years ago.

If only I could have found the courage to ask her to dance . . .

Without warning, my angel vanished.

A point of light pierced the mist and twinkled like a distant star. Advancing toward me, the light grew in intensity. I fell to my knees and reached out to touch what was now a glowing sphere the size of a human head. It was warm, soft, and smooth. In awe, I gazed upon its face. Fuzzy at first, and featureless, the face began to take shape . . .

Kimberly Turner!

You mean on a date? With you?

Bringing me back to reality, Ethan, who'd noticed my pre-occupation with the enchantress at the next table, elbowed me. "You like that girl, Ricky?"

"Ethan . . . she's . . . she's beautiful."

"So go talk to her!"

"I would, but . . . but I can't."

"Are you crazy? If you don't, I will!"

The waitress brought us our second round of shots. Slamming his, Ethan got up and swaggered over to introduce himself to the girl with golden hair. She looked up and smiled at him. I looked down and took an inventory of our table. Ethan had left me with half a plate of wings, a pitcher of beer, and a shot of Wild Turkey.

It's so easy for guys like Ethan . . . and Danny, of course—life's always been easy for Danny—I wish . . . I just wish . . .

Picking up my shot glass, I paused for a moment to inspect its rich amber contents before taking a gulp and chasing it with a mouthful of beer. I leaned against the wrought iron rail that separated me from the traffic below. Rush hour was over, yet the buzz continued . . .

The dog days of summer commenced with a meteoric rising of Sirius in the morning sky. Subject to the great star's whim, the winds shifted, and a violent procession of thunderstorms besieged Heartland City. August came and went. The thunderstorms ceased, and calm was restored. The storms in our office, however, showed no signs of letting up. Kidwell's abusive behavior continued unabated.

My late nights canvassing the bar scene with Ethan became more frequent. My drinking was nearly out of control. I came to work each morning with a splitting headache. The fog in my brain was so thick, I could barely log on to my computer. Performing the duties of an attorney became almost impossible.

How long can this go on?

As the 1992 regular season was winding down, the New York Mets called up Danny from the minors and inserted him into a major-league roster loaded with veteran pitching. While the Mets wallowed in fifth place in the National League East, he proved himself worthy of his promotion by earning a spot in the starting rotation and winning three games before the season ended. One New York paper touted him as "the only silver lining in an otherwise dismal season."

A celebrity now and larger than life, Danny came home to visit Mom and me for a couple of weeks in October. Together, we watched the Blue Jays beat the Braves four games to two in the World Series. It was good to see him, but we seemed to have little in common and not much to talk about other than baseball.

Before returning to the East Coast, he pulled me aside. "I didn't want to say anything, Ricky, but you look awful. What's going on?"

"It's nothing, really. It's . . . it's just that I've been working so hard. You know? I think I might be coming down with something . . . a cold, maybe the flu . . ."

"You're sure that's it?"

"Yeah, I'm sure."

"Okay." He picked up his suitcase. "Well, take it easy, buddy . . ."

When the holiday season came knocking, it brought with it a bracing northwest wind. Flurries filled the sky and coated the downtown city streets. It was the Monday before Thanksgiving, and the last straw was about to fall. Kidwell's attacks had become increasingly personal, and when I entered his office late that morning—still shaking the chill from my bones—he made the mistake of questioning my manhood.

"What kind of man are you, Williamson? Can you do nothing right? I send you to the courthouse to argue a simple motion to compel production of documents—documents we need to represent our client's best interests and that we are entitled to as a matter of law—and you fuck it up."

"In my defense, Mr. Kidwell, the other lawyer made a good argument."

"If you were a real man, you would've stood up to that other lawyer. You would've made your argument and defeated her. I heard she made mincemeat out of you."

Word travels fast in this town.

"And then . . . *and then*, just before ruling from the bench, the judge gave you one last chance to save face, to make the winning argument: 'Mr. Williamson, can you think of any reason I should grant your request, any reason at all these documents might somehow be *relevant* to your defense of this action?' Relevant! Why, he practically spoon-fed you the appropriate legal argument, yet you stood there and said nothing. You left the judge with no choice other than to rule against us."

I froze up. In the heat of the moment, I just froze up.

I knew the argument. I did. But I couldn't put it into words—just like in law school. Because of my incompetence, our whole case was very likely going down the toilet.

"Your performance is unacceptable. It reflects poorly on the reputation of this firm. It's an insult, a personal insult to me. What do you think they're saying on the courthouse steps about the kind of lawyers Jim Kidwell hires? They're questioning my judgment, Williamson. They're questioning my personal judgment. It's embarrassing. Shameful. I won't have it. This is unacceptable!"

Casting daggers at me with his beady little eyes, he took a breath and paused. By the hues of red appearing in his face, I could tell he wasn't finished with me. The worst was yet to come. I braced myself in the Kidwell hot seat and prepared to take my medicine.

"I told Chaz winning this motion would be a slam dunk. Now what do I tell him? Because of you, I'm going to look like an idiot in the eyes of the client."

"I'm sorry, Mr. Kidwell. I'm really—"

"Fuck your apology!" His face grew redder than I thought possible. "You have a responsibility to the client and to me as head of this firm. Make it right, Williamson. Be a man and take action. Make it right, goddamn it."

"What can I do? The judge has ruled—"

"'What can I do?'" he said, mimicking me in falsetto. "You sound like a little girl. A helpless little girl."

Little girl . . . little girl . . . little girl . . .

I'm on my hands and knees . . . in the murky waters of Parson's Pond . . .

Go ahead, Hen. Fuck him. Fuck him now. Fuck him while you can.

The hideously scarred face of Spencer Black materializes. His eyes are cold and lifeless. His breath is rancid.

Faster, Henry! Faster! Harder! Faster! Harder! Fuck this Williamson kid like the little girl that he is.

Returning to Kidwell's office, I found myself still in the hot seat, trembling uncontrollably. My head and neck burned with fever. My shirt was soaked with sweat. My heavy woolen suit was stifling. My throat tightened. I couldn't breathe.

"What do you have to say for yourself, Miss Williamson?"

"I can't . . . I can't—"

"I can't hear you."

"I can't . . . I can't—"

"This is pointless. You're wasting my time. Your performance as an associate attorney for this firm is unacceptable. Unacceptable!"

Grasping for my neck with both hands, I croaked, "I can't . . . I can't . . . breathe—"

"Jesus Christ, I hired a lawyer who can't even speak up for himself."

"I can't—"

"I don't understand a word you're saying, Williamson. I swear to God, you sound just like a little girl . . . or maybe, maybe you're . . . Are you a faggot, Williamson?"

His lips curled into a sadistic smile.

Faggot . . . faggot . . . faggot . . .

I raise the lid of my footlocker, and "FAGGOT" appears before me in big red letters. I slam it shut. Behind me, the room becomes filled with the fiendish sound of ten-year-old boys snickering.

"Oh my God! You are—"

"I'm . . . I'm—"

"—a faggot. That's it! You're a faggot!"

His words sliced into my soft underbelly like a newly sharpened fillet knife.

"I'm . . . I'm—"

"A faggot!"

He thrust the knife deep into my bowels where my fury had lain dormant for far too long.

That was it. I'd had enough. After a year and a half of unrelenting abuse, Kidwell had pushed me over the edge. Something inside me snapped, and the floodgates of hell opened. Exploding out of my chair, I launched myself over the top of his desk. The phone, the leather desk pad, his beloved red pen, everything went flying and crashed to the ground.

I grabbed him by the jowls. "I'm gonna kill you, you fucking son of a bitch!"

His chair toppled over backward, and I landed on top of him, pummeling his face with my fists. I hit him over and over again, bloodying him beyond recognition. The sight of the blood excited me and sent me into a fit of apoplexy.

Abandoning the assault on his face, I wrapped my hands around his neck and dug my thumbs into his windpipe.

"I'm gonna kill you, you fat fuck!"

"I can't . . . I can't . . . breathe—"

I strengthened my grip. "Speak up, Kidwell. I can't hear you."

"I can't . . . I can't . . ." His eyelids fluttered shut.

The next few seconds (or was it minutes?) faded into a blur . . .

At some point, the room became filled with people shouting and pulling me off Kidwell's barely conscious body. It took four men to drag me out of his office and wrestle me to the floor.

"Who's the faggot now, Kidwell?" I yelled at him from the hallway. "You want some more of this? Just say the word!"

He raised his head and peered over at me, sputtering and gurgling like an electric drip coffeemaker. I'd broken his nose so badly he was bleeding down the back of his throat and choking on a mouthful of blood. His neck was covered with horrible purple bruises.

The firm called an emergency meeting to discuss how to handle the situation. Kidwell recovered enough to attend the meeting and insisted that no one call the paramedics.

"It's not as bad as it looks," he said. "That little shit couldn't take Mickey Mouse in a street fight. He just got lucky. Sucker-punched me."

In the end, the partners agreed not to call the paramedics or involve the police, wishing to avoid an investigation that inevitably would unearth all the nasty details related to Kidwell's bullying and harassment of firm employees over the years. Instead, they called security to escort me out of the building with only a bankers' box containing my personal belongings. Without looking back, I made my way to the parking ramp, uncertain about my future, but for the first time in my life feeling empowered. It felt strange . . . and exhilarating . . .

I'm not a victim after all.

The next day, I received an overnight package from Kidwell, Hammond & Joyce that contained a generous offer of severance, contingent on my signing a nondisclosure agreement under which I'd be bound not to reveal the circumstances related to my separation from the firm. Anxious to get on with my life, I signed the agreement and in return received a year's salary and a favorable letter of reference signed by none other than James Kidwell himself. I was free . . . free and unemployed . . .

Tuesday, August 28, 2001

The mysterious boy I'd invited into my home that morning jolted me out of my trance with a full-throated sigh. Without opening his eyes, he rolled to one side, settled into the mattress, and resumed his peaceful slumber. No more than an arm's length separated us. Losing myself in the moment, I gazed upon his soft and untroubled features.

Was life ever so easy?

A heavy frown crept across my face, and the moment was lost. Not wanting to infect him with the negative emotions my memories of Jim Kidwell had stirred up, I quickly moved away from the bed.

Almost nine years had passed since my experience at Kidwell, Hammond & Joyce. Jim Kidwell was no longer a threat. Replacing him, another nemesis had come into my life. His name was Alexander Mountainfort, a business unit president for my current employer, Caste Enterprises.

The bedroom started to shrink. A wave of nausea rose into the back of my throat. It tasted of bile.

I've got to get out of here. Now.

Gathering David's wet clothes off the floor, I rushed out of the bedroom and down a flight of stairs into the dining room. Another flight of stairs, and I was in the basement. I entered a dust bunny–infested laundry room.

As I tossed the clothes into the washing machine, a thought that should have been obvious suddenly occurred to me.

This is crazy. What am I going to do with this boy? I can't take care of a child.

Back on the first floor, I slipped into my office. The hardwood floor creaked under my feet. A steel box I kept stashed in a desk drawer concealed a set of keys. Retrieving the box from behind a reserve of staples and Post-it Notes, I seized the keys and exited the house through the back door. The morning air had become as hot and thick as maple syrup. I scanned the vicinity to make sure I wasn't being observed. The neighborhood kids had returned to school. For them, summer was over.

The coast was clear.

Moving quickly, I proceeded to the door at the back of the garage. A toothpick was nestled in the doorjamb, exactly where I'd left it. *You can't be too careful.* I removed the toothpick, unlocked both the dead bolt and spring bolt, turned the doorknob, and stepped inside. It was a few degrees cooler than outside—only a few—and dark, except for a razor-thin beam of light sneaking in through a crack in the cardboard square ducttaped to the window above my workbench. A few stray dust particles entered the beam and swirled in a tumultuous dance. I shut the door behind me and flicked on the overhead light.

A rumpled utility blanket covered the workbench. My heart racing, I approached the bench and lifted one corner of the blanket, revealing a third-generation Glock 19 semiautomatic pistol (a compact version of the original Glock 17), chambered for the 9×19 mm Parabellum cartridge. Next to the Glock, two fifteen-round drop-free magazines had been meticulously arranged in parallel on the bench's grainy surface. With a flick of my wrist, I pulled away the rest of the blanket and unveiled a Model 6450 Colt AR-15 9 mm carbine semiautomatic assault rifle with collapsible stock and two thirty-round magazines. Stacked neatly along the back edge of the workbench, there were six boxes of ammunition containing 150 9 mm rounds for the Glock, and another 150 9 mm rounds for the Colt. The color of death, both weapons shone ominously under the light of a single dust-covered bulb hanging from the rafters above.

Breathing deeply, I wiped my sweaty brow and opened the workbench's top drawer. A downloaded copy of *The Anarchist Cookbook* lay there not quite so innocently, accompanied by a thick roll of duct tape and a spool of wire. I smiled a tight-lipped grin and closed the drawer.

Under the workbench, I'd stored the materials for assembling an IED, otherwise known as an improvised explosive device or, more simply, a bomb—one capable of producing a blast that would destroy the entire wing of an office building. An ordinary propane tank—the kind used for barbecuing—stood upright against the wall. A foot in diameter and a foot and a half tall, the white tank contained within its cylindrical walls twenty pounds of *"EXTREMELY FLAMMABLE PROPANE GAS."* Lined up next to the tank were one hundred boxes of two-and-a-half-inch roofing nails (to be used as shrapnel), a military-style canvas duffel bag (to conceal the tank), and a detonator, which would be linked to a cell phone for remote activation.

Beginning with my purchase of the Glock, I'd been stockpiling this arsenal for over six weeks. Everything was ready to go.

"Nothing's changed," I whispered out loud. "One more trip to the range, and Mountainfort and all those other bastards at Caste are gonna pay."

CHAPTER THREE

Tuesday, August 28, 2001

I LOCKED THE GARAGE AND RETURNED THE KEYS to the steel box before proceeding to the bedroom. David hadn't moved. He was still lying peacefully on his side. His eyes were closed. His lips were curved into a half-moon smile. His chest rose, crested, and fell in long, slow waves.

Reassuming my bedside position in my great-grandmother's rocking chair, I rested my elbows on my knees and leaned forward. The chair creaked, yet the boy didn't stir. I focused my gaze on his face and searched for signs of my long-lost childhood . . . There wasn't a line of worry . . . no creases, no wrinkles of doubt or concern . . . no, not a smidge of want, not a hint of anxiety.

Was I ever so innocent? So naïve? So trusting? Did I ever feel so safe? Did I ever sleep so peacefully?

He seemed vulnerable, so very vulnerable—delicate—like a newly hatched butterfly waiting for its wings to dry before taking first flight. And only inches from my grasp! Within my hands, I had the power to crush this butterfly—in one fell swoop—and determine its fate . . . and perhaps my own fate as well. It would be so easy to reach over with both hands and put an end to it all—the inevitable pain and suffering . . . a lifetime of misery awaiting him . . . After all, I knew how things were going to turn out. *I knew.*

I leaned in closer . . .

He doesn't belong here. He's a ghost . . . a ghost haunting my time, my place, my world. He'll only get in the way, cloud my thinking . . . and my thinking needs to be clear now.

I leaned in a little closer . . .

My heart thumping furiously, I raised my hands and leaned in closer still . . .

The Soulless Years: 1992–2001

"Time for another round, Ricky!"

"I don't know, Ethan—"

"*C'mooooon!* Bartender! Fresh horses!"

"Ethan, no, I think I've had enough. I'm . . . I'm not really feeling all that well. I'm gonna call it a night."

I tried to get up from the barstool. It was only nine o'clock, yet my head was buzzing, and my legs were like spaghetti.

"Don't go home." He flashed his winning smile. "The night is young!"

Surrendering too easily to his enthusiasm, I abandoned my lame attempt to get up.

"And there's tail everywhere!" he said, closing the deal. "Just look around."

I scanned the room. Ethan was right. The Sports Bar was packed to the gills, and there were beautiful women as far as the eye could see. It was the Wednesday before Thanksgiving, and the coeds were home from college for one final binge and then a quiet holiday with Mom and Dad before returning to school and revving up for finals.

Concert speakers hung menacingly from the rafters. "Rhythm Is a Dancer" filled the venue's cavernous space with an up-tempo dance beat. The sound originated from the speakers but seemed to rise from deep within the building's substructure. Adorned with portraits of local sports heroes, the walls shook. The buzz of windows tickled my eardrums like a swarm of ravenous mosquitoes. Each beat pounded a rivet into my head. Fortunately, the pain was dulled by alcohol.

In addition to three full-service bars, beer stations speckled the room, easily identified by red-and-yellow umbrellas and huge metallic tubs filled with ice and longneck bottles. The stations were attended by young women clad only in Daisy Dukes and tops that revealed both cleavage and midriff. Ethan and I sat at the largest of the three bars—a teardrop-shaped island situated at the room's epicenter. Behind us, a tidal wave of humanity descended upon an understaffed team of bartenders. Supported only by a hapless barback, they worked feverishly to keep up with demand.

Sitting there on the front line, we were in an enviable position, indeed. Arriving just ahead of the college rush, we had staked out our territory and ordered chicken wings, nachos, and a pitcher of beer. Above our bartender, a TV was tuned to an early-season NCAA basketball game.

Embracing the mega-sports-bar theme made so popular in the early '90s, the Sports Bar was a warehouse-converted nightclub featuring dozens of TV screens broadcasting live sporting events from around the world. The screens were on full display throughout the immense space—on every wall, behind each of the bars, and even in the restrooms. *Heaven forbid we miss even so much as a millisecond of our favorite team's march toward glory,* I thought with a grimace on my face that easily could have been mistaken for indigestion brought on by the wings, or more likely, the mountainous plate of Nachos Magnificos that had once been smothered with jalapeños, olives, onions, tomatoes, shredded lettuce, spicy ground beef, and some kind of melted cheese sauce resembling liquefied Velveeta or perhaps Cheez Whiz. Now, only an empty plate remained.

Kitty-corner from our island and clear across the room, a dance floor rose out of the crowd and took the form of a boxing ring, complete with padded posts, ropes, and even stools for those needing a break between rounds. Only females of the species occupied the ring. But a pack of hungry wolves, emboldened by liquid courage, had gathered. Salivating, they lurched forward. It was time to move in for the kill.

Ordinarily, I had no interest in dancing, yet in my boozy state, I was tempted—so very tempted—and even felt myself being drawn along with the pack toward the delectable prey inhabiting the makeshift ring. If I didn't take immediate action, it would be too late. Closing my eyes, I imagined myself gliding through the crowd, stepping into the ring, taking the first girl I saw by the hand, and busting a move—

"Ricky!"

My eyes popped open. I hadn't moved. My butt was fastened securely to the barstool. Across the full length of the room, a constellation of heavenly bodies glistened under flashing lights, moving together in synchronicity.

So far away . . . yet close enough to touch . . . If only, if only—

"Hey, Ricky! Snap out of it!"

I turned toward Ethan and tried to comprehend the words coming out of his mouth.

"I know why you're down." He placed a hand on my shoulder. "It's that stupid job. Listen to me and listen to me very carefully, amigo. Kidwell is an asshole. A serious asshole! You'll get another job, a much better job. But forget about all that for now. Tonight, let's set our worries aside and party. Bartender! Two Wild Turkeys!"

The drinks came.

Ethan raised his glass. "Carpe diem!"

"Carpe diem." I downed my shot of Turkey.

The rest of the night was a blur . . .

Stark naked. The following morning, I found myself dressed in nothing but a tangled morass of randomly strewn sheets and pillows. Next to me lay a young woman curled into the fetal position. She was a stranger to me—perhaps an apparition conjured by my subconscious in a forgotten dream. Sound asleep, she breathed as deeply as an ICU patient on life support.

She's alive! But is she real?

Focusing my sleep-encrusted eyes, I traced an imaginary line along the gently sloping landscape of her body—her long and graceful thigh, the elegant curve of her hip, the valley created by a torso that eventually ascended along her rib cage and into the roundness of a breast the size of a grapefruit, perfectly ripe and punctuated by an areola that eyed me with unabashed sass. As she breathed in, the breast rose in a magnificent arc toward the sky and hung there like a full moon at its apogee—momentarily suspended between heaven and earth—before falling downward and coming in for a soft landing. After four seconds at rest—*one one-thousand, two one-thousand, three one-thousand, four one-thousand*—the breast rose again, and the cycle repeated itself over and over as I watched in a state of utter enchantment.

Her plain-featured but pretty face was framed by a long wave of jet-black hair that cascaded over her snow-white shoulders. Her eyelids were painted a subtle shade of blue, like the Caribbean Sea at dawn. Except for rosy cheeks, her skin was fair. Her expression was calm, like that of a child.

Suddenly, her mouth stretched open, and she let out a well-rounded yet delicate yawn that was music to my ears. Smacking her lips together, she made a satisfied *mmmmmm* sound and fell back into an endlessly repeating sequence of breathing in and out . . . in and out . . .

I wanted to touch her and bring her sleeping eyes to life, but there was an invisible gulf between us I dared not cross. It should have been so easy to reach out and stroke her hair with my fingers, to draw her face toward mine, to press our lips together in a tender kiss. But the gulf was thousands of miles wide. We lived in different worlds that had collided—clinging together for only the briefest of moments—before separating into our respective positions at either end of an infinitely expanding universe.

Oh my God, what have I done?

I rolled onto my back and focused my gaze on a water stain emerging like a storm cloud from the ceiling of a studio apartment I'd never before visited and would never visit again. It was Thanksgiving morning, and I was terribly hungover—my head throbbing with pain, and my mouth as dry as the windblown sands of the Atacama Desert. It didn't help matters that the cluttered room smelled of alcohol, cigarettes, body odor, and sex.

A sudden wave of nausea rippled through my body. Terrified I was about to lose last night's nachos all over the bed, I clasped both hands over my mouth and swallowed. Fortunately, this preventative measure proved unnecessary, as the feeling quickly subsided.

First slithering out of bed and then gathering my widely scattered clothes, I managed to get dressed and find my way to the exit. Holding my breath, I turned the knob and eased the door open. Just before ducking out, though, I stole a final glance at Sleeping Beauty and threw her an invisible kiss . . .

Under a drab sky blanketed from one horizon to the other with thick, low-hanging clouds, I drove my Corolla, pockmarked with rust, through the deserted city streets toward home. My body craved nourishment, yet the mere thought of food repulsed me. When I got home, I would eat nothing but instead drink a tall glass of cold water, go directly to bed, and somehow rise in time to make it to my mother's house by three o'clock for Thanksgiving.

Requiring fresh air to prevent the nausea from returning, I cracked open the driver's-side window a couple of inches. The air was frosty yet still. Not a breath of wind. As I drove, the oppressively gray morning seeped into the car's interior, sank into my bones, and forced me to surrender to its will. Depressed and cold, I pressed the car window button, and the crack disappeared.

Up ahead, a traffic light turned from green to amber to red. As there were no other vehicles and no witnesses in the vicinity, I toyed with the idea of blowing through the intersection. At the very last second, however, I slammed on the brakes. They squealed in mighty protest. The tires fishtailed and skidded, leaving a thin veneer of rubber on the road. The Corolla came to a stop.

The red light glared down at me. A puff of smoke escaped from under the hood. The engine rattled and hummed to an unsteady beat. I gripped the wheel and contemplated the hopelessness of my situation.

This is not the life I want. What do I have to do to turn things around?

As I sat there waiting for an answer, images of Sleeping Beauty pushed their way through my alcohol-embalmed brain and into the hazy foreground of my barely conscious state of awareness. That perfect breast, her long black hair, her milky-white skin, her painted eyelids, her cheeks, those lips . . .

I only wish I knew her name . . . I'd give anything . . .

"Damn it, I'm so stupid!" I pounded the dashboard with my fist.

I should've woken her. I should've woken her and asked her for her name . . . and her number. But instead, I snuck out of there like a fucking coward! I should turn around and go back right now . . . with flowers . . . Yes, with flowers! That's what I'll do . . . except . . . except, I'll never find an open florist—everything's closed on Thanksgiving Day. Besides, it's too late now . . . much too late . . .

The light turned green.

I can't do this anymore. Somehow . . . somehow, I've got to get to the other side . . .

I stepped on the accelerator and was home in twenty minutes.

Christmas Eve . . . no, check that . . . Christmas Day now . . . well, strictly speaking, it's Christmas morning, early Christmas morning . . . 2:30 . . . 2:31 . . . No, not waiting for the jingle of Santa's sleigh bells or the prancing of hooves on the rooftop of my apartment building . . . gave up on that fairy tale long ago . . . In bed . . . alone . . . bottle of pills and a fifth of Jack on my nightstand . . .

"It's getting late, Ricky. Just when were you planning on leaving?"

"Leaving? But, Mom . . . it's, it's Christmas Eve, and I thought . . . I mean . . . I don't have any—"

"Listen to me, Ricky. This is my first Christmas with Norm, and I've prepared a romantic dinner for just the two of us. You understand, don't you, dear? We'll see you in the morning. We'll open presents then. Afterward, we'll have Christmas dinner together. Danny is flying in with his fiancée. Oh, but you knew that already. They should be here by two . . ."

Don't belong . . . don't belong . . . don't belong . . . nowhere . . . got no place in this world to call home.

Can't blame her—after all, you're not lovable. You get that, don't you? Now, maybe if you were her real son . . .

All alone . . . all alone . . . all alone . . .

Don't you wish you were dead? You got nobody. There's nobody in your life . . . and it's Christmas . . . Christmas . . . Christmas . . .

Wait a second! What about Sleeping Beauty? You know, the girl from Thanksgiving morning?

She could never love someone like you. Don't you get it, Williamson? You don't deserve . . . don't deserve . . . don't deserve . . .

Help me . . . someone . . . please help me!

Danny's found someone . . . of course Danny's found someone. Danny always gets what he wants—a major-league baseball career, lots of money, someone to love, someone who'll love him in return . . . an actress—glamorous type, young, vibrant, sexy, cover of People magazine, huge tits (bet they're fake), television and movies . . . Someday, they'll have children . . . and you'll be Uncle Ricky . . . you'll always be Uncle Ricky, standing alone in the corner with your hands in your pockets . . .

Even your mom has someone now . . . married just four months ago . . . to Norm—your stepfather—nice guy, don't you think?

"We'll see you in the morning. We'll open presents then."

Or not. What if they don't see you in the morning . . . on Christmas morning? After all, nothing's for certain. What if you don't make it through the night?

2:38 a.m. now . . . just want to sleep . . . and forget . . . forget everything . . . but no matter how hard I try, I can't—there's no sleep in this body . . . and no forgetting . . .

Whi-kisssh! Whi-kisssh! Whi-kisssh!

Hey! Listen, Ricky. Those newlyweds are at it again.

Thump-a-thump, thump-a-thump, thump-a-thump . . .

They're upstairs—right above you—lost in the rapture of each other, engaged in another session of yuletide lovemaking, and you're down here with your dick in your hand.

Thump-a-thump, thump-a-thump, thump-a-thump, thump—

Ahhhhh!

2:56 . . . 2:57 . . .

They have each other. You have nobody. Nobody! Wouldn't you do anything not to feel this way any longer? C'mon, be honest. Don't you wish you were dead? It'd be so easy, so ridiculously easy to bring this grand absurdity to an end—an absolute, final end. All you have to do is fill the bathtub with hot water and then slowly lower your pathetic body in . . . inch by inch by inch . . . watching your pasty skin turn pink, then red as a lobster . . . relaxing into, savoring the steamy heat—your nose and mouth barely above the waterline—taking your last few breaths on earth . . .

Ahhhhh . . . What a relief!

It's almost over now. Just reach for that freshly sharpened kitchen knife, its blade alive with the illumination of a million distant stars twinkling under the bathroom lights . . . That's it, you're doin' fine, you're doin' just fine, Ricky—

Stop it! Enough already. These thoughts in my head, these wild, crazy thoughts swirling around in my head . . . They're not me! They're not me! They're not—

You don't wish to be dead?

No! I want to live! I'd rather bear those ills I have than fly to others that I know not of . . . Yes, okay, yes, I admit it. Like Hamlet, I'm a coward . . . a coward living parasitically on the face of Mother Earth, breathing her air, drinking her water, eating her food . . . contributing nothing, caring for no one, only myself—my miserable, self-absorbed, loathsome self . . . but wanting more out of life, much more . . . wanting to love another, to dive headfirst into my broken heart, to find the love that surely must be buried within, and share it with somebody special . . .

Is there . . . Is there anybody out there? Anybody who feels—

3:17 a.m.

Is this night ever going to end?

I was up all night, going back and forth between wanting to end it on the one hand and holding on for dear life with the other.

I held on.

It must have been just before dawn when I finally dozed off into a sweet, dreamless oblivion filled with nothing, *nothing* at all— no thoughts tormenting a once-tempestuous mind, no competing voices echoing back and forth inside a weary head, no sound whatsoever, no light, no past, no future, no me . . . just a clear and open space of pure nothingness . . .

I slept straight through Christmas morning and most of the afternoon, getting up only once to go to the bathroom.

The sun cast long, thin shadows that appeared as prison bars on the interior wall of my bedroom. Peeling myself from the mattress, I made my way to my feet and staggered into the kitchen for a sandwich. In the soft amber twilight, I took a greedy bite of my pastrami and rye and wiped an errant smear of mayo from the corner of my mouth. In the adjoining room, a blinking red light beckoned. With a deep sigh, I went over to the answering machine, pressed the Play button, and listened to no fewer than a half dozen messages from my mother. She sounded worried, frantic.

"Ricky, where are you? Are you all right? Don't you know it's Christmas Day? Danny and Courtney are here. Everyone wants to see you. They're all wondering where you are. Please, please call!"

Instead of calling, I returned to the kitchen and finished my sandwich, chasing it with a can of Pepsi. *Now what?* I stared hard at my plate, clean except for a few randomly scattered caraway seeds. My apartment succumbed to the dark of night. Still, I held my stare. After at least half an hour of first straining my eyes to count and recount the seeds and then poking at them blindly with a finger, I got up from the table, found my way to the telephone, and called my mother back.

She answered on the first ring. "Ricky? Thank God. Is it really you?"

"Yes, it's me."

"Where on earth have you been?"

"My apartment. I'm just gonna stay home today."

"But, Ricky, it's Christmas—"

I hung up the phone and went back to bed.

With no job to pry me out of bed, I slept in each morning during the week between Christmas and New Year's and never once left my apartment, not even to check the mail or take out the trash. I became the lone wolf endlessly pacing back and forth within the strict confines of my one-bedroom lair. I was numb. I felt nothing—neither good nor bad, happy nor sad, alive nor dead. I simply existed, going through the motions of daily life with spiritless disinterest. I ate when I was hungry, drank when I was thirsty, and slept when I was tired. I masturbated frequently but indifferently. I didn't bathe or groom. My hair became greasy and matted; a patchy beard appeared in the mirror. Every day, I wore the same tattered pair of sweatpants and hooded sweatshirt with holes in the elbows. The bed was left unmade. The dishes piled up in the sink.

Rising later each morning until finally waking at noon, I was left with only a few short hours of dreary daylight. At night, I would slip under the covers, scoot close to the window, and howl at a crescent moon hanging precariously over the courtyard.

When not engaged in either pacing or howling, I sat idly on the sofa and stared into empty space. Sometimes the television set was on, sometimes not. When it was on, I barely noticed the parade of commercially acceptable but mindlessly inane trash passing before my vacant eyes.

Knock, knock.

This sudden and unfamiliar sound jolted me out of a trance.

"Who's there?"

"It's your mother."

It was late in the afternoon of Thursday, December 31. New Year's Eve. The very last shadows of 1992 were creeping into the living room and filling the space with a somber haze. I hadn't been expecting a visit, certainly not one from my mother. Having been glued to the sofa all afternoon watching enormous snowflakes float past the icy windowpane, I was unsure of my legs. Haltingly, I planted one foot on the floor and then the other before proceeding to the door.

"What do you want?" I asked, not out of spite but a genuine sense of curiosity.

"I'd like to speak with you."

I opened the door a crack, allowing a whiff of fresh air to enter my apartment for the first time in a week.

"Ricky, will you please let me in?"

With a tug, I swung the door open, returned to my post, and lay down with my feet up and head supported by a cushion. She followed me in, shook the snow off her coat, and sat in a wingback chair next to the sofa. I didn't look at her. Rather, I kept my eyes focused on the ceiling.

After she settled in, there was a long silence. I could feel her eyes poring over me and my wildly disheveled appearance. A horn blared. Brakes screeched. I braced for impact, but there was none. A near miss.

"The roads are icy," she said.

"Yeah."

She took a deep breath. Then, without further ado, she began to speak. I felt certain she was going to apologize for kicking me out of her house on Christmas Eve. Instead, she proceeded to explain the reasons for her actions—to justify herself to me! I didn't say a word. I simply listened while maintaining my steady focus on the ceiling.

"Please try to understand it from my point of view, Ricky. After your father died, I was alone. Almost twenty years. And then, after giving up any hope of ever being happy again, I found someone—someone who means an awful lot to me. Norm makes me feel special, Ricky. He's a good man, and he treats me well. That's important in a relationship. And rare. Honestly, I didn't think I'd ever remarry. But I did. I fell in love and got married.

"For the first time in a long while, I'm happy. I feel so, so grateful . . . so blessed to be with Norm, and I want to take full advantage of the time we have together. I've learned the hard way that time is precious. From now on, I want to make each moment of my life count. I deserve this, Ricky. I deserve to be happy, and I don't think it was unreasonable or even selfish to want to be with my husband on Christmas Eve and enjoy a romantic dinner with him."

I said nothing. I felt nothing.

"Ricky, are you listening to me?"

I nodded.

"Your actions affect others, you know. You really hurt Danny and me when you didn't show up on Christmas Day."

She was seeking an apology from me. *Not gonna happen.* I turned onto my side. The sofa's backrest was within inches of my face, muffling the sound of each breath.

"Please don't shut me out, Ricky. I know I've made mistakes, but I'm still your mother, and I love you."

As she continued, her voice became increasingly shrill.

"Can't you understand that I'm a human being with feelings? I get sad and lonely, just like you do. I missed your father so much . . . so, so much. I still miss him. He was the love of my life. We were so happy together—all of us—and then he was gone. *Gone.* I didn't think I could survive without him. So, I drank. I drank and cried myself to sleep every night . . . softly . . . into my pillow . . . so you boys wouldn't hear . . ."

Then I did feel something. For the first time in a week, I felt an emotion—a wave of sadness surging through me, rising to the surface, searching for a way out. I tried desperately to control it, to hold it in. It was no use. Teardrops escaped from the corners of my eyes and formed a string of pearls that rolled down the side of my head and fell into the sofa's cottony fabric. With my back turned toward my mother, all evidence of my inner state was hidden from her view. She couldn't know what I was feeling. She couldn't know how much I wanted to turn around and embrace her.

"Then, after many, many months and years of grieving, finally . . . finally, the pain of losing your father started to loosen its grip. Bit by bit and gradually over time, I began to heal. Eventually, I learned to survive and function in this world without your father. But, Ricky, I was so lonely, so very, very lonely for so many years. I'd actually given up on the notion of ever falling in love again until I met Norm.

"Ricky, are you listening? Are you? Show me a sign you can hear me. Please, please talk to me. Say something. Anything! Anything at all . . ."

Unable to respond, I remained firmly entrenched in my bunker. Safe. But alone. *Alone.*

Following an interminable silence, a deep sigh of resignation filled the room. It was over. She gathered her things, lifted herself out of the chair, and plodded across the hardwood floor. Each footstep fell heavy on my heart. Still, I couldn't speak. I couldn't move.

When she reached the door, she paused, placed her hand on the knob, and turned it. The hinges creaked—

"Wait. Don't go."

Springing from the sofa, I ran across the room and into her outstretched arms. In tears, we stood there by the door, shaking with emotion in each other's embrace.

"I'm sorry, Mom. I'm so sorry . . ."

After the tears dried, we had a good, long talk. We even shared a laugh over the hopeless state of my beard. She invited me to her house for dinner, but I politely declined, explaining that I wanted to get to bed early and start the new year fresh. With an understanding smile, she kissed me and left.

No longer a caged wolf, I felt lighthearted and spry as a dancer. Spinning away from the door in my stocking feet, I executed a world-class pirouette and stuck the landing with arms stretched triumphantly toward the balcony. The sold-out theater exploded in applause. I took a bow and found myself facing the living room window of my once-again-empty apartment.

Before I had an opportunity to contemplate my next move, the telephone rang. It was Ethan inviting me out for a New Year's Eve celebration he guaranteed I would never forget. I begged off.

"Aw, come on now, Ricky! Don't leave me high and dry. It's New Year's Eve. You've got to come out. I'm tellin' ya—"

"Not this time, Ethan."

I hung up the phone without giving him a chance to finish his sales pitch.

Having now declined two invitations, I had the evening to myself. I was alone yet free. With no interest in staying up to watch the ball drop from Times Square, I lit a candle, prepared myself a simple meal of split pea soup and saltines, and went to bed well before midnight. Sleep claimed me as soon as my head touched the pillow . . .

It's raining. Hard. I'm standing in a forest surrounded by lichen-infested trees reaching for me with their crooked branches. My path is blocked by a fallen oak. I take a step backward, but it's too late. They have me in their clutches, strangling me . . . A sudden clap of thunder, and the rain comes to a stop. The trees withdraw. I'm safe . . . for the moment . . . Soaked to the bone and freezing cold, I gather wood for a fire. I start the fire by rubbing two sticks together,

just like Chad—from Camp Abenaki Valley—taught us so many years ago. Staring into the blazing fire, I speak to my father.

Daddy, I know I'm not living the life you had in mind for me. I know you must be disappointed. But I'm ready now to turn things around. Daddy, if you're listening, I need your help. What's my next move? Please show me the way. Give me the strength and confidence I need . . .

I sit by the fire all night, waiting for an answer . . .

When day breaks, I stand up, stretch my aching body, and move away from the smoldering embers. There's somewhere I need to go, something I need to do. Instead of returning to the water's edge, I step over the fallen oak and go deeper into the forest . . .

In the morning, I rose with the sun and hopped out of bed. Restless from a week of being cooped up in my stuffy apartment, I first emerged from my self-imposed confinement to take out the trash. Opening the building's back door, I was welcomed into the world by a blast of fresh arctic air and brilliant sunshine reflecting off mountains of snow plowed to either side of the alley. Temporarily blinded by the light, I staggered backward before righting myself and stepping into four inches of crystalline powder. There I stood for a few moments, taking it all in and gazing spellbound into a limitless sky.

On the power line high above, a host of chattering sparrows paused to take note of my presence. They regarded me for only a second or two before inviting me, with a flourish of song, to proceed. Obliging them, I trotted through the new snow to the dumpster and heaved my trash bags over the edge.

Well done, well done, well done, the birds seemed to sing.

I returned inside.

Invigorated by the fresh air and sunshine, I worked feverishly all day and for the entire balance of the weekend, scrubbing and scouring every inch of my apartment. When I was finished, it sparkled like a diamond. The following week, I cleaned myself up with a shave and a haircut, bought a new suit, updated my résumé, and started searching for a job.

Early that spring, I was offered a position as in-house legal counsel for SteadFast Components, a locally based manufacturer of computer hardware parts. Its newly christened world headquarters resided in a Heartland City suburb, Golden Meadow, about a thirty-minute commute from my apartment. Although my first instinct was to jump at the offer with a resounding yes, I bit my tongue and took a few days to think it over.

On its face, SteadFast seemed like the perfect opportunity for any ambitious young professional wishing to make headway into the business world. Founded in the late '40s at the beginning of the postwar economic boom, SteadFast was a solid company with excellent prospects for growth in both domestic and international markets. The world headquarters building was a beautiful, state-of-the-art facility with a breathtaking three-story glass atrium that allowed natural light to flow into the building's wide-open interior spaces and fill the hearts of employees and visitors alike with warm feelings of community and goodwill. No expense had been spared in its construction.

The people at SteadFast were friendly. They'd made me feel at home throughout the interview process. There were opportunities for international travel and career advancement. The pay and benefits were competitive.

Yet I couldn't help thinking my father would have been less than proud of a decision to pursue a career as an in-house corporate attorney, a soldier in a battalion of legal professionals dedicated to managing risk and protecting company assets against foreign invaders, while facilitating the smooth and orderly flow of commercial transactions necessary for maximizing profits and shareholder value. Although he never actually said so, I believed he had something more heroic in mind for me—something other than sitting in a suburban office building and dreaming up legal theories to validate company interpretations of arbitrary rules of commerce, which he would have described as "illusions shared by agreement."

Sitting on my sofa with the offer letter cradled in my hand, I listened as my father's sonorous voice filled my head.

When a critical mass of people in society decides to share the same illusion, that illusion becomes fact, law, or doctrine. In effect, we agree to play by the same rules, but we don't always choose a game worthy of us. When we choose to play a game based purely on the profit motive, life becomes dull and passionless. When we choose to play a game based on higher ideals such as freedom, peace, and love, life takes on a brilliant luster.

What kind of game was I about to play? Was it a game worthy of me? Or was I about to sell my soul to the devil in exchange for a lousy buck?

The career path before me was a far and lonely cry from the ideals of social justice my father had held so dear and that were embodied so elegantly in his favorite fictional character, Atticus Finch. The idea of fighting, as Atticus did, for the rights of the weak and disenfranchised held some romantic appeal for me, yet there was one small problem. As I learned from my experience at Kidwell, Hammond & Joyce, I was terrified of courtrooms—a deathly affliction for an aspiring trial attorney. Actually, it wasn't courtrooms per se but public speaking in any forum that terrified me.

What kind of hope could I have offered the falsely accused Tom Robinson in Harper Lee's *To Kill a Mockingbird*? Atticus Finch may not have been successful in defending him, but Ms. Lee's Depression-era tale of life in a small Southern town did send a message that inspired Americans of good conscience to rise up in support of the civil rights movement. Like Harper Lee, I wanted to make a difference. A real difference. Yet I felt trapped. Trapped by a stifling fear on the one hand and the lure of security offered by a tedious daily routine in corporate America on the other. I wanted to do something big. But how much of this was ego and how much was an authentic desire to help others? I wanted to live an extraordinary life, yet how many times could I repeat this worn-out mantra before losing all credibility with myself, God (if there was one), and my long-deceased father?

Daddy, I know this isn't what you had in mind for me, but I can't sit around in my apartment for the rest of my life. I need to reenter the world. I need to start earning a living. I'm going to take the job.

I accepted the job offer that afternoon and began work on a Monday, settling into the unremarkable yet profitable life of a dutiful corporate soldier.

At first, I kept mostly to myself and resisted becoming part of a mainstream culture that shared little in common with my father's high ideals. I took lunch at my desk. I politely declined invitations to join my colleagues for happy hour. I did what was asked of me but didn't go the extra mile. Before long, however, I became a willing if not eager model employee, following the herd through the bountiful pastures of economic prosperity that prevailed through the remainder of the decade.

I bought a house. And a car—a 1993 Audi 90 CS Quattro Sport. Bright red, it came with all the latest bells and whistles, including a 2.8-liter V6 engine, five-speed manual transmission, and a sunroof. I developed a strict routine of waking up early each morning to beat rush hour traffic and arrive at the office by six thirty. I became capable and efficient in my job. Transactional law suited me much better than a litigation practice, and I thanked my lucky stars I was no longer working for the litigation-savvy boutique of Kidwell, Hammond & Joyce.

I was busy. Very busy. Without a personal life to offer up in sacrifice to the corporate altar, however, I barely noticed the excessive workloads and long hours, accepting them as normal.

I found peace in my work and in my life . . . a precarious peace . . .

The '90s passed like sand through my fingers on the southwest Florida beaches of my childhood, a world inhabited by my brother, my mother, my father, an old banyan tree, a Donald Duck inner tube, and an angel—an angel with equal doses of love and pain residing in her boundless eyes . . .

In my grown-up world—inhabited by lawyers, paralegals, legal secretaries, administrators, managers, executives, sales personnel, customers, and suppliers—the dawn of a new millennium was approaching. Fears of some unimaginable catastrophe, to be caused by the notorious Y2K bug, weighed heavily on everyone at SteadFast. Our customers were demanding warranties to protect against claims of loss of data or some other end-of-the-world scenario. Consequently, I spent countless hours in front of the computer, drafting language to appease their concerns. Of course, the year 2000 arrived quietly and without the coming of the widely predicted global apocalypse.

In those first few days of the new year, I took inventory of my situation at SteadFast. I felt challenged. From time to time, I even felt stimulated by my work. But with no promotions and only incremental increases in salary during my seven years with the company, I grew restless in my job. I thirsted for more . . .

More came with surprising speed. On the morning of a cold and cloudy Valentine's Day, our CEO summoned all WHQ employees to report for a previously unannounced meeting, to be streamed via webcast to off-site employees throughout the world. Mystified, I joined my coworkers in descending upon the auditorium and taking our places in the steeply inclined stadium seats. From the last row, I commanded a view of almost nine hundred people. An anxious hush fell over the crowd. Our CEO took the stage and found his way into the spotlight. A technician in the control booth gave him the thumbs-up. Clearing his throat, our fearless leader dispensed with a series of insipid pleasantries before informing us that an agreement had been signed the night before—an agreement under which electronics giant Caste Enterprises would acquire SteadFast.

Monday, February 14, 2000

CASTE TO ACQUIRE STEADFAST COMPONENTS FOR $2.1 BILLION

PALO ALTO, CALIF. (AP) – Caste Enterprises (NYSE: CEN) announced today it will acquire SteadFast Components (Nasdaq: SFCI) for $2.1 billion in a $28.50 per-share all-cash deal expected to close in the second calendar quarter of 2000.

Caste, a Silicon Valley–based manufacturer of a wide array of high technology electronic components with over $25 billion in annual revenues, has been following an aggressive strategy over the past three years of acquiring businesses to grow its Computer Electronic Solutions business segment into a global market leader. The acquisition of SteadFast should bolster the position of Computer Electronic Solutions as a key supplier of computer hardware components to manufacturers of home and business computers throughout the world.

According to Caste's CEO, Thomas O'Brien, "SteadFast is a perfect complement to our existing portfolio of businesses. The combination of SteadFast and Caste will create economies of scale that will enable us to move at lightning speed as we drive an expanding range of high-quality products through a global network of distribution channels to meet our customers' insatiable demand for world-class hardware solutions."

The transaction is structured as a tender offer to be followed by a merger of the two companies and is subject to customary closing conditions . . .

The auditorium buzzed with speculation. Surely, workforce reductions would be required to eliminate redundancies and allow Caste to take full advantage of the promised economies of scale from combining the resources of the two companies. The only comfort our CEO could offer was that our jobs were safe at least until the closing date of the acquisition. After that, Caste management would take over and begin making all executive decisions.

Then, in the spring of 2000, the dot-com bubble burst. Tech stocks declined in value. Many companies failed outright. Yet somehow, Caste's acquisition of SteadFast managed to move forward, closing on June 6.

On the very next day, the new management team flew in from various parts of the country and assumed control of our company, taking up residence in the recently vacated executive wing, which overlooked the pond and its marshy grasses and cattails. As the team moved into their offices, a bald eagle sat in a nearby tree, glaring into the glass paneling. It was unclear whether the eagle was engaged in a "first to blink loses" stare-down with his own image—perhaps mistaking it for a territorial foe—or scrutinizing the activities of his new neighbors. In either case, the formidable bird of prey remained in the tree all morning, motionless and silent, watching, watching, watching . . .

Throughout the remaining months of 2000, the dot-com crash continued as one internet start-up after another bit the dust. Overall confidence in the technology sector dwindled, and our business suffered as orders for computer hardware components plummeted. Panic-stricken, Caste management initiated a series of massive layoffs, euphemistically referring to this course of action as a "rightsizing program." The first round of layoffs hit SteadFast on the last Wednesday of June.

Wednesday, June 28, 2000

CASTE ANNOUNCES STEADFAST LAYOFFS

PALO ALTO, CALIF. (AP) – Today, Caste Enterprises (NYSE: CEN) announced elimination of 40 percent of the workforce of its recently acquired SteadFast business. In all, over 2,000 jobs will be slashed worldwide, including 356 at SteadFast's Golden Meadow facility.

Since Caste's acquisition of the computer hardware components manufacturer, demand for SteadFast's products has weakened, due at least in part to the bursting of the so-called dot-com bubble earlier this year. Analysts questioned whether the SteadFast deal should have been completed, given the uncertain business climate, but Caste company officials remained optimistic and moved forward with the transaction, publicly stating they believed the prevailing market conditions to be no more than a temporary adjustment.

According to Caste's CEO, Thomas O'Brien, "This rightsizing effort is necessary to ensure the long-term profitability of the SteadFast business. We stand firmly behind our acquisition of SteadFast Components and look forward to growing the business for many years to come."

Golden Meadow employees were notified first thing in the morning and ordered off the premises by the end of the day. Emotions ran high. Tears flowed. A dissonant chorus of wails echoed throughout the cavernous facility. Voices rose in anger. Shouts were exchanged. Threats of violence were made. Downsized men and women stalked out of the building, returning before the end of the day to gather their personal items under the watchful eyes of armed security guards, hired to ensure company property was protected against sabotage, vandalism, and theft.

A survivor of the massacre, I went to bed that night with a terrible headache and a stabbing pain in my stomach . . .

Leaving the fallen oak behind, I descend deeper and deeper into the forest . . . somewhere I need to go . . . something I need to do . . . The air's so thick, I can barely breathe. It's so dark, I can barely see . . . yet I proceed, navigating my way from one twisted shadow to the next . . .

Have faith, Ricky . . .

The beat of a distant drum echoes in my ears . . .

Da-doom, da-doom, da-doom . . .

It fills my skull and rattles the fillings in my teeth . . .

Da-doom, da-doom, da-doom—

It stops. A blood-curdling cry tears through the forest like a siren . . . and another . . .

Run, Ricky!

I break into an all-out sprint . . .

Don't stop. No matter what happens, no matter what you hear, keep running!

Soon, cries are coming at me from all directions as I run like a decapitated chicken through a tangled maze of trees, roots, and underbrush . . .

This isn't right! I've given over twenty years of my life to this company.

I can't afford to be laid off! My oldest starts college this fall.

Gone by the end of the day?

Just who in the fuck does Thomas O'Brien think he is? Taking over our company, turning our lives upside down . . .

You're firing me?

Eliminating my position? Is this some kind of sick joke? I've got bills to pay.

Letting me go? With no notice? This is horseshit!

You're sorry? Are you kidding me? To hell with your apology, and while you're at it, to hell with you and this company. Better yet, to hell with Caste Enterprises, and to hell with Thomas O'Brien!

One by one, unseen friends, colleagues, and coworkers are picked off . . .

Keep running, Ricky!

Fueled by raw fear, my legs carry me still deeper into the forest, leaving the desperate, angry cries far, far behind . . .

I'm alone now . . . still running . . . the only sounds in the forest are the crunching of leaves and snapping of twigs under my feet. My lungs gasp for air . . . I slow down, and the beat of the drum returns—very faint, but gradually growing louder . . .

Da-doom, da-doom, da-doom . . .

The next round of layoffs was announced just four weeks later, on the last Wednesday of July, "Black Wednesday," as these days came to be known around the office. This time, one thousand jobs were cut, bringing the total number of remaining SteadFast employees to just under two thousand worldwide. Five hundred more people were downsized out of their jobs on the third Wednesday of September. After that,

the workforce was "fine-tuned" by a series of smaller downsiz-
ings in the final three months of 2000 . . . always on a Black
Wednesday . . .

By the end of the year—when the smoke had cleared—just over
1,000 of the 5,000 SteadFast people employed before the Caste
takeover remained with the company. Only a paltry 253 continued to inhabit our beloved glass palace in Golden Meadow,
which felt more like a ghost town than a place of work. Even the
bald eagle had disappeared from his post outside executive row.
Word soon spread that Caste would be putting the building up
for sale and relocating us to a much smaller and more suitable
facility down the road.

The floggings will continue until morale improves.

Those few of us remaining with the company became angry,
resentful, and cynical. In the name of improving corporate effi-
ciency and increasing bottom-line profits, the company had laid
off 3,900 people, leaving an undermanned platoon of demor-
alized soldiers responsible for managing ever-increasing workloads and impossibly high expectations. We worked longer days,
including weekends, with no corresponding increases in pay.
We were on call 24-7 via a new mode of communication—a
device called the BlackBerry.

We couldn't keep up with the work. It was too much. Yet
the implicit message was that we should be thankful to have
a job. Meanwhile, CEO Thomas O'Brien was rewarded for
implementing his rightsizing program with an increase in
annual pay to $30 million in salary, bonuses, stock grants,
and options.

Loyalty became a thing of the past. Employees felt allegiance neither toward the company nor to each other. An every-man-for-himself mentality spread throughout the organization. Like dogs in the ghetto fighting over a bone, employees were willing to do whatever it took to survive, including betraying each other to senior management.

I learned this lesson the hard way and discovered the importance of exercising discretion when leaving messages on voice mail, for such messages easily could be saved and forwarded to anyone in the organization.

Late one Friday afternoon, I made the mistake of responding to a sales manager's abrupt demand for legal support with an equally abrupt voice mail asserting I would be unable to attend to his matter until after the weekend. When Monday morning came, an irate president of the Computer Electronic Solutions business unit—one Alexander Mountainfort—was waiting for me in my cubicle. Informing me that lawyers were a "dime a dozen," he came within a whisker of terminating my employment but was suddenly called away on a more pressing matter. I'd dodged a bullet, and in the process, I'd learned to watch my back. Dealing with people at work had become a minefield to be navigated with extreme caution.

Expecting another bullet to come along at any moment, but numb to the possibility, I settled into a mindless routine and grew quiet, submissive, and resigned. Painting a grim smile on my face, I assumed the role of a good corporate soldier and carried out my orders without complaint. I became exactly what management wanted me to become—a hypocrite and traitor to my soul . . . and to the memory of my father . . .

After a brutal winter of below-zero temperatures and four-teen-hour days confined within the perimeter of my ten-by-ten cubicle, I decided I'd had enough. Spring had arrived, and I was as restless as a caged animal. So, I worked up the courage and requested a meeting with my boss, a veteran corporate lawyer named Art Charrington, to discuss my future with the company.

Sporting high-end designer glasses on the bridge of his protruding beak and a grizzled but well-groomed beard upon his chin, Art carried the title of vice president and associate general counsel with a thinly veiled air of exaggerated self-importance. A transfer from Caste world headquarters in Silicon Valley, he clearly didn't care for our winters, or our springs, preferring to spend as much time as possible on airplanes bound for sunny California.

Having scheduled an appointment through his secretary, I caught Art between trips, and we sat down together in his executive row office on a cold, rainy afternoon in the first week of April 2001. Fidgeting nervously before this imposing Caste executive, I expressed my interest in opportunities to advance. I'd been working in the same job for eight years and was now ready for a new challenge. I was even willing to relocate.

"Opportunities to advance!" he exclaimed from behind his desk, his eyes first growing wide at the very absurdity of the idea before darting frenetically about the room in an apparent attempt to find a place to hide.

I guessed he was on his fourth or fifth cup of coffee.

"Well . . . yes . . . yes, of course. I'm glad you took the initiative to request this meeting, Richard. Very glad, indeed. And let me assure you—there will be many opportunities for advancement within the Caste organization, especially for someone with your experience and abilities. A great many opportunities. I only ask that you be patient."

The opportunities would never materialize. Of course they would never materialize. Art Charrington had no interest in advancing my career. He needed me to stay put and continue supporting the SteadFast business. He didn't wish to be bothered with SteadFast. To him, we were an annoyance. My career aspirations were an annoyance. This meeting was an annoyance. He had much more important concerns waiting for him back at the mother ship in Silicon Valley.

"I hate to cut this short, Richard—"

It's Ricky, you self-involved prick.

"—but I have a plane to catch. Feel free to schedule another meeting through my secretary when I get back."

She has a name. It's Catrina.

"Thanks for stopping by."

He slipped his laptop into a travel case with one hand while reaching for his coat with the other and was gone.

The summer of 2001 arrived with a fury of wild thunderstorms that bred a procession of tornadoes, which threatened to march right through but instead skirted the northern border of the Heartland City metro area. Miraculously, there were no fatalities, and property damage was limited to the loss of only a few homes in the outer-ring suburbs. In the aftermath of this vicious assault, the entire region was subjected to an extended period of stifling heat and demoralizing humidity—the type of weather that drained one's body of the will to live. The air was so laden with moisture that even the roses in my backyard sagged under its oppressive weight.

On the day after a tornado warning had driven all SteadFast employees into the basement of our Golden Meadow facility (plans to sell the building and move us out were delayed due to a bureaucratic snafu in Silicon Valley), I attended a meeting led by the president of Computer Electronic Solutions, Alexander Mountainfort—the same executive who'd ambushed me in my cubicle that winter.

Arriving early, I took a seat near the door and checked my phone. *June 28.* It had been exactly one year since the first lay-offs were announced.

Familiar faces populated the conference room. To Mountainfort's right sat the vice president of CES product management, Brian Otterness, whom I knew well and liked. A legacy SteadFast employee, Brian was in his late forties, tall, blond, and possessed with above-average intelligence and good looks. In his younger days, he must have been quite a ladies' man, but that was before twenty years of marriage, two teenage kids, a receding hair-line, and an all-consuming love affair with a career that buried him up to his neck in promises, commitments, and one unrealistic deadline after another. Somehow, he managed to stay on top of it all. Barely. Although extremely competent in his job, Brian did possess one small weakness—he lacked the killer instinct to advance to the next level. In short, he was too nice. Sitting to Brian's right was one of his direct reports, a product manager named Julia. Also in attendance were the following individuals: the financial controller of CES, the vice president of manufacturing operations, a global supply chain manager, and the head of the proposals group.

Presiding over the meeting with an air of absolute authority that was not to be challenged, Mountainfort was dynamic, self-assured, and smoothly articulate. Coming to SteadFast through the acquisition, he brought with him a hard-driving, unyielding, and results-oriented management style. Believing fear to be the most powerful and effective motivator, he squeezed as much as he could from his people in blood, sweat, and tears. If you performed to his expectations, he'd acknowledge your efforts. Get on his bad side—as I had—and he wouldn't hesitate to dress you down in public, or worse.

Wearing vintage pince-nez spectacles and a thick walrus moustache, Mountainfort was an intimidating yet admired leader who bore more than a slight likeness to Theodore Roosevelt. I wondered whether he was aware of his resemblance to our twenty-sixth president.

Mountainfort called the meeting to order.

"Due to the prohibitive costs of domestic manufacturing," he said, "the company has decided to move all manufacturing operations offshore. The first phase of this initiative is to outsource at least half of SteadFast's manufacturing operations to contract manufacturers. The second phase will be to identify offshore plants for acquisition. The purpose of this meeting is to kick-start phase one.

"First, we need to create a list of potential contract manufacturers from such locales as China, Taiwan, Thailand, the Philippines, Singapore, and Hong Kong and invite them to submit bids. The RFP will be sent out within two weeks."

He glanced at Maria Lopez, who'd served as senior manager of proposals since long before I'd started with the company.

Maria nodded, her head jiggling like that of a bobble-head doll.

"The contract manufacturers must respond to the RFP by the end of July," Mountainfort said. "Otherwise, their bids will not be considered. From among the bids received, we'll choose one contract manufacturer to act as test pilot for phase one of the initiative.

"At this point, we'll need assistance from legal to negotiate the contract and finalize all paperwork. This task must be given absolute priority, and it must be completed by Labor Day at the very latest."

He peered at me out of the corner of a spectacled eye as if expecting me to object.

I held his gaze but said nothing.

"Once the relationship with the first contract manufacturer is established and the program is up and running, we'll use it as a model for entering into agreements with additional contract manufacturers."

Mountainfort paused and scanned the room with his steely pale blue eyes. "Is everything I've said clear so far?"

One head after another bobbled in the affirmative. I imagined the group expressing their solidarity like Governor Le Petomane's cabinet in *Blazing Saddles*, with an emphatic chorus of *harrumph!* The lone dissenter, I kept my harrumph—and my bobble—to myself.

Satisfied everyone was on board, Mountainfort continued, "As we transition more manufacturing abroad, we'll phase out of existence most, if not all, our domestic-based plants by the end of next year—calendar year 2002. I will rely on our VP of operations and his team to work with HR to oversee this process.

"Well," he said, once again scanning the room for dissidents, "that's all I have for now, except to say we should've done this years ago. With the high cost of labor, governmental regulations, and taxes, it quite simply doesn't make sense to manufacture goods domestically. Hell, most of our competitors already have their own manufacturing operations in Mexico, India, and China. We're behind the eight ball a little, but with some hard work and focus, we'll get it done. Any questions?"

"What about the workers in our American plants?" I hadn't intended to speak; still, the words came. "They have lives . . . families to support."

What the heck was I doing? Was I insane? I knew there was no room for discussion, that Mountainfort didn't tolerate being second-guessed, that Caste was a hierarchical organization with a strict top-down management philosophy.

"Well, I'm very sorry about that," he said in a tone that made it clear he wasn't the least bit sorry.

The human element meant nothing to him. I could see . . . I knew—had known for a while—that SteadFast had been absorbed into a cold-blooded culture run by an end-justifies-the-means mentality. In fact, there was little, if anything, left of SteadFast.

"This is business. It's survival of the fittest. If people get hurt along the way, well, then, that's just too damn bad. Not everyone's going to make it, Williamson. Some need to be sacrificed for the greater good. Now that might sound harsh or unfeeling to a bleeding-heart liberal like you, but that's just the way it is. Like it or not, that's the world we live in. If we want the SteadFast business to be competitive and thrive, then we need to take full advantage of every opportunity—and I mean *every* opportunity—to trim the fat from our operating budget."

His eyes lighting up as he spoke, he pounded the table with his fist. Tiny beads of sweat appeared at his temples. The corners of his mouth bent upward into a crooked smile. He was actually enjoying this little rant.

"There's been talk of our Connecticut plant unionizing. Unionizing! We need to get out in front of this thing before those goddamned labor unions drive us out of business. We need to take action now!"

"All they want," I said, "is a fair wage and decent working conditions for their members."

An angry shade of crimson surged into Mountainfort's pudgy cheeks.

"Whose side are you on, Williamson? You're our lawyer, right? Christ, you sound like a fucking socialist."

For the remainder of the meeting, I sat quietly in my seat. Seething. I wanted to leap up, grab Mountainfort by the throat, and choke the life out of him. But I'd tried that once before and was lucky to escape without being charged with a crime. Still, I had to do something. I couldn't let him get away with it. But what could I do against this powerful executive who'd just humiliated me in front of my colleagues? I wanted to respond to his "socialist" comment; I even opened my mouth, yet no words came out.

What's wrong with me? Why can't I stand up to authority?

On the drive home that evening, my grip on the steering wheel produced white knuckles before finally loosening, one grudging finger at a time. With each passing mile, the ache in my hands lessened. My shoulders relaxed. My heartbeat eased into a gentle cadence. About halfway through the commute, I glanced at the rearview mirror, and there was Alexander Mountainfort, glaring at me through his Theodore Roosevelt specs. I blinked, and he disappeared.

If I could just keep driving, all memories of Mountainfort and Caste would eventually recede into nothing more than a tiny speck . . . and I'd be free . . .

The stress from my confrontation with Mountainfort drained out of my body, through the Audi's chassis, and onto the highway. If anyone wished to clean up the toxins I'd just left behind, they would need to wait until after rush hour. My arms and legs became as limp as overcooked noodles. My brain turned to mush.

The brake lights of the vehicle ahead of me flickered.

Back at summer camp, I was a pretty good shot—

Like a blip on a radar screen, the thought vanished. No longer flickering, the brake lights became steady beams of red. Traffic came to a halt. It would be stop-and-go for miles.

On an impulse, I took the next exit—Chandler Boulevard—and pulled into the parking lot of the county sheriff's office. Without stopping to think, I marched through two sets of doors, entered a sparsely furnished lobby, and approached a deputy sporting a shiny badge, a khaki uniform, and a caterpillar moustache. A pane of bulletproof plexiglass separated us. Pressing a button and leaning into a microphone, he asked me to state my business.

"I'd like to apply for a handgun permit."

He deposited an application form in a tray and pressed another button. The tray popped open. I seized the form and completed it.

Two weeks later, after returning home from a long day at work, I found my permit waiting for me in the mail. The very next day, I visited a gun shop and purchased a Glock 19 semi-automatic pistol. At that point, I had no specific plans for the Glock, but I did start making regular trips to a nearby shooting range.

After first mastering the Glock, and then growing bored with it, I bought a rifle—a Colt AR-15 9 mm carbine—at an outdoor gun show in the blistering heat of a colorless Saturday afternoon in early August.

A few days later, I learned we had awarded the offshore manufacturing business to Doltz Technologies, a contract manufacturer in Shenzhen, China. Per Mountainfort's orders, Brian Otterness assumed the role of project team leader. One of Brian's first action items was to send me an email with contact information for Doltz's lawyer.

From: *Brian Otterness <brian.otterness@caste.com>*
To: *Ricky Williamson*
Subject: *Doltz Contract Negotiations*
Attachment: *Zhang.Ying.vcf 56.7 KB*
Date: *August 8, 2001 08:34:27 CDT*

Mountainfort wants the contract negotiated posthaste. Please contact Doltz's lawyer and set up the first conference call. I've included her contact information in the attached file. Let's try to get this thing done without traveling to China. My son will be on the varsity soccer team this fall, and I've already missed too much.

I took a deep breath and replied that I would get on it immediately.

An unusually candid exchange of emails revealed that Doltz's lawyer, Zhang Ying, was from a small village about two hours northeast of Beijing. Her parents were farmers. The first of her family to travel outside China, she attended law school in the United States, graduating from NYU in 1989. After a short stint with a New York law firm, she returned to China to establish her own practice. Currently, she was officed in Hong Kong, representing clients in the manufacturing sector throughout the Asia Pacific region, including mainland China.

We scheduled our first teleconference for Monday, August 13, at 6:00 a.m., Heartland City time, to account for the thirteen-hour difference.

Armed with a Venti-size Starbucks, a hard copy of our one-hundred-page template, and a red pen, I met Brian in a third-floor fishbowl conference room. It was before dawn, and the building was dark. Brian flicked on the room's overhead light. A warm glow filled the fishbowl and sent our shadows meandering down the deserted hallway toward executive row. After getting settled, I called Zhang Ying, and we began negotiating the contract, issue by issue and page by page. Making good progress, we reached a logical stopping point three hours later and agreed to continue our conversation on Thursday, as it was getting late in Hong Kong.

After Thursday's marathon session, which lasted almost four hours, we reached the document's halfway point and agreed to call it quits for the day.

Exhausted, I returned to my cubicle to gather my thoughts. Something didn't feel right. Zhang Ying had insisted on discussing each issue ad infinitum, posing one hypothetical after another and dwelling on unlikely outcomes. Yet in the end, she'd been accommodating. Too accommodating. She'd made concessions on key legal points without making the customary arguments. She was making my job easy! But why? It was as if she were a reluctant advocate, simply going through the motions, not representing her client with the zeal required by our American rules of professional responsibility.

Her heart wasn't in it.

Although she spoke with the ease and grace of a consummate professional, there was something under her words. She was hiding something. I was sure of it.

Leaning into the tightly wound springs of my office chair, I closed my eyes, half expecting to see some ghostly image appear and impart its otherworldly wisdom to me. An angel perhaps, or the restless spirit of my father . . . I saw nothing of the kind. Rather, I heard something . . . something awful flooding my consciousness with feelings of dread and despair . . . a sharp, high-pitched wail like that of an infant deprived of food and water. The sound reverberated inside my skull and penetrated my brain and my soul. And there was pain—too deep for words . . . I grabbed my head with both hands in a feeble attempt to make it stop. Yet the sensation grew and grew. Somewhere, someone was suffering . . . suffering terribly . . .

After what seemed like hours but was probably no more than seconds of clock time, the pain subsided.

What was I to do? I glanced at my watch. It was almost noon. I certainly couldn't go to management with nothing more than my intuition. Instead, I decided to go to the proposals group and ask to see their Doltz files.

Not knowing what I was searching for, but certain I would recognize it when I saw it, I skipped lunch and spent the afternoon digging through bankers' boxes filled with materials related to Doltz's business, including financial and accounting records, projections, personnel records, operational and logistical reports, strategic analyses, product descriptions, and so on.

There's much more material here than would be required for an RFP.

I took a step back to survey the two dozen or so boxes stacked before me.

And all these documents are at least two years old. What's going on here? What happened two years ago? This level of detail would only be necessary if Caste were conducting due diligence; for example, to evaluate a potential acquisition.

I frowned. A deep furrow split my brow. Then it hit me between the eyes with the force of an exploding bullet.

Of course! It's obvious, isn't it? Caste must have been in the process of buying this company and then held on to these boxes when the deal fell through!

It was just after five o'clock when each member of the proposals group collectively powered down their computers and left for the day. Yet I continued my search. I needed to know why Zhang Ying was so indifferent to the cause of her client. I needed to know what she was hiding.

Hours passed. The only sound was the hum of the HVAC system. The sun had long since set over the marshy wetlands outside the window behind me. Only the building's security lights lit the proposals area. Nursing a stiff neck and feeling utterly discouraged, I pulled an ordinary-looking document out of a file folder and discovered a vague reference to:

An investigation of the company's alleged labor practices involving—

The rest of the sentence was blacked out. It appeared as if someone, in great haste, had used a Magic Marker to blot out the remaining text. There were no further clues. I wanted to continue, but I needed to get some sleep.

The following morning, I got to work early, logged on to my computer, and resumed my investigation. Searching the internet for anything related to "Doltz" and "labor practices," I came across a large number of hits, most of them directly on point. Reviewing one appalling account after another, my eyes grew wide in shocked disbelief.

What am I doing here? I ought to be in China, finding a way to help them . . .

Finally, after spending the entire morning and part of the afternoon glued to my monitor, I wrote up a summary of my findings along with an unequivocal recommendation that we immediately cease all efforts to establish a business relationship with Doltz Technologies. Printing out a draft and proofing it first, I emailed the summary to Alexander Mountainfort and Brian Otterness with a CC to my boss, Art Charrington. Then I powered down my computer, turned off my phone, and left work early to blow off steam at the shooting range.

Those bastards. Those fucking bastards! If Caste was looking at Doltz as an acquisition target, they must have known . . .

After a couple of hours at the range, I went home and stewed all weekend long, without leaving the house and without checking my email for the inevitable backlash against my strongly worded recommendation, which in Caste-speak would surely be interpreted as gross insubordination.

Come Monday morning, I found myself in the hot seat, at the end of a long racetrack-shaped conference table. Alexander Mountainfort sat at the head of the table, presiding over a nine-person star chamber. As usual, Brian Otterness occupied the seat to Mountainfort's right. All other members of the court were senior people from executive row. Only Art Charrington was absent. He was in California.

I hid my trembling hands in my lap and cast a desperate glance across the room. The door beckoned. But there was no clear route of escape.

Reading from my summary, I recounted the appalling facts.

"In conclusion, innocent children are suffering . . . suffering horribly and needlessly. We cannot . . . we must not be a part of it."

Peering up from my summary, I was met not by the looks of horror and indignation I'd hoped for but by nine stony faces suspended in unbearable silence. In that agonizing moment, which hung over my head like a French guillotine, I became certain these sharply dressed, highly compensated executives were already aware of the facts I'd just delineated. They simply didn't care.

In 1999, the International Labour Organization had issued a report detailing Doltz Technologies' use of child labor in Shenzhen. Impoverished and illiterate children, often orphans, worked fifteen-hour days, seven days a week, performing only the most menial and mindlessly repetitive tasks in Doltz's factories. These children, while being exploited for profit, were robbed of the opportunity for an education and a future.

According to the ILO report, the children were paid, if at all, below China's minimum wage and far below what would be considered minimum wage in America. Some of the children had been forcibly removed from their homes in the middle of the night and sold into indentured servitude before ending up on Doltz factory floors throughout the country. Many were beaten for failure to meet production quotas. Others were victims of rape and sexual abuse. Many of the girls—some as young as nine—were forced into prostitution in the squalid neighborhoods surrounding the factories. Inside, conditions were dirty and dangerous. Injuries and work-related illnesses were common. In the summers, it was unendurably hot, primarily due to outdated and poorly maintained HVAC equipment. On more than one documented occasion, children had swooned, only to be subsequently punished.

Following publication of the ILO report, Doltz cleaned up its act—or so everyone was led to believe—until recently when the Fair Labor Association opened a new investigation into Doltz's despicable child labor practices.

Finally, someone spoke. It was Peter Van Kamp, vice president of manufacturing operations. His slicked-back hair gleamed in the fluorescent light.

"An investigation? So, there's no proof. No actual evidence of any wrongdoing."

"Anything conclusive?" said Chester Markeson, vice president of finance and controller of the CES business.

Haven't they been listening? Are we actually going to talk about this?

"No," I said. "Nothing conclusive. Not yet anyway. But consider their history. Before moving forward, we should look into this independently."

Once again, the faces around the table turned to stone.

Meeting these cold stares head on, I summoned the courage to continue. "We should conduct our own investigation, require Doltz to open their factories to us. In the meantime, we need to stop—"

"No, no, no, no, no," Mountainfort said disdainfully. "We're not going to stop. We can't afford to stop. We're on a very, very tight schedule. Every day that passes bites into the bottom line. We need to transition to an offshore model and do so immediately. We've already awarded the business to the lowest bidder. It's too late to turn around now."

"I agree with you, Alex," interjected the vice president of communications and public affairs, "but just to play devil's advocate, if this new investigation reveals Doltz is using child labor again, we could find ourselves in the middle of a public relations disaster."

Mountainfort responded without missing a beat. "You're right, Sheila. To be on the safe side, we should take steps to distance ourselves from this child labor thing. Why don't we set up a dummy corporation in Shenzhen—"

A dummy corporation?

"—whose sole purpose for existing will be to purchase components from Doltz. We'll name the dummy Component Purchase Corp, or CPC for short. CPC will export the purchased components to either SteadFast or distributors for resale to our customers throughout the world. The dummy could even drop-ship the components directly to the customer's manufacturing locations, if that's what the customer wants. Regardless of how it works, we keep the Caste name out of it. We set up the dummy as a wholly owned subsidiary of SteadFast, not Caste. In this way, we disassociate Caste from whatever might be going on in Shenzhen."

Obviously pleased with himself, Mountainfort turned to Brian Otterness. "What do you think, Brian?"

A dummy corporation?

"What do I think? I think it could work," Brian said enthusiastically.

Regardless of whatever his personal feelings might have been, Brian was Mountainfort's yes-man.

The executives murmured their general agreement.

"Good. It's settled." Mountainfort turned to me. "Make it happen, Williamson."

Make it happen? Make it happen? You don't understand what you're saying. You cannot take a fundamentally flawed idea—one so completely lacking in integrity—and dress it up to make it appear legitimate. Well, you can try, but it's not right!

"But . . . but . . . there's the . . . the ethical issue . . ."

Ironically, Caste Enterprises was in the middle of a high-profile internal marketing campaign to roll out the company's updated *Guide to Ethical Conduct* and educate employees regarding Caste's unwavering commitment to doing business with integrity. In support of the campaign, the legal department had been tasked with traveling to Caste locations throughout the world and training Caste employees on business ethics. Apparently, the campaign's message hadn't reached the people in this conference room.

"Don't bother me with your opinion of the ethical issue. That's not your job. Just tell me one thing: Is it illegal?"

"Illegal? No . . . no, not technically, I don't think . . . but the child labor . . . innocent children are suffering—"

"We don't really know what's going on over there, Williamson."

"That's why we need to investigate—"

"It's not our responsibility," he said in a low, cold-blooded tone. "We cannot be held accountable for what may or may not be happening in China."

"But—"

"No more buts. Make it happen. Fast!"

But it should be our responsibility. It should be, it should be, it should be . . . Goddamn it! What's wrong with you, you callous bastard? Can't you see? Innocent children are suffering. And you talk of trimming the fat, of profits and bottom lines! Well, I'll tell you what—tell you what, I'll tell you—I won't be a part of this. You can set up your own dummy corporation. I won't be a part of this . . . this deception . . . this legal sleight of hand.

You already are.

I cannot allow this to continue.

Oh, but you will.

I won't.

You will, or you'll be out on your ass.

I won't.

You will.

I will?

A condescending smile . . .

Wait a second. I know you! We've met before . . . a long, long time ago . . . and then again . . . and again . . . and again . . .

Whi-kisssh! Whi-kisssh! Whi-kisssh!

Oh, Daddy! I wanna do the right thing, I swear to God I do. I'm tryin', I'm tryin' really, really hard, but they're doing it to me again . . . and it hurts, it hurts real, real bad . . .

Whi-kisssh! Whi-kisssh! Whi-kisssh!

Please make them stop! Daddy? Can you hear me? Are you there? Is anyone there?

Dooong . . . Dooong . . . Dooong . . .

It's my own damn fault . . . not strong enough . . . can't stand up to . . .

Here I am, sitting in this room with you and your fellow conspirators, a mere breath away from executive row, but not part of the club, not invited to the party, not earning your respect . . . or your millions . . . Day after day after day, I wait submissively outside your door with papers for you to sign . . .

Oh, have you been waiting long? He'll be right with you, Mr. Williamson . . .

No respect, no respect, no respect, no, no, no, no . . . not for a feckless wimp like me . . . All you want from me is my rubber stamp. To you, I'm nothing but a . . . a . . . a worthless—

FAGGOT

Faggot? Faggot? I thought you learned your lesson. I'll show you who the faggot is! This time, I'm gonna kill—

Another condescending smile . . .

You don't think I have what it takes, do you?

Same smile. No response.

No . . . no, of course you don't. It's my own damn fault . . . all of it . . . it's on me. I let it happen. I let you fuck me. Me. A whimpering, pathetic, helpless little victim . . . but no longer! No longer!

I looked around. The conference room was empty. The meeting was over, had been over for quite a while now. I was alone. Knowing what had to be done, I got up and withdrew, leaving my summary lying there flat on the table.

That week, I rounded out my arsenal by loading up on ammunition and procuring the materials for a bomb capable of taking out executive row. I'd had enough. More than enough. My quest for justice, my personal war against tyranny, had begun . . .

The following Monday, the twenty-seventh of August, Mountainfort descended upon my cubicle to remind me of the urgency of closing the Doltz deal. He spoke in a patronizing yet soothing tone designed to lull the unwary into a false sense of security. I wasn't among the unwary.

"Where are we in negotiating the contract with Doltz?"

"Actually, it's been a few days since I've spoken with their lawyer."

"I sense your heart isn't in this."

"I'll set up a conference call with her for tomorrow morning."

"You need to be a team player and get on board with the program, Williamson."

What? And sell my soul to the devil just to strike a lousy deal?

No. Do what you're paid to do—support your client by providing world-class service and facilitating the business.

How eloquent. How very eloquent. You can dress it up however you want—

It's your choice, Williamson. After all, lawyers like you are a dime a dozen.

Are you threatening me?

I'll be straight with you, Ricky. You've become a liability. You're good for one thing and one thing only. Covering your ass.

Covering my ass? Covering my ass? Can you hear—

"Don't worry, sir. I'm on board. One hundred percent. I'll get the job done. Trust me."

Tuesday, August 28, 2001

He doesn't belong here. Not in this place . . . not in this time . . .

Leaning forward in my great-grandmother's rocking chair, I was no more than a whisper's distance from the boy I'd pulled out of Lake Weston that morning. Dry and comfy now, he lay sleeping peacefully in my bed. My hands hovered over his throat . . .

I've got to stop. I'm too close!

Fearing he would hear the beating of my telltale heart, I did stop. Then, lowering my hands, I shifted my weight and retreated. The one-hundred-year-old oak rocker responded with a petulant *creeeeeak*.

The boy opened his eyes and smiled at me, his face shining as brightly as a diamond in the sunlight streaming through my bedroom window. His radiance danced into every corner of the room and imbued the morning with possibility . . .

He stretched his skinny arms above his head. The sleeves of the absurdly oversize T-shirt I'd lent him unraveled and fell haphazardly about his shoulders. He opened his mouth into a gaping crater, and a boyish yawn emerged. His eyelids squeezed together and opened, revealing an infectious cheerfulness that dared me to defy it. Apparently undisturbed by the unfamiliar surroundings, he seemed to know he was exactly where he belonged. He hadn't a care in the world.

I want what you have.

"I feel great!"

He expressed this sentiment with such uninhibited abandon that I laughed, in spite of myself, out loud. The cast-iron shell that had encased my heart for so long melted away. The past receded, and all my darkest, most angst-ridden thoughts evaporated in the boy's radiance.

"I'm so glad to hear that!" A feeling of youthful exuberance welled up from somewhere within me. "Your clothes are in the wash. They'll be ready soon. What would you like to do today?"

Together, we're going to make it right . . .

CHAPTER FOUR

Tuesday, August 28–Thursday, August 30, 2001

WEARING A WINSOME SMILE that shone with the same radiance I'd witnessed earlier that morning and dressed in his freshly laundered T-shirt and blue jeans, the boy, whom I'd named David, appeared in the kitchen doorway. Pausing for only the briefest of moments, he strolled in and joined me at the chopping block. Together, we prepared a lunch of club sandwiches with pickle spears and potato salad on the side. An excellent assistant, he handled the serrated bread knife with expert facility, cleaving the neatly stacked double-decker sandwiches into perfect quarters. We attempted to enjoy our meal on the deck, but a fiery noonday sun chased us back inside, where we found refuge from the heat under a runaway ceiling fan in the dining room.

After lunch, I took David shopping for clothes and a few other essential items, including a baseball glove, which emanated a rich, leathery scent that magically transported me back to my Little League days in South Orange . . .

Craaack!

Relying on nothing but blind instinct, I dive to my left and snag a whistling line drive, just before landing—stretched out from head to toe—on the grainy base path between second and third. A cheer rises from a crowd of astonished parents and other onlookers. Surely, my heroic feat robbed the hitter of extra bases! A wide grin blooms across my face as I make my way to my feet and wipe the dirt from my uniform. Preparing for the next hitter, I sneak a peek into the crowd. The sting of bittersweet tears fills my eyes. If only he were here . . .

Done with shopping and back at home, I found my old glove and a tattered ball hidden in a dark, cobweb-infested corner of the basement.

"Wanna play catch?"

Grateful for his new glove and looking forward to the opportunity of breaking it in, David beamed from ear to ear. Grateful for the opportunity to revisit my childhood, I beamed too. We bounded upstairs and out the front door.

Protected from the sun by the shade of a towering ash, we tossed the ball back and forth and talked of baseball and of the days of Hall of Famers Carl Yastrzemski, George Brett, Johnny Bench, Tom Seaver . . .

Neither one of us wanted the day to end, so after an hour of catch and a light supper of gazpacho soup and pretzels, we flung ourselves into my car and rode to the bluffs along the Mississippi River.

With sunset near at hand, our whimsically contorted shadows grew long as we hiked the bluffs, in search of the perfect spot. Along the way, we passed a biker, a jogger, and a young couple holding hands and sauntering down a narrow path that faithfully followed the precipice over the winding contours of the river below. Otherwise, we had the realm to ourselves. Prompted by a light, southerly breeze, the leaves in the branches above our heads broke into a sweet melody that suffused the air like a thousand winged gossamers set free into the adolescent night. Not to be outdone, an orchestra of crickets tuned their instruments for an evening performance of Vivaldi's Concerto in G Major.

Bathing us in delightfully resonating harmonies, the music followed us as we proceeded north, keeping the river to our left and far, far below us. We were in no particular hurry—we'd find our spot whenever it presented itself to us. In the meantime, we enjoyed the evening and each other's company without exchanging so much as a word, each of us honoring the other's introspective nature.

Stealing a glance at the boy, I marveled at how calm and relaxed he appeared. He moved along the increasingly rugged path with unparalleled ease and grace. Smiling confidently, he walked tall and proud with shoulders thrown back, as if to declare:

Come, world! My heart is open. I'm ready to accept whatever you may have to offer, be it good or bad, pure or defiled, virtuous or evil.

There's no anxiety, no fear in his eyes. My God, he's at peace! How did he get this way? How is it possible? After everything he's been through . . .

I was reluctant to interrupt the crickets' concerto; nevertheless, I felt compelled to speak.

"You seem so . . . so happy, David."

"I am happy, Ricky. Happy and filled with joy, just to be here, sharing this picture-perfect evening with you."

"Don't you miss your home, your friends, your family?"

"I do, but I'll be going back soon enough. You see, Ricky, I've come to appreciate and feel deep gratitude for each moment of my life—*each and every single moment*—as a precious gift. And now, I'm feeling grateful for the miracle of being here with you—the rolling river below us and the sounds of the approaching night above and all around us. After all, this beautiful moment will soon be gone and replaced by another . . . then another . . . and another . . . until we've breathed our last breath."

What's this boy's secret? Is he a philosopher, a priest, a guru?

As if reading my mind, he flashed me a knowing smile. "I'm no one special, but not too long ago, I had a remarkable experience, one that taught me a valuable lesson: each of us has the power within to choose happiness and live in a state of joy, regardless of our circumstances."

He sounds more like my father than a ten-year-old boy.

"You see, Ricky, just before you found me lying unconscious at the edge of that lake, I had an encounter with my father."

"With your . . . your father? But . . . but that's impossible. I mean, I thought you said he died."

"Yes, he did. He'd been gone for over two years, but somehow, somehow he came back to me . . . and took me by the hands—"

"He actually touched you?"

"Yes, and when he did, I felt a strange sensation pass through my hands and fill my body from head to toe. I'm not sure I can explain it, but in that moment, something extraordinary happened to me. It was as if I'd received—in one fell swoop—the gift of all my father's earthly knowledge and the wisdom of his eternal spirit."

"Oh my God."

"As a result of that experience, I now see the world through a new set of eyes. Everything has changed. Everything. I'm no longer bound by the past. I'm free, Ricky—free from all my old beliefs, misconceptions, and fears. Free . . . free to choose a life of joy and happiness . . ."

We found our spot. Or rather, it found us.

A pair of young maple trees framed a striking panoramic view of the great river flowing south from our right to left. Between the maples, a patch of plush grass invited us to rest. Accepting the invitation, we plopped down less than a stone's throw from the edge of a cliff that dropped precipitously to the riverbank. Settling into the warm grass, I leaned on an elbow and turned my gaze westward. The sun lingered over the rippled tree line on the opposite side of the river. Rich soil and moss intoxicated me with their earthy aromas. My shoulders and neck relaxed, and my head swayed in the breeze. David sat cross-legged and as still as a statue of the Buddha, taking in the day's last few rays of sunlight and listening to the sounds of the earth with all his being . . .

The last sliver of sun fell from sight, and the sky transformed itself into a blazing menagerie of red roses, lavenders, and violets. Catching me unawares, the spectacle quieted my mind and filled my soul with awe . . . and hope . . .

A single tear rolled down David's cheek, leaving behind a silvery trail.

"Thank you," he whispered.

Holding us spellbound, the sky gradually faded one lazy hue at a time into a hazy, bittersweet darkness. The last vestiges of a day I would never forget were now gone . . . forever . . . and forevermore . . .

The evening's first star appeared overhead. The river gurgled. Lightning bugs came out to play hide-and-seek. Mesmerized, we watched these weightless creatures as they frolicked in the airspace above our plushy island of grass, appearing only momentarily as tiny dots of incandescent light before disappearing under the untraceable cover of darkness.

"Hold still," David said in a firm but gentle voice. "Don't move a muscle."

"Okay. But why? What is it?"

"Quiet. There's a lightning bug on your shoulder."

"There is? I don't see any—"

"Ssssshhh."

He placed an index finger on my shoulder. It tickled, but I remained still. Then, as if obeying an unspoken but nevertheless clear and irresistible command, a lightning bug crawled onto the boy's finger and into his hand. Handling the tiny critter with loving care, he raised his open palm skyward, and we watched with fascination as it took flight, flashing its golden taillight at us before vanishing into the night.

"How on earth did you—"

Then, I remembered . . .

The boy winked at me before casting his gaze into the sky, where the stars were multiplying into a brilliant array of thousands of mystical points of light.

. . . that night with Danny . . . so many years ago . . . after the championship game and just before the fireworks . . . But this . . . this boy . . . here and now . . . it doesn't make any sense. It's . . . it's impossible. I must be dreaming . . . Okay, fine, I'm dreaming, but for the first time in my life, I feel . . . I feel . . . whole . . . whole and complete. Before this morning, there was something missing—I felt empty inside, like an eggshell without a yolk, but no longer. Oh, and by the way, if I am dreaming, I don't ever want to wake up . . .

Continuing to study the sky, the boy delved into his pocket, pulled out a small object, and rolled it around in his hand.

"What's that?"

He opened his hand, revealing a heart-shaped stone. "This stone? It's been in my pocket for as long as I can remember. I don't know where it came from exactly, but it makes me feel safe, the way my father used to make me feel. What about your father, Ricky? Can you tell me about him?"

My father's face appeared before me, obscured by a watery veil of tears.

Daddy?

"He's always in my thoughts," I managed in a tremulous whisper.

"I can see you're in a lot of pain, Ricky."

Fighting to maintain control and fidgeting desperately inside my skin, I looked away from the boy. The young maple's trunk appeared as a silhouette in the faded twilight. A ragged clump of weeds rose from its base. A long, papery strip of bark dangled. I tugged at it until it tore.

"I'd like to help you." He placed a tender hand on my shoulder.

How can you possibly help me? You're just a boy.

"No . . . no, thanks," I croaked, holding back a tsunami of tears. "Don't worry about me. I'll be fine."

"Do you have a favorite memory of him?"

How you doin', sport—

"I'd rather not . . ."

"Okay." His eyes shone with compassion. "I understand."

I want to let you in. I just don't know how.

So there we sat, staring into the star-painted sky. In uninterrupted silence. A thirty-five-year-old man whose light was badly in need of rekindling and a ten-year-old boy whose torch burned brightly . . .

Ten or twenty minutes passed. Perhaps an hour. Impossible to know for certain, as time was losing its grip on me. Without exchanging a word—and in perfect synchronicity—we rose from the grass and slowly made our way to the car.

At home, I inflated an air mattress. It would be like having a sleepover. When I was a kid, my friend Joey and I spent the night at each other's house all the time. Joey liked baseball, bubble gum, monsters, going to the movies, making a killing selling lemonade at the train station, sleepovers . . .

Sleepovers. Whatever happened to sleepovers?

I offered the boy my bed. But no. He'd called dibs on the air mattress. I protested. He insisted. The matter settled, he left the room to brush his teeth. It was almost midnight by the time we tucked ourselves in.

With a start, I woke from a dream. I'd traveled back to Camp Abenaki Valley. We were at Parson's Peak for a Sunday evening campfire. Danny, Willy, Sam, Miles, Jihad, Henry, Spencer . . . The dream was so real I could smell the smoke and feel the fire's heat, even from my perch in the amphitheater's top row. Below me, a clean-shaven man with dark skin, wiry curls, and round spectacles emerged from the fire's flickering shadows. Removing the spectacles, he wiped his brow and shot me a penetrating gaze.

Are you listening, Ricky?

Replacing his specs, he strummed a chord or two on his guitar and began to sing a bittersweet melody.

I glanced at my alarm clock. It was just past three. I was awake now, yet the music continued. *Is it in my head? Or in the house?* I peered over the edge of my bed. The air mattress was empty. The boy was no longer there.

He must be downstairs . . .

I listened to the melody, trying to pinpoint its origin.

Yes! He's downstairs, and he's singing Don McLean's "Vincent."

Unable to sleep, he must have found my old six string in a forgotten corner of a forgotten closet. It was an instrument I'd purchased years ago with the best of intentions. Yet I never learned to play.

When did he learn to play? And sing so well!

After a brief pause, he broke into a lively version of Cat Stevens's "Peace Train."

The following morning, I called work and claimed another sick day. My gastrointestinal condition hadn't improved. My secretary, Carol, warned me that Mountainfort was on the rampage. He wanted to know my whereabouts. *Immediately.*

I thanked her, dropped the phone, and put my head in my hands. Mountainfort and his devious schemes would have to wait. Taking deep breaths, I purged myself of every thought of the man.

When my head was clear, I retrieved the phone and went to settings. The device was already in do-not-disturb mode. Having thus confirmed the barrier between my world and the world of Caste Enterprises, Alexander Mountainfort, and that shady deal with Doltz Technologies, I turned to David. The state fair was in the middle of its annual two-week run. I suggested we make a day of it. He readily agreed.

After a leisurely breakfast of bagels and orange juice out on the deck, we hopped into the Audi and hit the road.

Parking about a mile from the fairgrounds, David and I continued our journey on foot. With each passing block, we were joined by fellow pilgrims uniformed in caps, sunglasses, T-shirts, and shorts. As we neared the main gate, the avenue became increasingly difficult to navigate. Moving at a snail's pace, a sweaty, jam-packed mass of humanity funneled us toward the entrance, through the turnstiles, and into the 320-acre fairgrounds. One hundred thousand men, women, and children were in attendance. It was hot. And sticky. Neither David nor I minded, though. We were just happy to be there. Together.

Then, like a pod of ravenous humpback whales hunting krill, the fairgoers closed in and threatened to swallow us whole. I felt suddenly overwhelmed and agitated. David appeared fully at ease with himself, at peace with the world and all its glorious imperfections and flaws. Life seemed to flow through and around him, a cascading river of sparkling energy. Impetuous waves of complaining kids and irritated parents were mollified by his approach, yielding to his will and parting like the Red Sea at Moses's command. Even an obnoxious gang of drunk, cigarette-smoking teenage boys was pacified into submissive tranquility as he passed. One of them stopped to wheel a disabled veteran across a busy intersection. Another assisted a young girl separated from her parents.

In awe of the miracle I was witnessing, I followed in David's footsteps as one tamed group of insurgents after another allowed us to proceed unimpeded. Every now and then, he would come into incidental physical contact with someone—a light brushing of arms—and that person's face would transform into a radiant halo of light, as if he or she had been touched by the almighty yet lovingly gentle hand of God.

This boy . . . this wondrous boy has received more than just the gift of his father's knowledge and wisdom . . . much more . . .

Working our way south at first and then along the fair's grid from east to west, we entered the dairy building and encountered a ninety-pound block of butter carved into the likeness of the newly crowned Dairy Princess. A life-size bust, she stared at us with a peculiar intensity, as if pleading to be released from her predicament. Other likenesses on display included Tom Cruise, Oprah Winfrey, and our president, George W. Bush.

From the sterile chill of the climate-controlled dairy building, we strode into the heat of the livestock barns. The pungent odor of manure competed with the sweet scent of hay for supremacy. The atmosphere was made tolerable only by the industrial-grade floor fans placed throughout. Horses, cattle, goats, sheep, and chickens greeted us with a neigh, a moo, a baa, an unintelligible stream of clucks. On our way out, a baby goat nibbled at the hem of David's shorts, imploring him to stay.

In the swine barn, we made the acquaintance of a smug, one-thousand-pound boar named Ernest, and we beheld a sow named Lizzy giving birth to a litter of piglets. Unable to pull ourselves away from the wonder unfolding before our eyes, we remained still for almost two hours. Twelve pint-size beings had come into the world, squirming and scrambling for their first meal, which Lizzy provided, too exhausted to offer any resistance.

After doubling back along the boulevard adjacent to the barns, we quickly made our way through the agriculture building and emerged on a street lined with food vendors. From curb to curb, hungry fairgoers wrangled with each other for position in line. Clamoring for a bite to eat, they weren't unlike the newborn piglets we'd just witnessed in the swine barn.

The following delicacies were for sale: corn dogs (on a stick, of course), hot dogs, french fries (by the bucket), cheese curds, elephant ears, mini doughnuts, pickle dogs (pastrami and cream cheese wrapped around a pickle on a stick), teriyaki ostrich on a stick, deep-fried candy bars rolled in powdered sugar and served on a stick (on a stick was a big thing at the state fair), and many, many others.

Moving strategically from one booth to the next, we collected our food and sat at a nearby picnic table, just vacated by a young couple herding their three preschool-age children in the direction of Kiddy Land. Famished, we wasted no time in digging into our treasure trove of goodies. I had a Pronto Pup smothered with ketchup and mustard, and for dessert, a deep-fried Snickers bar on a stick. David had an About-a-Mile-Long Hot Dog, a Bucket o' Fries, which he graciously shared, and a bag of mini doughnuts for his dessert. Washing down our hearty, if not nutritious, meals with ice-cold lemonade, we lingered at the table in a state of perfect contentment. The branches of a leafy tree floated over our heads like a band of lute-playing guardian angels sent to protect us from the sun's late-afternoon rays.

A voice erupted from a speaker perched atop the booth of a local radio station. From behind a plexiglass window, a heavily bearded man—more animal than human—with dark sunglasses and wild hair howled into a microphone and cued the next song on his playlist. The song's first few notes rose above the din—created by a blending of sounds from all over the fair, from the deep, sonorous mooing of cows to the raucous shouts of revelers in the beer garden to the high-pitched squeals of terrified boys and girls negotiating a steep descent on the midway's wooden roller coaster, a rickety fifty years old.

The song, Lifehouse's "Hanging by a Moment," had held dominion over the airwaves that summer. The summer of 2001. It was a summer that would mark the end of our country's innocence—a precarious innocence to which we'd been clinging for far too long. Something wicked was looming. The world, as we knew it, was about to change . . . forever . . .

For now, however, we had this moment.

"Have you ever been in love, Ricky?"

"In love?"

"Yeah, you know, like in the song. In love."

"Well . . . yes . . . at least I thought so at the time. There was this one girl . . . She didn't feel the same way I did, though."

"What was her name?"

"Kimberly . . . Kimberly Turner . . ."

Losing track of time, we walked the fairgrounds for the remainder of the afternoon. It was after nightfall when we finally entered the buzzing chaos of the midway, home to hundreds of rides, carnival games, and other attractions. Lighting up the night with all the magnificent splendor of a dancing aurora borealis, the midway rekindled my soul with childhood memories of family visits to the amusement parks of Coney Island.

Overrun by thrill seekers of all ages, shapes, and sizes, the midway was divided into two quarter-mile-long corridors that ran in parallel to each other. At the near end of the corridors were the carnival games. At the far end were the rides—dozens and dozens of them—brilliantly adorned with lights of all colors, flashing, bobbing, and swirling at dizzying speeds. Rising above a steady stream of up-tempo pop music and echoing up and down the corridors, an amplified voice could be heard whipping the passengers of some unidentified ride into a frenzy.

"Do you wanna go faster?"

"Yeeeaaahhh!"

"Do you *really* wanna go faster?"

"*Yeeeaaahhh!*"

Reigning over this chaotic kingdom of lights and noise, a Ferris wheel stood firmly planted at the midway's epicenter. The wheel was of classic design—a king lavishly appareled in glittering vestments of canary yellow, tangelo orange, and flaming red. All other rides cowered in his shadow as he transported his charges toward heaven.

Frozen in a state of childlike awe, we gaped up at the divinely appointed king. Time stood still. The lights ceased flashing. All noise faded into the background. David gave me a nudge. I snapped out of my stupor, and we plunged into the fray.

Taking my hand, the boy led me through the overly congested corridor and toward the games, where we encountered a dog pound of carnies, each wearing a derby, a red-and-white-striped shirt, and a vest. Collectively, they barked at us as we passed the Ring Toss, Frog Launcher, Whack the Gopher, Stand the Bottle, Balloon & Dart Throw, Skee-Ball, and Basket Toss. At the Milk Bottle Toss, a commanding bellow stopped us short.

"Step right up!"

The voice belonged to a stubby man with porkchop sideburns. A few stray wisps of hair escaped from under his derby. His pockmarked face glowed with perspiration.

"Step right up and prove your manhood! Knock down all three bottles and win one of these humongous prizes."

He motioned toward a wide variety of stuffed animals and pop culture icons hanging from the booth's ceiling.

"My manhood?" I said. "Okay, you've got yourself a customer."

I paid the man and received two hard-rubber baseballs in return. Without wasting any time, I took aim at the bottles, which were stacked in an awkward pyramid, and knocked them over with my first throw.

"We got a winnah!" the carny cried out so all passersby could hear.

"I'll take that one." I pointed to an oversize Bart Simpson doll.

I relinquished my prize to David, who turned to his right and handed it to a boy of no more than four years of age. Wide-eyed, the boy gazed with profound amazement upon the stuffed Bart. Then, clinging to the doll, which was almost his height, he scampered to his parents, who'd been watching the scene with great interest. The couple thanked me and vanished into the crowd with their son. They didn't seem to appreciate or even notice David's role in the giving of the gift.

Next, we took a grand tour of the rides, passing two roller coasters, the fun house, the bumper boats, the Zipper, and the Octopus. Finally, we arrived at the base of the Sky Diver—a Ferris wheel–like ride. Yet much more menacing than a Ferris wheel. The ride's passengers were enclosed in steel cages equipped with steering wheels that allowed them to barrel-roll the cages clockwise and counterclockwise while simultaneously rising and falling with the Sky Diver's natural circular motion as it painted an arc in the sky. Somehow, David talked me into giving it a try.

The operator ushered us into a cage and locked the door, sealing us inside and perhaps sealing our fates as well. Slowly at first and then more quickly, we rose upward. Beyond terrified and white-knuckled, I grasped the steering wheel for dear life as we ascended higher and higher.

When we reached the apex, the cage lurched and came to a stop. Below us, the midway twinkled like a Christmas tree. Fairgoers skittered about like ants. A gust of wind rocked the cage.

"Oh my God!" I shrieked. "I'm gonna die!"

"This is fun!" squealed David. "Turn the wheel, Ricky. Let's get this thing spinning!"

My grip on the wheel tightened.

"Are you okay, Ricky?"

The steel cage plummeted toward earth.

Again, we rose. We dived. We rose. We dived. Someone was screaming. On the fourth ascent, my voice turned hoarse, and I realized the screaming was coming from me.

Finally, the machine slowed and came to a merciful halt. With David's assistance, I staggered out of the cage. My knees smacked the pavement. A couple of teenage girls tittered. I got up and dusted myself off. Ashamed of having made such a spectacle of myself, but grateful my feet were once more planted firmly on the ground, I began to regain my wits and recover from the ordeal.

Unfazed by the experience, David regarded me with some concern. Apparently deciding I'd be okay, he then smiled. Mischievously.

"Come on!" He darted toward the House of Glass.

I tried to follow, but my legs hadn't yet fully recovered, and I stumbled. By the time I reached the attendant's stand, he'd disappeared inside.

He's gone!

In a blind panic, I dashed into the House of Glass and groped through its maze of mirrors, glass panels, and flashing white lights. One dead end after another blocked my way and forced me to retrace my steps. Meanwhile, the voice of a demented clown taunted me. It seemed to come from everywhere . . . and nowhere . . .

"Aaaah-ha-ha-ha-ha-ha! Around and round you go, searching for a way out . . . that I alone know . . . Aaaah-ha-ha-ha-ha-ha!"

I floundered from one chamber to the next, receiving multiple bruises from collisions with the glass. A storm of footfalls rained down all around me, clattering the aluminum floor. Yet no one was visible. Only my own deformed, frantic image in the mirror . . .

I've lost him!

With me one moment and gone the next. It was as if he'd never existed in the first place. Perhaps he'd been nothing more than a figment of my imagination, a hallucination (had I gone mad?) . . . or, as I'd guessed earlier, a ghost or some other kind of spirit—

"Aaaah-ha-ha-ha-ha-ha!"

My face flushed. My neck prickled. My hands became cold and clammy. My heart pounded so loudly I could hear it reverberating off the glass walls that were now closing in on me.

There's no way out. I'm trapped!

Inch by inevitable inch, the walls grew closer and closer. The clown's maniacal laugh rang in my ears. Louder and louder. My breath came in short, desperate gasps. It would be over in a matter of only seconds. I was going to die . . . alone—

Tap, tap, tap . . . tap, tap, tap . . .

It was David. He was outside the House of Glass, tapping the front panel with the tips of his fingers. Grinning innocently, he waved at me.

I let out a sigh of relief, and my vital signs returned to normal. The walls magically receded.

He's fine! And I'm free!

Feeling sheepish, I found my way to the exit and joined the boy outside.

"You escaped this time," said the demented clown. "But if you should ever come this way again . . . Aaaah-ha-ha-ha-ha-ha!"

We had just agreed to call it a day when we came across a man with a bow tie and waxed handlebar moustache. He was standing on a wooden box at the entrance to a large canvas tent, gray from years of exposure to the elements. A crowd of curious onlookers gathered. Gesticulating passionately, he attempted to lure us in with well-rehearsed promises of "peculiar oddities and bizarre displays of superhuman feats." There were fire-breathers, sword swallowers, contortionists, Tiny Tim (the world's smallest living man), Bertha (the world's fattest lady), Gorilla Woman, Lizard Man, Cobra Girl, a man with two heads, a four-legged woman, and finally, the show's main attraction . . . the cryogenically preserved body of the one and only Eddie the Lobster Boy!

Drawn in by the man's hypnotic croon, we stopped to listen to him pitching these outrageous yet intriguing claims. After a few moments, we moved on. It wasn't until some minutes later I noticed David's smile had faded. How quiet he'd become. For the first time since his arrival, he seemed pensive, melancholy . . .

In silence, we hiked to the car and drove home.

Question: What do the worlds of the state fair midway and corporate America have in common?

Answer: They're both worlds of illusion.

Not willing to tempt fate by playing hooky a third consecutive day, I let David sleep in and hit the road early. At work, I settled into my cubicle and spent most of the day digging out from under an avalanche of emails. *Impossible!* It was impossible to focus. My thoughts continuously returned to David and our remarkable time together. Finally, after nine hours of agonizing over the wisdom of leaving a ten-year-old unattended, I left work and was home by five o'clock.

After parking the car in the driveway, I removed the keys from the ignition, sat back in my seat, and let out a sigh. I was fortunate to make it through the workday without a visit from Mountainfort. But it was only a temporary reprieve. A late-afternoon email had informed me there would be an important conference call with the senior executive team in Palo Alto to discuss the status of the Doltz deal. The real purpose of the call was to put me in the hot seat, determine the reasons for the delay, and take whatever measures were necessary to motivate me to set up the dummy corporation and finalize the contract.

The call was scheduled for the following morning.

An angry knot festered in the pit of my stomach. I took a deep breath and let it out. The air fizzled through my teeth like a slow leak in a bicycle tire. I didn't want to think about the damned call, nor did I want to enter the house and face the boy until I could paint at least a passable smile on my face. Clenching my jaw, I pushed all work-related thoughts out of my head and stepped out of the car.

A random tune popped into my head. Whistling nervously, I hurried past the garage's south-facing window—the one I'd boarded up that night in early August while my neighbors slept. It had been so late, and I'd been so careful . . . so stealthy . . . so quiet . . . so masterful in my planning . . . in assembling my arsenal . . . there was no stopping me—

A sharp pinch and tug at my earlobe . . .

Ricky, my love—

—no stopping me . . . unless someone were to discover . . . If revealed, the secret behind that window would cost me everything—

—haven't these past few days taught you anything?

—my freedom . . . my life . . .

Ricky—

Just act natural . . . someone might be watching . . .

Approaching the back door, I fumbled for the house key and slipped it into the lock.

A face appeared, framed inside one of the door's four glass panels. My heart leaped into my throat. It was David's face, but it wasn't David. David was gone. This face, devoid of any expression of life, stared straight through me and into another world, as if its owner were in a deep, unrecoverable trance.

He knows.

I glanced over my shoulder at the garage. No signs of forced entry. No visible signs that anyone had been inside. I took a closer look. The toothpick was nestled securely in the doorjamb.

Pivoting toward the house, I turned the key and opened the door. Still in a catatonic state, the boy stepped backward and allowed me to enter. He was awake and capable of performing simple motor functions, yet he didn't seem to be conscious in any ordinary sense of the word. The sparkling radiance that had once lit up his features was gone. Face-to-face now with this senseless automaton standing rigidly in the mudroom, I scanned its lifeless eyes for some sign of the boy I'd come to know as David. But I found nothing. Only a blank stare that chilled me to the bone . . .

"David." I grasped him by the shoulders and gave him a gentle shake. "Hey, David! Are you okay? Snap out of it."

His body softened, and the sparkle returned to his azure-blue eyes.

"Hi, Ricky. Welcome home! How was work?"

"How was work? What do you mean, 'how was work?' How are you? Boy! Did you ever have me worried."

"Worried?" he said with all the pureness of heart and sincerity of an innocent child. "Why?"

"I thought you'd left me."

In response to my words, his face burst into an enormous smile. He flung himself into my arms and hugged me with all the warmth and passion of the loving son I never had. Disarmed by this outpouring of unconditional love, my heart melted. Tears filled my eyes. I returned his embrace and lost myself in the moment. Mountainfort and my war against tyranny became a distant memory. After all, what were they compared to this?

I'm not alone anymore.

You were never alone. We're connected—all of us. We're one. Separation is nothing more than an illusion created by the human mind.

We moved into the kitchen and prepared for dinner.

"I just had an idea, David. How about we go to the movies tonight?"

"Movies? I love movies. More than anything!"

"I know. How about a drive-in?"

"Sweet!"

After dinner, we drove out to the hinterlands and visited one of the few drive-in theaters still in operation. Pulling into a vacant stall, we hooked up the speakers and treated ourselves to a triple feature of *Shrek*, *Jurassic Park III*, and Tim Burton's *Planet of the Apes*. David loved *Shrek* (especially the donkey) and was riveted by the dinosaurs in *Jurassic Park III*, but finally he succumbed to sleep twenty minutes into *Planet of the Apes*.

We were about halfway home when the boy stirred and then woke from what had appeared to be a sound and impenetrable slumber. He sat up in his seat and gazed out the passenger's-side window. Lit only by the moon and stars above, the county road buzzed by at a decent clip of seventy miles an hour. Without looking at me, he spoke in strange, unnaturally low tones that blended into the rhythmic sound of the tires pounding the pavement below us.

"My time here is limited, Ricky. There's something I need to do. Something important. Once it's done, I'll be going back . . . for good."

"Going back? But you could stay—"

"No, Ricky, I can't."

He leaned into the door and pressed his cheek against the window. A thin cloud of vapor blossomed on the glass, advanced upward, and receded.

"David . . . David . . . David, are you still awake?"

No response.

Until just now, I didn't realize how lonely I was before this boy came into my life, and now . . . and now, he says he's leaving . . .

Friday, August 31, 2001

What's that?

A heavy curtain of trees parts, revealing a sliver of flickering light. A log cabin materializes . . . and a window . . . A thin, dimly lit candle sits on the sill and beckons to me. Its flame flutters help- lessly in the wind. If only I can get there before it goes out . . .

Da-doom, da-doom, da-doom . . .

My heart beats wildly. My lungs gasp for air. A fiery dose of lactic acid attacks the muscles in my legs and cramps them in a vise grip of agony. I will myself to ignore the pain and continue toward the light . . . I'm getting closer . . . almost there, but I make a fatal error—foolishly, I risk a glance over my shoulder. Expecting to see the war-painted faces of fierce cannibals, I see nothing; yet I can feel them breathing down the nape of my neck, setting the tiny hairs there ablaze . . . A root leaps up from the forest floor and catches my foot, sending me into a free fall . . .

I raise myself from the underbrush and reset my sights on the cabin, but it's too late—the faceless savages are upon me . . . their bony, gnarled hands are all over me, clawing at my flesh . . . I begin to scream—

I woke up in David's arms.

"It was just a dream, Ricky. Everything's gonna be all right. I promise."

You can't promise that. You don't know what I know . . . or do you?

"It was only a dream."

Under the spell of David's soothing voice, I fell back to sleep—this time, into a mercifully dreamless abyss—and slept through my alarm, only waking when David lifted the spell with a light touch of his fingertips on my cheek. It was almost ten o'clock.

The meeting! I'm going to be late!

With lightning speed, I leaped out of bed, got dressed, ran a comb through my hair, and bounded into the Audi.

I drove into the parking ramp in Golden Meadow with just minutes to spare before the ten-thirty meeting. Caste executives would be calling in from Palo Alto. There'd be hell to pay if I were late. Without stopping for coffee, I ran directly to the fish-bowl conference room on the third floor. Taking a deep breath, I placed my hand on the door and paused . . .

I cannot allow Mountainfort's scheme to move forward. I'll give them one last chance. If they won't do the right thing, I'm going to take matters into my own hands and put an end to this nonsense!

I entered the room. Brian Otterness was punching a code into a speakerphone splayed over the table like a giant tarantula. Mountainfort sat erect in a chair at the fishbowl's far end, his formidable arms folded into an X across his chest.

"Nice of you to join us, Mr. Williamson," he said, his voice oozing with sarcasm. "Have a seat."

The door swung shut behind me, and I took the very same seat from which I'd delivered my report detailing the atrocities committed against children in China. The executives at that meeting had received the news with cold indifference. They had no interest in what was happening in Doltz's factories. To them, it was nothing more than an annoying inconvenience.

It had been during that same meeting that Mountainfort had dismissed my concerns and proposed setting up a dummy corporation to cover up Caste's involvement with Doltz, a company that had, according to the ILO, used child labor. There'd been nine people other than me present. This week, there were only two others in the room. Mountainfort would be speaking for the team.

"Thank you," said an electronically generated voice in the dialect of a well-educated, middle-aged English woman. "Your call is already in progress. There is one other participant on the line."

"Hello. This is Brian Otterness in Golden Meadow. With me in the room, I have Alexander Mountainfort and Ricky Williamson."

There was a significant pause during which the speaker-phone transmitted only background noise, including a door opening and closing, the shuffling of feet, muffled voices, and a flurry of chairs.

"Hello? Brian? This is Art Charrington. I don't think we've ever met. I'm Ricky's boss. My apologies for the delay; we're just getting organized here."

More background noise. A single chair skated across a floor in a Palo Alto conference room. The phone became quiet. I imagined a huge floor-to-ceiling window with a picturesque view of rolling emerald hills as far as the eye could see . . .

"Okay, good. We're all here now. With me are Manny Cunningham, Paul Feinsmith, and Ed Squire."

The vice president of global operations for the entire Caste organization, of which SteadFast and Computer Electronic Solutions were only a small part, Manny Cunningham was a twenty-five-year veteran of the company, with a reputation for being every bit as hard-driving and demanding as Mountainfort. I'd read Manny's bio. A graduate of Stanford Law School, he had abandoned a promising law practice to pursue a career in manufacturing. Paul Feinsmith was Caste's vice president of global strategy and business development, and Ed Squire was its vice president of sales and marketing. All three men reported directly to the company's chief executive officer and chairman of the board, Thomas O'Brien.

Art continued, "The purpose of this meeting is to identify the reasons for the delay in closing the deal with Doltz
Technologies and determine appropriate corrective action measures. After the meeting, I'll provide an update to my boss, who
will, in turn, brief Mr. O'Brien."

Art's boss was Caste's general counsel and corporate secretary, Arlen Wright, who reported to Thomas O'Brien.

"Let's get started. Most of us are familiar with the outsourcing program and our selection of Doltz as an offshore contract
manufacturer. But I'd like to make sure we're all on the same
page. Alex, would you be so kind as to provide us with a brief
chronology of the facts and events leading up to this meeting?"

Starting with the June 28 kickoff meeting, Mountainfort
reviewed the process of selecting Doltz to act as a test pilot for
the outsourcing program, the subsequent contract negotiations,
and finally, the August 20 meeting, during which the child labor
issue was discussed and the dummy corporation idea proposed.
What Mountainfort failed to mention was that, two years earlier, Caste had explored the possibility of acquiring Doltz. Due
diligence had been conducted. Accordingly, the company's
executive team knew all about the child labor scandal when it
awarded Doltz the business back in early August.

"Mr. Williamson discovered some unpleasant history in
Doltz's past related to the use of child labor in its factories, and
he should be commended for his efforts. But that issue has been
resolved for quite some time now."

I wanted to speak up, to inform the group of the Fair Labor
Association's recently opened investigation, yet Mountainfort
plowed ahead.

"Here's the bottom line: the contract negotiations are taking too damned long. There's been absolutely no progress since the August 20 meeting. And what about the dummy? It's been more than ten days now, and we're still waiting for legal to set up the dummy corporation so critical to the program's success. Still waiting! Gentlemen, we need legal to get into the game. We need legal to commit to getting the job done and getting it done ASAP. Every day that passes is a lost opportunity to win back market share from the competition."

"I understand Mr. Williams—uh, Ricky—was out of the office for two days this week," said Ed Squire.

"Yes," confirmed Mountainfort.

"I took a couple of sick days," I said, genuinely beginning to feel ill.

"We cannot afford any more delays," said Squire. "If you're on your deathbed, you call in and complete this deal from home! Understand?"

Coming to my aid, Paul Feinsmith interrupted the blood-thirsty sales executive with a sharp clearing of his throat.

"Hold on a second, Ed," he said. "I've got a question. Alex, can you explain to me the purpose for this so-called dummy corporation?"

At this point in the discussion, I grasped on to the slimmest of hopes that this voice of apparent reason would prevail.

"It's just a precaution, Paul," Mountainfort replied, "to shield Caste from any future problems that might arise."

Before Feinsmith had a chance to challenge this glib expla-nation, however, Manny Cunningham jumped in. With all the skill and finesse of a seasoned prosecutor, he started in on me, as if cross-examining a witness.

"Mr. Williamson, am I to understand you still have issues with Doltz and with the setting up of the dummy corporation?"

"Yes, sir, I do."

"Is Doltz engaged in illegal activities?"

"No, not so far as I know. But as I told Mr. Mountainfort and the other CES executives last week—"

"Is the dummy corporation illegal?"

"No, not technically."

"Good."

If you only would allow me to clarify my position, I think you'd find it—

"Very good."

—compelling . . .

While setting up a dummy corporation isn't technically illegal, in this case, it most definitely would be perceived as an intentional misrepresentation of facts designed to deceive not only our customers but also other stakeholders, such as our investors, the American government, the general public, and of course, the United Nations and its International Labour Organization. As you well know, the only reason we're considering setting up a dummy is to cover up our business dealings with a company that uses child labor in its factories. Child labor! This type of deception won't be easily forgiven. If there's ever an investigation into the activities of this dummy corporation, Caste's reputation will be damaged, and sales will suffer as a result. The very survival of the company could be threatened—

"Very good, Mr. Williamson." Cunningham's voice was condescendingly dark and ominous, yet it had a strange calming effect, like that of a snake charmer's pungi. "You're doing just fine."

"But—"

"As long as it's not illegal, I'm okay with it."

"But—"

"You have a problem with the ethics."

"Yes, sir."

"That's not your concern."

"But—"

"Thank you, Mr. Williamson." Cunningham concluded his examination.

"No offense to you, Art," he said. "I have all the respect in the world for you and Arlen Wright. Your organization performs a valuable service for this company. But I don't want to hear any holier-than-thou pronouncements from the lawyers' pulpit. Not today. I'm not in the mood."

"You can set your mind at ease, Manny," said Art. "Speaking for Arlen and the entire legal department, we are here for the sole and express purpose of serving you and supporting the business. The business always comes first. Always. I know from time to time, legal has been perceived as an obstacle, but make no mistake about it, you have our full and complete cooperation in this matter."

Our full and complete cooperation? Are you kidding me, Art? What about the company-wide rollout of the ethics campaign? Isn't that your baby? C'mon, don't be shy. Of course it's your baby, Arthur! You can't fool me. In fact, I have it on good authority that you dedicated the last six months of your career to developing a compliance program—one designed to ensure all employees understand their ethical obligations as dutiful members of Caste's happy family of businesses.

Armed with a respectable budget, a staff of three, and a mandate to create a world-class culture of compliance, Art

Charrington began by enlisting the marketing department to produce glossy brochures with catchy yet meaningless slogans and buzz phrases, such as:

Understand your ethical obligations. Be part of the solution, not the problem!

And:

At Caste, we're proud of our absolute and unwavering commitment to doing business with integrity.

As well as the ever-popular:

Doing business with integrity. The right way. The Caste way.

He developed state-of-the-art PowerPoint presentations with all the bells and whistles. He launched a training program to spread his message of "doing business with integrity." He introduced the company's *Guide to Ethical Conduct* to Caste employees around the globe. To ensure ongoing compliance, he engaged an outside firm to develop an online course to be completed by all employees on an annual basis.

So, do you stand by your ethics program, or are you simply paying lip service to a hollow idea? Is Caste really committed to business ethics, or are we just going through the motions? Did some consultant advise you that an ethics program is essential to portraying the right kind of image to the investing public? You know what I hate, Art? Hypocrisy! I hate that we have become so very good at telling people exactly what they want to hear. Without meaning a word of it! And when it matters most, we abandon our principles as easily and quickly as dropping a piece of hot coal from our charred hands.

And what about our mutual friend, Mr. Manny Cunningham, who doesn't want to hear any holier-than-thou pronouncements from the lawyers? Well, why the hell not? Isn't your program designed to ensure we all conduct ourselves in a manner beyond reproach? And isn't it the legal department's job to ensure all Caste employees comply with the rules set forth in the company's ethics guide? Or perhaps the rules don't apply to the executive team? As we're learning today, they most definitely don't apply when a deal is on the line and profits are at stake.

Hypocrisy! Hypocrisy is alive and well at Caste Enterprises! The seeds of corruption are rooted in the very fabric of the company, in the hearts and minds of its executives . . . and these seeds must be eradicated before they have a chance to sprout and flourish . . .

Little did I know at the time, but the seeds of corruption were germinating not only just beneath the surface of Caste's well-tilled fields in the dog days of that summer of 2001 but also in fertile soil throughout corporate America. In the following months and throughout the remaining years of that first decade of the new millennium, one seed after another would sprout and emerge from the earth in the form of corporate scandals that would ravage Wall Street and disgrace our country with head-lines of accounting fraud, corporate espionage, bribery, insider trading, securities fraud, embezzlement, kickback schemes, and more. Falling prey to the insatiable greed and treachery of their once-trusted corporate officers were such companies as Enron, Adelphia, AOL Time Warner, Global Crossing, Halliburton, Tyco International, WorldCom, HealthSouth, Freddie Mac, AIG, Lehman Brothers, and many others. In executive suites and boardrooms across the country, the wisdom of the human heart was eclipsed by a cold-blooded, calculating logic fueled by a torrid lust for extravagant wealth and power.

For God's sake, Art, this one's not even a close call. Mountainfort's scheme is clearly in violation of Caste's own ethics guide. What do you want me to do? Turn the other cheek? Stick my head in the sand? Play ball? Well, I won't do it! Maybe there's nothing I can do to end the suffering of children in China, but I refuse to be a part of it, and I will not allow these heartless executives to pretend it doesn't matter.

Aren't you ashamed, Art? I am. That we live in a civilization capable of exploiting its children for profit should be repugnant to our moral sense. Yet here we are on a beautiful Friday morning, poised on the edge of another Labor Day weekend, discussing—in callous disregard for the lives of children—how to expedite the Doltz deal. And for what? What is it really for? I'll tell you what. For nothing other than to increase shareholder value and line the pockets of the Caste executive team with millions of dollars in stock options.

"I'll take care of setting up the dummy corporation from this end," said Art. "I know counsel in Hong Kong who can handle this expeditiously. In the meantime, let's get Williamson on a plane to finish negotiating the contract with Doltz."

"Excellent!" said Mountainfort. "Williamson, book yourself a flight to China right away."

"B-b-but . . . this is Labor Day weekend."

"Fine. Enjoy the holiday. Just make sure your ass is on a plane to China come Tuesday morning. And don't bother coming back until the contract has been finalized."

"Close the deal, Williamson."

"Yeah, get it done, Ricky."

The speakerphone crackled.

"Alex? Alex, this is Art. Before I let you go, I wanted to remind you that Manny and I will be in Golden Meadow on Tuesday on some unrelated business . . ."

Isn't that interesting? Art Charrington, Manny Cunningham, and Alexander Mountainfort are going to be in Golden Meadow on Tuesday.

There's only one sane response to an insane situation . . .

My mind was made up. Originally, I had targeted September 11, but time was no longer a luxury I could afford. I left the conference room, went home, and started the holiday weekend early.

Saturday, September 1–Monday, September 3, 2001

The weekend commenced with a heat advisory. The air was unfit to breathe. The local news outlets urged residents of Heartland City to stay indoors. I lowered the blinds and fell into a hopelessly morose state, plodding from one dimly lit corner of my bungalow to the other. A faucet dripped. The refrigerator wheezed. The house lurched. An aging air-conditioning unit powered up and struggled to keep pace with the rising temperatures. The boy, who must have sensed my inner turmoil, respected my space. Careful to avoid a collision, we went about our business like two lonely, overburdened barges on the Mississippi, lumbering past each other in the night.

Forgoing sleep, I locked myself in the garage and worked into the wee hours of the morning. The heat was intense, yet my focus remained sharp and my fingers nimble as I finished assembling the last and most lethal weapon in my arsenal. The bomb was ready.

When I wasn't moping around the house or locked away in the garage, I was at the shooting range. Inhaling toxic clouds of gunpowder, I conjured up likenesses of Alexander Mountainfort

. . . Art Charrington . . . Jim Kidwell . . . and a sixteen-year-old boy named Spencer . . . *Spencer Black* . . .

I fired with deadly precision at the target's bull's-eye. Mountainfort's face exploded. Blood and flesh and bone splattered the floor. Another face appeared . . . I took aim and squeezed the trigger . . .

They're gonna pay. Bang! All of them. They might have me outnumbered, but come Tuesday, I'm gonna be prepared. And when I complete my mission—Bang!—the world will wake up from its collective slumber—Bang!—and take notice . . .

Bang! Bang!

They will remember Ricky Williamson and what he stood for . . .

Bang! Bang! Bang!

It was Monday evening, and Labor Day was coming to a swift and unceremonious close. I had just returned home from a final stint at the range, open for business 365 days a year. On this day, like most, it had been packed to the gills with sharpshooters of both genders and all ages. Honing their skills. Together, we were preparing for a new world order. Our time had come.

After checking the garage to make sure my arsenal was secure, I entered the house.

It was quiet.

Too quiet.

A firm and steady voice, not much louder than a whisper, cut through the stillness like a machete through an overgrown mass of rotting vegetation.

"I know what you're planning, Ricky."

No emotion. The voice had simply stated a fact. An incontrovertible fact.

"You don't have to do it. We can end this here and now."

I followed the voice into the living room. Naked from the waist up, the boy stood in a shadowy corner. His skinny arms were folded across his chest. His luminous eyes pierced the shadows and came to rest on me. Two azure stars—twins—shining from a distant galaxy. Constant. Resolute. The day's last few rays of light filtered through the venetian blinds and cast tiger stripes across the amber hues of the hardwood floor at the boy's feet.

Unfolding his arms, he stepped into the light and turned his back to me. A grotesque landscape of mangled ridges and valleys came into view. A gasp sprang from my throat. I should've been prepared, yet for some reason, I'd expected the smooth and unblemished skin of a healthy ten-year-old boy.

Unable to tear my eyes away from those hideous scars, which covered most of his back, I uttered, "My God, what happened to you?"

"You know what happened, Ricky." He turned to face me. "You were there. We share the same scars, the same secrets. I'm not showing you these wounds to upset you but to make a point. To demonstrate how powerful you can be. How powerful you are. You see, within us, we have the ability to choose. We can choose a life of freedom, joy, and peace, regardless of our scars, regardless of the past.

"The past cannot control us, Ricky. The past is nothing but a feckless phantom haunting the dark and dusty hollows of our overly susceptible minds. The past has no real power, only illusory power. It can determine the direction of our lives only if we allow it to define who we are."

In shock and unable to process the boy's words, I felt a bilious attack of outrage rising from deep within my gut. I swallowed hard. The anger continued to rise . . .

"Who . . . who did this to you?"

"You know who did this. There's no need to pretend anymore."

Whi-kisssh!

The hickory branch sliced through the cool Maine air. I braced for impact. The searing heat of the first blow ignited a fire across my back. I winced against the pain and choked back a sob. My knees buckled.

Whi-kisssh!

I staggered to the floor, and the sobs came in waves.

"S-S-Spencer . . . Spencer Black," I spluttered. "Henry Hatfield. Their two henchmen—those, those, those *freaks*— they were so big—those twin brothers, Theodore and Thaddeus. Jim Kidwell. Alexander Mountainfort and all those other bastards at Caste. I'm gonna make them pay. I've got a plan to get even—"

"There's no getting even, Ricky. Revenge is not the answer. There's only one remedy, only one path to peace—"

"It's not just about revenge!"

Forgiveness . . .

Tears of rage filled my eyes. "It's . . . it's about justice . . . *justice* for all those innocent children—"

"Please listen to me, Ricky. I need you to listen as if both our lives depended on it. I don't have much time left. We need to focus. It's not about justice for those children. There's nothing you can do for them."

"But—"

"This thing you're planning to do tomorrow, it isn't necessary. Something else is possible. Something extraordinary. Something beyond extraordinary . . ."

The boy—young Ricky—paused and gazed deeply into my eyes, as if that *something* were to be found somewhere within me.

He continued, "You'll need to do something you've never done before. You'll need to take a leap of faith, to let go of the past and pursue dreams worthy of you . . . worthy of us, worthy of our father, our mother, and all our brothers and sisters around the globe . . ."

I made my way to my feet and fell into his arms.

"Perhaps someday, Ricky, you'll tell our story."

CHAPTER FIVE

Tuesday, September 4, 2001

S OMEHOW, I BREAK FREE FROM THE FACELESS SAVAGES *and resume my sprint toward the cabin. The candle still flickers in the window, but its wick is dwindling . . . I'm almost out of time . . .*

I reach the cabin, grab the rusty doorknob, and freeze. A wave of foreboding knocks the wind out of me like a swift kick in the solar plexus. Something terrible is waiting for me on the other side. I can feel it in my bones . . . But there's no time for delay. The savages are only seconds behind me, their drums matching, beat for beat, the tempo and ferocity of my pounding heart.

Da-doom, da-doom, da-doom . . .

It's all around me. The beat's crushing weight—it's more than I can bear. Whatever's behind this door can't be any worse than the incessant beating of those drums . . . those infernal drums! I try to turn the knob, but my hand swells—like a water balloon—to two, three times its normal size. It's distorted beyond all recognition as a

*human hand and completely useless to me. I take a stab at the knob
with my other hand. It too swells up. In a panic, I use my forearms to
turn the knob, and the door swings open with a sharp creak.*

The drums stop. The candle goes out.

*I stagger into a black box of a room, lit only by a hazy moon
casting diffuse beams through the cabin's only window and onto the
splintered planks at my feet. The room is empty, except for a ladder
that leads to a loft. Whatever's up there is hidden by a canvas sheet
hanging from the ceiling. I take a step toward the ladder, and the
floor opens. Crying out, I spiral downward through the twists and
turns of a seemingly never-ending wormhole . . .*

*. . . until, at long last, I land with a hard thump on a cold dirt
floor. I'm in a dungeon, rank with the smell of mold and echoing
with the sound of water dripping down its jagged stone walls. A
thin ray shines from above—the only sign of hope in this dank and
sepulchral hole I've fallen into.*

You want another one?

*A man with skin the color of faded copper, a black beard, and a
vaguely familiar face steps into the light. He strikes a match, ignites
a cigarette, and, between puffs, bares a bone-chilling grin. At his
feet are the tangled and bloodied bodies of a woman and two adolescent girls.*

He cackles fiendishly under his breath.

Hello, Ricky.

Jihad?

*The woman stirs and lets out a pitiable moan. Her eyes flutter
open. She's alive!*

Ricky? Is that you? Help us, Ricky. Please help us.

*She raises a bruised and broken hand from the floor and
extends an open palm.*

There's still time . . .

Kimberly?

Reaching for her outstretched hand, I move toward her—

A sonic boom fills my ears, and the dungeon bursts into a mass of flames. Above the explosion's din, I hear the man with coppery skin laughing maniacally . . . and then . . . silence, darkness . . .

4:13 a.m.

Resting safely in the basket of a hot-air balloon, I floated upward. The darkness lifted. A white dove with bloodred eyes flew by. Below, surrounded by clouds of smoke and debris, a woman reached out to me with an open palm. She needed my help. There was nothing I could do for her. Almost entirely obscured by the smoke, her face contorted into a desperate grimace. Her chest heaved, and she gasped for air. Her lips moved but made no sound.

Rising from the nethermost regions of consciousness, I drew upon all my faculties to stay focused on her receding face. Was it? Could it be? Kimberly? The image shrank to the size of a button and disappeared.

At the summit of consciousness, I became aware of my physical body. Cold sweat covered my skin from head to toe. From deep within my core, I trembled like autumn's last leaf clinging for dear life in the face of a harsh wind and pitiless November rain. My eyes flittered open. The hardscrabble lunar landscape of my bedroom's textured ceiling materialized. No trace of the woman. She was gone.

This is it. Today is the day. In a few short hours, it'll all be over.

Attempting to maintain control over the raw energy surging through my body, I resisted the urge to spring out of bed. Instead, a cautious peek over the edge . . .

Illuminated by the alarm clock's greenish glow, the boy lay sprawled on the inflatable mattress. His eyes were closed. His mouth drifted open in a silent snore. Sleeping soundly. Peaceful as an angel. *Young Ricky.* Was it possible? It had been seven days since I discovered his body floating among the cattails and reeds of Lake Weston . . . seven days . . .

. . . and twenty-five years since that night at the pond . . . twenty-five years . . .

In any case, it would be over soon.

I crawled out of bed and tiptoed around the inflatable mattress. At my dresser, I delved into a drawer. It produced a pair of underwear, athletic socks, a T-shirt, and blue jeans. A casual-dress day at the office. Given the circumstances, the fashion police weren't likely to put up a fuss. With my clothes tucked under one arm, I used the other to feel my way through the darkness. My senses charged with electricity, I maneuvered around the unconscious boy with the precision and balance of a ninja. Exiting the bedroom, I crept down the staircase without in any way disturbing the integrity of the nascent morning's peace.

4:46 a.m.

I had just completed a final inventory of my arsenal. All boxes on my list were checked. Squatting, I lifted a bulky canvas duffel bag off the floor and lowered it into the Audi's trunk. My muscles strained and quivered under the bag's considerable weight . . .

The door at the back of the garage swung open. The boy stepped inside. Startled by his sudden entrance, I fumbled the bag. It slipped out of my hands and dropped to the bottom of the trunk—a distance of only four or five inches, but it was enough to make my heart stop, for the bag was packed with roofing nails, a propane tank bomb, and a detonator.

I thought I locked that goddamned door. No . . . I'm sure I locked that goddamned door.

As if to mock me, the door slammed shut. The walls shook. I nearly jumped out of my skin. The boy, unperturbed by the loud bang produced by the door, remained perfectly still. His pointed gaze harpooned me from across the full length of the garage. The only source of light—a solitary bulb swinging back and forth like a pendulum in the rafters—cast a pale yellowish glow across his face. Gravely serious, yet calm.

That unventilated and musty old garage was hot. Very hot. Although it wasn't yet five in the morning, I perspired profusely. My T-shirt clung tenaciously to my chest and shoulders. The air was thick and rancid. Trying to recover my wits, I took a deep breath. It was like sucking on a filthy bar rag. Not in the least bit bothered by the unfavorable atmospheric conditions, the boy maintained a cool and composed demeanor, waiting for the right moment to speak.

My stomach growled. I had attempted a light breakfast of half a bagel and a banana. After a few nibbles, though, I realized it would be impossible to keep anything down. So, wisely deciding to forgo food, I'd proceeded to the garage to make my final preparations.

Returning to the task at hand and avoiding the boy's gaze, I picked up the AR-15 9 mm carbine semiautomatic assault rifle from the workbench and carefully placed it in the trunk next to the bomb. Its jet-black finish gleamed. I smiled. Polishing the weapons had been well worth the effort.

"You don't want to do this," the boy said.

"I don't? Just watch me."

I began depositing magazines and ammunition into the trunk beside the rifle.

"You know this isn't right."

"Oh yeah? Well, what're you going to do about it? You can't stop me. You're not even real."

"I'm more real than you think."

"How could you be real? How could you possibly be real? You look just like . . . just like . . ."

"Just like who, Ricky?"

"Just like . . ."

I turned away from the boy, returned to the workbench, and loaded a box of fifty rounds of ammunition into the car.

"I know what you're feeling, Ricky." He moved away from the door and approached the workbench. "I can see your pain, your loneliness . . . I want to help."

"You can't help me," I muttered. "No one can help. It's too late for that."

I continued loading the ammunition into the car.

"Don't do this, Ricky. It's not who you are."

"How would you know who I am? Do you have some special insight into my soul? I've come too far—much too far—to allow a figment of my imagination to stop me now."

"A figment of your imagination . . . Is that what you think?"

"Of course that's what I think!"

"Well, it's true that I have no special insight, no mystical powers of perception. But I do have a pretty good idea why you're doing this. You feel betrayed by the world for all the wrongs you think have been done to you, and this is your chance to get even."

I stopped, thrust my hands into my pockets, and spied a crack in the floor where the concrete had shifted. An ant emerged from the crack, raised its antennae, and skittered away. The empty crack gaped up at me.

When did that happen? Have I been sleeping? Yes, I surely must've been sleeping. But . . . but how did it happen? What combination of forces is capable of creating such a crack? How many years of imperceptibly small, incremental changes are required to—

"And there's something else, Ricky. You feel responsible for the fate of those children in China. You think you're in a position to do something about their situation, and you feel obligated—"

"Yes."

"And you identify with them. You know what it feels like to be a victim, to have your childhood snatched from you. You feel their misery. You're carrying it around like a physical sickness—a metastasizing cancer eating you alive from the inside out. You've created a world for yourself not unlike theirs, Ricky. It's almost as if you were in China, slaving away in those sweatshops right alongside them—those innocent children suffering at the cold, indifferent hands of the corporate machine, day in and day out . . . those beautiful children . . . your brothers and sisters . . ."

"Yes."

Finally, someone who understands.

"You believe you can save them."

"Yes . . . no . . . I don't know . . . maybe."

"Well, perhaps you can. But not this way. Not this way, Ricky. Violence is not the answer. It cannot cure the world of its ills. Violence only begets more violence."

"I can't just stand by and let it continue. I have to do something!"

"Relax, Ricky. Breathe. You've been carrying the weight of the world on your shoulders for far too long. It's time to let it go."

"But—"

"Let it go, Ricky. It's much too great a burden for any one man to bear. Let it go. Let it go and be free. Yes, you can be free, but you have to be willing—"

"But I . . . But they . . . But you . . . you don't understand."

"I do understand. Believe me, I understand. And I care. I care about the lives of each and every one of those children. It breaks my heart to think of them being sacrificed—not so much like lambs but mongrel dogs wandering the streets for scraps, and for no reason other than to bolster corporate profits. It's an abomination. It's morally reprehensible. But taking out your anger on the executives at work won't solve the problem. It won't bring the children relief."

"Maybe not immediate relief, but someone has to start somewhere. Men like Mountainfort are a fundamental part of the problem. They don't see human beings; they see only opportunities for profit. Mountainfort and his gang are willfully turning a blind eye to the suffering of children, and they should be punished for it."

"Why do *you* need to be the one to punish them?"

"Because of what they've done to me."

"What have they done to you?"

"What have they done to me? How can you even ask such a question? They've made my life a living hell—that's what they've done to me."

"How?"

"How? I'll tell you how. They denied me opportunities to advance. Opportunities I'd earned! They . . . they took advantage of me. During the layoffs, they forced me to work insane hours with no increases in pay."

They betrayed me.

"They ridiculed me."

They ambushed me.

"They cross-examined me in meetings."

They beat and raped me.

"They humiliated me in front of my colleagues. They threatened to have me fired. Time and time again, those bastards disrespected me."

"So?"

"So, I have to make them pay."

"Why?"

"Why?"

I was getting confused now, losing my focus . . . Before I met this boy—who was so wise beyond his years, who'd become my teacher, my friend, my best friend, my only friend—I'd been so sure what needed to be done. Everything had been so clear.

"I don't know exactly . . . I told you already. They disrespected me. They humiliated me. Time after time, they humiliated me. They made me feel insignificant. They robbed me of my dignity, my honor. Yes! My honor! It's a question of honor!"

"Honor? My dear Ricky, what is honor? Can you show it to me? What does it look like? Where is it? Is it hiding in the corner? Under this workbench? No? Is it in the air we're breathing? Is it floating around in the space between us? No, of course it isn't. Honor is just an idea. And like all ideas, honor has no inherent reality of its own. It was made up by humans to give us a false sense of security, of self-importance, of being morally superior, of always being in the right. And we hold on to our honor with all the tenacity of Wile E. Coyote pursuing the Road Runner—a fruitless exercise, wouldn't you agree?"

The Road Runner? I used to be a roadrunner—that's what they called me in school—but that was before . . . before . . .

"Wouldn't you agree, Ricky?"

"I dunno. I guess so."

"You say they robbed you of your honor—"

"They did! They robbed me of my honor."

"Well, maybe they did and maybe they didn't. But rest assured, nothing of any true value can ever be taken from you. And yet, every day, hundreds of thousands of young men roam the streets of this country's cities, willing to kill and be killed defending their honor. Nations go to war for honor. Innocent bystanders and civilians get caught in the cross fire and are slaughtered in the name of honor. Politicians refer to them as 'collateral damage.'

"It's high-minded-sounding words like *honor, dignity,* and *respect* that serve as the building blocks for the stories in our heads about who we think we are and who we think we should be. In and of themselves, these stories aren't a problem, but beware not to take your personal story too seriously. And know that your story is neither true nor false, good nor bad, right nor wrong. It's just a story.

"Here's the thing," he said, pausing for dramatic effect, "it's your desperate clinging to this story that's responsible for all the suffering in your life.

"Don't you see, Ricky? By clinging to your story as if it were real, you've been making yourself miserable. And for what? To defend a made-up idea like honor? Give it up, Ricky. Give it up and be free. There's so much more to you than the ideas and thoughts in your head. You can be free of them. It's simple. Just be aware of them when they arise and recognize they're not who you are. Don't give them power. Let them go. You'll discover something remarkable. Beyond the realm of these ideas and thoughts lies your true self—fully conscious, present, at one with all creation . . . infinitely powerful . . .

"You don't need to follow the same old script that's been written into the collective consciousness. By following this script, humans have created modern civilization. All its conveniences and technical marvels. Yet what price have we paid? Watch the nightly news. An escalating stream of conflicts between nations. Hostilities between races and members of different religious groups. Violence on our streets and in our schools. Terrorism is on the rise. The very real possibility of global war threatens civilization's very existence. It doesn't have to be this way. You can bring something new into this world."

"And what's that?"

"Love. *Your* love, Ricky."

"Okay, I've heard enough."

I removed my hands from my pockets and loaded the last fifty rounds of ammunition into the car.

"You're very articulate for a ten-year-old boy, even an imaginary one." I slammed the trunk shut. "Now, if you'll excuse me, I have a job to do."

I returned to the workbench. Two items remained: the Glock 19 and a long black leather trench coat, just like Neo's in *The Matrix*. I holstered the Glock and threw the coat through the driver's-side window. It landed in a heap on the passenger's seat. Time to go.

"Ricky!" said the boy. "The threshold! Do you remember the threshold?"

The threshold?

I stopped dead in my tracks. "What did you say?"

"The threshold. Do you remember that night at the end of the dirt road—the one leading out of Camp Abenaki Valley?"

The heat in the garage bored into my skull, stifling my ability to think straight.

Camp Abenaki Valley?

"It was late. There was a brilliant moon in the sky. You had just made it through the Tunnel of Doom. Your toes were no more than an inch or two from the edge of the state highway. You were standing there, wrestling with an important decision."

"Camp Abenaki Valley . . . the Tunnel of Doom . . . the state highway . . . Yes . . . yes, I remember. How could you possibly know—"

"You know how."

"I do?"

"I'm *you*, Ricky. I've come to you from the past. Your past."

"That's . . . that's impossible . . . It doesn't make any sense. There's no proof."

"Ricky, we share the same scars."

He had me. Hot tears filled my eyes.

"You've always known."

"Yes."

"You've known ever since you found me on the shore of that lake."

"Yes."

"Okay. Good. Now, tell me what you remember."

"They were going to kill me. To shut me up. Spencer and his gang. They chased me into the Tunnel of Doom. It was dark . . . so dark I had to feel my way along the side of the road. Somehow, after what seemed like hours, I made it to the end of the tunnel—well, just about to the end—when I came face-to-face with Burning Sky. I thought he was a myth. But he was real. He was on horseback, coming at me with his bow and arrow drawn. I closed my eyes and braced for impact, but he passed right through me. Then Spencer appeared. I kicked him. Hard. So hard he fell to the ground and couldn't get up. I ran. I ran out of the tunnel and right up to the intersection of the dirt road and the state highway."

"What happened next?"

"Nothing. Nothing happened. I was a coward. I stood there for the longest time trying to summon the courage to move forward. But I couldn't. Something powerful held me back. I was only a step, a mere step from crossing the threshold, yet I didn't . . . I couldn't do it . . ."

"Go on."

"The wind whispered in my ear, encouraging me to take that

step—that one little step that promised to change my entire life. But I refused to listen."

"What did the wind say?"

"*Have faith.*"

"Yes. That's right, Ricky. Have faith."

"Yes, well, faith never came. I never stepped onto the highway. I never crossed the threshold. Instead, I turned around and returned to my cabin."

"What about Spencer?"

"Spencer? I don't know. He was gone."

After a long silence, the boy smiled and leaned forward. "Have you ever wondered how your life would have turned out if you had crossed that threshold?"

"Every day . . . *every* day . . . every single day . . ."

"Listen to me, Ricky. What if I were to tell you that you did cross that threshold?"

"What are you talking about? I wanted to step forward onto that highway, to begin my journey home, but I couldn't and didn't. So, I returned to my cabin."

"No."

"No?"

"No. You didn't return to your cabin."

Not yet, anyway.

"I distinctly remember—"

"Ricky, look at me. I'm here to tell you that you *did* cross the threshold. That night, you fell under a powerful spell to make you believe otherwise. To make you believe you returned to your cabin. To make you believe you woke up the next morning still at Camp Abenaki Valley. To make you believe you continued living that life—the life of a powerless victim who grew up to be tormented by the likes of Jim Kidwell and Alexander Mountainfort. The spell made you believe in a life of fear. It made you believe you weren't worthy of love. It made you believe you weren't capable of crossing the threshold."

The boy's eyes lit up, and he continued, "The truth is you did cross the threshold. You crossed the threshold with me, and together, we began a life-transforming journey. I'm here before you now to free you of all your illusions."

"Okay, that's it. I've had enough."

"You see, Ricky, none of this is real."

"Enough! I'm not listening to any more of this nonsense."

"I'm here to help you, Ricky." He took a step toward me. "The life you've always dreamed of . . . it's within your reach . . ."

"Stop right there."

I removed the Glock from its holster and pointed its barrel straight at the boy's chest.

Without losing his composure, he took another step.

"You don't have to do this, Ricky," he said evenly. "You're standing on the threshold again. You have a choice."

"A choice!" I gripped the pistol with both hands. "That's a laugh! What kind of choice do I have? What kind of choice did I ever have? I never had a choice. The script for my life was written from the day I was born."

"That's not true, Ricky. You want proof?" Another step. "I'm your proof."

"That's far enough! You want to find out if this gun is loaded?"

"I'm not afraid to die, Ricky. Are you?"

I placed my finger on the trigger.

"Ricky—"

"Quiet! No more words. I'm done listening."

Taking one final step, the boy spread his arms wide—as if preparing for flight—and moved to embrace me. My finger fell away from the trigger. The gun rose over my head, and I watched—as if from the sidelines—as its butt came crashing down on his temple. His body crumpled to the floor like a rag doll.

Oh my God. What have I done?

There was no blood. There should have been blood. Lots of it. I'd heard head wounds produced lots of blood. I bent down to inspect the boy's body for signs of life. After a careful search, I detected movement. A flutter of the eyelids, a twitching of the nose. His breath came in a labored spasm and then settled into an easy rhythm. He sat up and gazed at me with his big blue eyes.

"It's okay, Ricky. I'm fine. You can't hurt me."

Certain I'd just heard the words of a ghost, I stood straight up and backed away slowly.

"I'm . . . I'm sorry, I'm so sorry, but I-I-I have to go. I d-d-don't have a choice. I really don't."

I holstered the Glock, jumped into the car, and fired up the engine. The garage door opener should've been clipped to the visor. It wasn't. *Shit.* Groping for the device, I found it sitting in the passenger's seat under the trench coat. Clicked it. Nothing. Clicked it again. Coughing and sputtering, the door clambered upward.

Come on! Come on, already . . . one one-thousand, two one-thousand . . . Finally!

Backing out of the garage and down the driveway toward the alley, I stole a glance through the windshield. The boy stood up. Our eyes met. He looked at me not with anger or even disappointment but with compassion and the faith of an angel . . .

I'm sorry, Ricky. I failed you . . . but there's still time to make it right . . .

You failed me? I just clobbered you over the head with the butt of a pistol . . . and you failed me?

There's still time to make it right . . .

5:29 a.m.

After backing into the alley, I shifted the car into drive and began my final commute. The route was so familiar I could have navigated it blindfolded. Over the course of my eight-year career at SteadFast/Caste, the Audi had worn a groove into the roads from my house to Golden Meadow—a groove so deep all I needed to do was tap the accelerator, and the car would get me to work with little or no active participation on my part. Traffic was light. The mad rush to the suburban office parks following the holiday weekend hadn't yet begun. As I merged onto the freeway, I reminded myself of the illicit nature of my cargo. It would be imperative to drive at or below the posted speed limit so as not to attract the attention of the state highway patrol.

It was dark. The sun wasn't due to rise for at least another hour. Above, a thick veil of clouds moved in, obscuring the moon and stars. *I'm all alone.* I clenched my jaw and grasped the steering wheel with both hands . . .

What's that? It sounds like . . . It's Mom! She's crying! I open the door . . . On the nightstand, there's a lamp with a discolored shade radiating a wide circle of pale yellow light. Within this circle, Mom is sitting on the edge of her bed, head in hands . . . weeping . . .

What is it, Mom?

Ricky, come sit by me . . . Your father died last night . . .

Spiraling downward into an abyss, I land feetfirst on a hard, flat surface, my toes hanging over the edge . . . Below me, a tiny point of light twinkles against a backdrop of utter darkness. The only star in the universe. The light begins to pulse, and with each pulse, it grows larger and larger . . . Soon, I'm staring into the image of a golden sun reflecting off a pool of aqua blue. It's beautiful, blinding . . . my head spins . . . waves of nausea ripple through my body . . . I want to jump, yet I'm held hostage by fear. All I'd have to do is take one step, one teensy-weensy step, and I'd be falling headfirst into the unknown . . . the glorious unknown . . .

And hot! I couldn't remember it ever being this hot and sticky so early in the morning except . . . except for the summer of 1976 during my five-week internment just outside a sleepy little town in southern Maine . . .

The water evaporates . . . the sun vanishes . . . I'm staring down . . . down . . . down . . . into nothingness . . . until finally, a new image comes into focus . . .

My feet are planted in the grainy dust of a dirt road, no more than an inch or two from the paved surface of the state highway: Maine State Route 4. On the other side of this threshold lies a new beginning, a fresh start . . . It's so close I can smell it, taste it . . . But I'm stuck; something's holding me back . . .

The truth is you did cross the threshold. You crossed the threshold with me, and together, we began a life-transforming journey . . .

You're standing on the threshold again. You have a choice.

I rolled up the windows and turned on the air conditioning. Devoid of all emotion and numb to physical sensation, I continued the commute on autopilot, focusing only on the narrow slice of highway illuminated by my headlights. A few random drops of rain appeared on the windshield.

There's still time to make it right . . .

5:56 a.m.

As I approached the Caste corporate campus, my breathing became deep and slow. My mind grew quiet and still. Past the campus, which was coming up on my left, a plethora of cloned office parks and strip malls littered a rolling expanse of meadow. Beyond, the western horizon loomed. A jagged streak of lightning split the sky in two. A towering curtain of purple clouds appeared. Darkness returned, leaving no trace of the spectacular display.

A wave of thunder rolled across the meadow. The Audi's windows quivered. I turned off the main road and onto the campus grounds. The winding private drive led me through well-manicured landscapes lined with flowering summer shrubs and deciduous trees. I came to a stop at the parking ramp's entrance. The gate rose. My foot nudged the gas pedal, and the vehicle lurched forward. Driving the entire length of the structure and taking a U-turn, I parked in a spot nearest the exit.

I lowered the windows and killed the engine. The thick, heavy air of the impending storm rushed in. I took a breath. It tasted of fennel and sweet basil. Surprised at how relaxed I felt, I sat back in the driver's seat, closed my eyes, and went over the plan in my head.

Step one: Carry duffel bag and its contents to executive row.
Step two: Plant bomb in an empty cubicle or closet.

Step three: Return to car and wait for Mountainfort and the other executive officers to arrive. Most, if not all of them, will be at their desks by seven thirty or eight at the very latest.

Step four: Detonate bomb remotely from car, using cell phone.

Step five: Armed with semiautomatic pistol and assault rifle, enter building and take out any and all hostiles (a.k.a. "executive officers") that might have survived the bomb's blast.

The plan was elegant in its simplicity. That it didn't account for what would happen to me afterward was of little or no concern. The final countdown was about to begin. My long, hard struggle would soon be over . . .

Unacceptable! Totally unacceptable. What kind of man are you, Williamson? Can you do nothing right?

Let me assure you—there will be many opportunities for advancement within the Caste organization, especially for someone with your experience and abilities. A great many opportunities. I only ask that you be patient.

Not everyone's going to make it, Williamson. Some need to be sacrificed for the greater good.

Whose side are you on, Williamson? You're our lawyer, right? Christ, you sound like a fucking socialist.

We should take steps to distance ourselves from this child labor thing. Why don't we set up a dummy corporation . . .

You need to be a team player and get on board, Williamson. After all, lawyers like you are a dime a dozen.

Enjoy the holiday. Just make sure your ass is on a plane to China come Tuesday morning. And don't bother coming back until the contract has been finalized!

I smiled.

Enjoy the holiday . . .

After double-checking my holster for the Glock, I swung the door open and jumped out, leaving the trench coat behind for the time being. Trying to appear casual, I ambled to the rear of the car yet couldn't resist the impulse to stop and glance over my shoulder. The coast was clear. I opened the trunk.

There's no turning back now.

I hoisted the duffel bag out of the trunk and slung it over my shoulder. The canvas strap dug into my trapezius. I winced in agony. Between the roofing nails (at least a thousand of them) and the steel tank containing twenty pounds of propane gas, the bag was a very heavy load. I adjusted the strap, slammed the trunk shut with my free hand, and staggered toward the door leading out of the parking ramp.

Lowering my unencumbered shoulder, I pushed open the door and was met by a strong breeze. It had broken free from the storm and was now dashing and swirling around the three buildings that made up Caste's Golden Meadow campus. Another wave of thunder, less distant than the previous one, was followed by a rogue splattering of raindrops on the walkway between Buildings B and C. Under the cover of darkness— sunrise was still thirty minutes away—I bypassed Building C and made my way to the side door of Building B. Swiping my security badge and turning sideways to accommodate the bag, I stepped inside the glass palace.

The climate-controlled facility was pleasantly cool . . . and quiet . . . quiet, that is, except for the air conditioning's steady background hum and the sound of my footsteps echoing off the concrete floor and rising into the atria three stories above . . .

Some need to be sacrificed . . .

"Who's there?" I said.

You sound like a fucking socialist.

A fucking socialist? The voices had followed me into the building—

Lawyers like you are a dime a dozen.

—or perhaps they'd been there the entire time, waiting for the right moment to pounce—

Make sure your ass is on a plane to China.

—waiting for me in the maintenance closet on my left or the copy center coming up on my right.

And don't bother coming back until—

I stopped. The voices stopped. The HVAC system cycled down and came to rest. I peered over my shoulder and up into the shadowy atria.

"Hello?"

The building was empty. It was most definitely empty. There wasn't a living soul anywhere on the premises. I was alone.

Resuming my trek, I headed down the corridor that connected Buildings A and B. Passing the kiosk where I usually grabbed my morning coffee and danish, I checked my watch. It was six fifteen. Juanita, a good-natured and pleasantly plump unmarried mother of five, would be arriving at any moment to open the kiosk for business. Gaining momentum, I emerged from the corridor. Building A's glass elevator came into view. Huffing and puffing, I arrived at the sliding doors and pressed the Up button.

A few moments later, I was on the third floor, striding past the fishbowl conference room and down the carpeted hallway toward executive row.

Executive row was lit by a limited contingent of overhead light fixtures, kept on overnight for security purposes. These lights cast a dull and lifeless glow, creating the illusion of an endless underground mining tunnel. On my right, lined up like a troop of pickax-wielding miners reporting for duty, were the glass-fronted executive office suites, unlit and dark. Somber.

A flash of lightning illuminated the glass palace. A deep rumble of thunder followed. The storm was still a couple of miles away.

A perverse sense of excitement swelled within my breast. Fueled by adrenaline, I moved at a good clip, no longer noticing the duffel bag's weight. All my pain disappeared. I had become the master of the universe. I was flying. I was actually flying!

Halfway down executive row, I cut the engines and came to an abrupt landing in front of Mountainfort's office. In the reception area, two secretarial cubicles stood guard in front of the office's glass wall. One of them had been empty for quite some time.

This is gonna be a cinch.

With the agility and stealth of a cat burglar in the dark of night, I navigated the circumference of the empty cubicle before sneaking in through the office-facing side. My heart pounding furiously, I gently—ever so gently—set the duffel bag on the floor. I took a knee and unzipped the bag. A giddy laugh sprang into my throat. Swallowing and biting my tongue to prevent any further mirth, I recomposed myself. Then, with all the focus and skill of a world-class neurosurgeon, I commenced the process of activating the detonator.

When the operation was complete, I sealed the bag and carefully slid it under the cubicle's desk, almost completely hidden from view. I backed out of the cubicle. Someone would have to be looking pretty hard to find it, I decided. Satisfied no one would discover the duffel bag and its contents in the next couple of hours and feeling much lighter now, I retraced my steps down the hallway toward the fishbowl.

I heard a sound. A voice . . . another voice . . . a rising murmur of voices . . .

The building was coming to life. The first wave of morning commuters had begun trickling into the glass palace. Afraid my casual clothes would attract attention and invite unwanted questions, I kept my head down and quickly descended the stairs to the first floor. In the corridor, Juanita was setting up shop. Without looking up, I breezed by the kiosk and proceeded to the exit at the far end of the building. Outside, a light but steady rain prompted me to dash across the walkway from Building B to the parking ramp.

6:33 a.m.

Inside the ramp, I returned to my car. A few other vehicles now speckled the vicinity. Jumping into mine, I fell into the driver's seat, closed my eyes, and let out a long whistle.

Ho-ly shit! Everything's falling into place. Like clockwork. Now, I wait . . . for an hour, maybe longer . . . better make it an hour and a half, just to make sure all targets are in place. And then . . . and then, all hell's gonna break loose . . .

The storm intensified. The wind howled. Rain pelted the ramp's top level and flowed into the drainage system, roaring through its pipes with the ferocity of white water raging down a class V river. Within seconds, the system was filled to capacity. The excess rain cascaded in sheets over the outer edge of the ramp and sprayed across the Audi's hood. The windshield became a blur.

I closed my eyes and breathed in the storm.

I sensed a presence. Someone was in the car with me. I opened my eyes and gasped. In the rearview mirror, a man with coppery skin, a black beard, and an ivory turban was glaring at me. Red, spiderlike veins riddled the whites of his eyes.

I know this man. Where have I seen him before?

A crack of thunder shook the parking ramp's foundation, and a triumphant smile burst across his weatherworn face.

Justice, my brother! The time for justice is now at hand. Yours is indeed a noble cause—a noble and heroic cause in the war against tyranny. This is your moment of truth. It's your sacred duty to make the evil transgressors pay for their crimes. These men, these decadent American businessmen, these exploiters of innocent children, they have no honor, no integrity—just a self-indulgent, insatiable desire for material gain and extravagant wealth. It's up to you—and you alone—to set things straight. Do it, Ricky. Do it now, and you'll find what you've been searching for your entire life. But you'll only attain your reward if you act quickly. Corporate America is corrupt and becoming more corrupt with each passing day. You know this to be true. You've seen it with your own eyes. So, send them a message. Send them all a message. A message that will be heard across the country and throughout the world. Do what you came here to do!

Jihad?

Allahu Akbar!

Yes . . . yes, I'm gonna kill those bastards. I'm gonna kill them. Now.

I reached for the cell phone.

Don't do this, Ricky.

I returned my eyes to the rearview mirror and saw not the man with the black beard but the boy whom I'd come to know as David. Yet his name wasn't David. His name was Ricky. He was me at the age of ten.

Young Ricky's skin was smooth and vibrant. His face was lit by a warm glow that formed what appeared to be a halo over his head. A halo.

Don't do it. It's not who you are.

"It is who I am," I said. "It's who I've become."

I flipped open the phone. The screen glared at me, daring me to take the next step. Matching its glare, I fell into a hypnotic trance, and the rest of the world receded . . .

My finger begins to move toward the keypad . . . and stops. Something's happened. Something very strange. There's no sound. No sound at all. No thunder, no wind, no rain . . . no sound whatsoever. I glance up. The windshield and hood are bone-dry. It's as if there never were any rain . . . as if the storm never happened . . . I return to the screen. *Focus now, Ricky.* I bite my lip. Hard. The taste of blood seeps into my mouth. Clenching my jaw, I enter the code that's programmed into the bomb's detonator.

"One one-thousand, two one-thousand, three . . . come on, come—"

Kaboom!

The explosion tears murderously through the silence. The sound of shattering glass follows, ringing across the meadow like a grand ensemble of thousands of bells falling from heaven.

Out of the cacophony, a melody emerges . . . a joyful melody . . . a celebration.

I fight to suppress an early childhood memory that's rising up . . .

It's Christmastime in the village of South Orange, circa 1970. The Williamson family is strolling down South Orange Avenue. The sidewalks overflow with holiday shoppers and merrymakers. I'm holding Daddy's hand; Danny is holding Mommy's. We come across a handbell choir of young men and women dressed in costumes representing the finest attire of nineteenth-century England, Dickensian-style. Assembled on the front steps of town hall, they're performing "Carol of the Bells." Their voices produce puffs of steam that waft upward and hover over the crowd before dispersing into the sky. The bells sail through the crisp December air. Ding-dong, ding-dong . . .

We stop to listen . . .

Even though I'm parked well clear of the blast, the earth beneath me has shaken the parking ramp's foundation just enough to entice a sprinkling of white, powdery dust to fall from above. Like a thin layer of snow, the dust covers my windshield . . .

A light sprinkling of snowflakes covers the sidewalk at our feet. Seized by a flash of dread, I squeeze Daddy's hand and try to focus on the song's uplifting melody. He pulls me close, and the feeling begins to pass—

Enough already! I have a job to finish.

Checking my holster for the Glock, I grab my black leather trench coat and leap out of the car. I throw on the coat and open the trunk. The assault rifle is loaded and ready to go. I snatch it up and stuff my pockets with boxes of extra ammo and spare magazines. *Invincible now.* Clutching the rifle to my chest, I make a mad dash from the ramp to the roundabout in front of Building A. This is the grand entrance to the palace, where visitors from all over the world are received.

The building is still standing, but much of the glass is gone. A few jagged shards hang precariously from the exposed frame of the façade. The once mighty edifice is now held up only by a twisted network of mangled steel rods and beams protruding awkwardly from the poured concrete of the ravaged structure. A blackened steel arch occupies the spot where a pair of towering glass doors once presided.

Glass fragments crunching under the heels of my combat boots, I rush through the arch and begin shooting indiscriminately. At anything that moves. A splash of blood, and a body falls . . . and another . . .

Navigating the debris, I work my way methodically toward executive row, leaving bodies in my wake . . .

Thirty minutes later—that's all it takes to complete my mission—I'm back on the highway, weaving through rush hour traffic toward home. When I arrive, I park the car in the garage—safely out of sight—and rush inside. The boy is waiting for me in the living room. The blinds are drawn. It's dark. Furiously wringing my hands together, I begin pacing the room, back and forth . . . back and forth . . .

"I did it! Oh my God, I did it! I set off the bomb and destroyed executive row. Then, then I went into the building and ran around shooting everyone in sight . . . I got Mountainfort . . . I'm pretty sure I got Mountainfort . . . and Charrington and Cunningham . . . and, and . . . Kidwell—"

"Kidwell?"

"Yeah, yeah . . . Jim Kidwell . . . and, and . . . Spencer—"

"Spencer?"

"Spencer Black. I shot him right between the eyes—"

"Ricky—"

"—and, and I just kept shooting . . . I shot at everything that moved . . . and, oh God, the blood . . . all the blood . . . and bodies lying on the floor . . . and people screaming . . . and the fire alarm . . . it was so loud . . . and it wouldn't stop. It wouldn't stop! I can still hear it. Oh God, I can still hear it . . . in my head . . . it won't stop. Please God, make it stop!"

I fall into the boy's arms, whimpering and drooling like a helpless infant. He guides me to the floor. I curl into fetal position.

"So, so many of them were blinded by the flying glass. They were st-staggering, staggering around in wh-wh-what was left of the building, f-f-feeling their way with their arms stretched out in front of them, tripping over the rubble, getting back up, desperately searching . . . searching for someone to help them. They were easy targets and, and . . . I-I-I . . . I shot them dead."

"Ricky! Listen to me. There's still time to make it right. Do you understand what I'm saying?"

"Make it right? Are you insane? There's no way to make this right."

"Trust me, Ricky. We can fix this if we act fast. Quick, go pack a bag."

"Pack a bag? Where will we go? I can't escape from this. By now, they've put out an APB. The roads will be crawling with police. They'll be looking for my car. They'll be pulling over anyone and everyone who matches my description. By noon, I'll be in jail . . . or dead . . . No, no, no . . . it's no use. It's over.

Everything's over. I need to turn myself in. That's what I need to do . . . turn myself in . . . turn myself in—"

"Stop it, Ricky! Pull yourself together. You need to trust me. If you do exactly what I tell you, everything will be okay."

I stare at him in disbelief. Yet something in his tone makes me realize I'm in capable hands.

"Are you with me?"

Stifling a sob, I nod.

"Good. Now, go pack a bag."

Within ten minutes, we're on the road, heading east.

"Where are we going?" I ask.

"Back to where it all began."

A siren wails. Another one . . . and another . . . Soon, my head is filled with a deafening chorus of sirens. A glimmer appears in the sideview mirror and balloons into a galaxy of flashing blue and red lights. The police! Dozens of squad cars. Must be the entire force. It took them less than an hour to find us. I pull over, reach for my pistol, and place the muzzle in my mouth. Finally, it's going to be over. I let out a sigh of relief, and—

"No, Ricky! Don't!"

6:38 a.m.

I came to with a jolt.

Where am I?

I was still in the parking ramp. A car alarm was blaring. I peered over my shoulder. Fred Sonenshein, a middle-aged clerk from accounting, waved at me with a sheepish grin and mouthed the word *sorry* as he scurried back to his car to turn off the alarm.

The rain dwindled. The storm was passing.

The cell phone! It was still flipped open in my hand. I returned my eyes to the screen. 6:38 became 6:39. I snapped the phone shut and pocketed it. Droplets of rain covered my car's windshield. Not a trace of dust.

It wasn't real! It was all in my head. A trial run. That's what it was. A trial run. I get another crack at it now. I'll wait here until eight, just to make sure everyone's arrived, and then . . . and then—

Oh God, the blood . . . all the blood . . . and the bodies . . . and the screaming . . . and people blinded by flying glass . . . their arms stretched out . . . searching . . . searching for someone to help them . . .

I checked the rearview mirror. No bearded man urging me to proceed with my quest for justice. No sign of young Ricky calmly instructing me to abandon the plan. It was just me. Just me staring back at me with my own eyes . . . my own miserable, battle-weary, bloodshot eyes . . .

Where's the life . . . the spark . . . the joy?

My lids were swollen and heavy; my lashes were crusty. Under my eyes, puffy bags were accentuated by dark semicircles. Deep valleys crossed my forehead. Wrinkles subdivided my brow into two uneven plats. My hair was a jungle. Stubble speckled my face. An oily film covered a complexion stained by an epidemic of red blotches.

A madman in the mirror, an FBI mug shot.

Oh my God, look what I've become. This isn't the way things were supposed to turn out. There's something very, very wrong with—

Yes, my love. Something's wrong. And together, we're going to make it right.

My angel . . . you've come back to me . . .

I've always been with you.

A single tear rolled down my cheek.

A distant rumble of thunder, and the rain ceased. A cool breeze blew in through the window and ruffled my hair. The clouds gave way, and the morning's first rays of sunlight slipped into the parking ramp, casting new shadows, creating new possibilities . . .

A new day.

"The bomb. I've got to go after that bomb. Right now. Before Mountainfort gets to work."

6:50 a.m.

Springing from the car, I ran out of the ramp and into Building B. The second wave of commuters had begun to arrive. Leaving behind a trail of wet footprints, a cluster of thirtysomethings advanced on the kiosk. Juanita looked up from the register. A brilliant smile lit her face, and she waved at me. Without breaking stride, I waved back and continued my sprint down the corridor toward Building A. At the elevator, I pressed the Up button and took the opportunity to catch my breath.

During the painfully slow ascent to the third floor, I closed my eyes and prayed Mountainfort hadn't yet arrived. The elevator came to a stop. The doors slid open. My prayer had been in vain. Mountainfort was early. He was in the fishbowl, meeting with Brian Otterness, Art Charrington, and a man I assumed was Manny Cunningham, much smaller in stature and less fearsome than I'd imagined. At least Mountainfort wasn't in his office. That would've made things much more complicated.

My heart racing, I lurched out of the elevator and made a beeline past the fishbowl.

Good. I don't think they saw me.

Proceeding down the hallway toward a live propane bomb capable of obliterating the entire building, I resisted the impulse to run. On my right, all cubicles along executive row were empty. It was too early for the secretaries. They wouldn't be in for another hour. I halted in front of Mountainfort's office. The light was on. The office was empty. No one was around.

Thank God!

Taking just seconds to deactivate the bomb, I rezipped the duffel bag, slung it over my shoulder, and headed back down the hallway. The bag's weight caused me to swerve. I corrected course and forged on. There was no way to exit the executive wing without passing the fishbowl. The shadows of its four occupants crawled along the floor like crooked fingers probing for me in the dark. Trying to shrink myself into invisibility, I decided against taking the elevator and hightailed it for the stairs.

I think I'm gonna make it!

"Hey, Ricky!"

It was Brian Otterness.

"Hey, Ricky, what's your hurry?"

I pretended not to hear.

"Hold on there, Ricky. Where are you going?"

I kept walking.

"What's in that bag?"

"My running gear."

"That's an awfully big load for running gear."

I was almost to the stairs.

"Come back here, Ricky. Mountainfort wants to see you. You're supposed to be on a plane—"

"I'm sorry, Brian. I'm in a hurry."

There's someone waiting for me at home.

Parking the car in the driveway, I ran into the house and fell into the safe harbor of young Ricky's warm embrace. There was no longer any need to think of him as David. I knew who he was. I'd always known who he was. He was me.

His skinny arms pulled me in and held me close. The war was finally over.

"I couldn't do it."

"I know."

The tears began to fall.

"I'm sorry. I'm so very sorry . . ."

"I know, Ricky. I know you are. It's okay. Everything's okay. Now, you can begin to live the life you were meant to live."

"The life I was meant to live? What does that mean? My whole life's been based on nothing . . . nothing but self-pity, fear, anger, desire—an all-encompassing, obsessive desire to get even with my enemies. Now that it's over . . . I, I don't know . . . I'm . . . I'm lost. Without my enemies, I'm lost. I don't know what's next. I don't know what to do with my life. Now what? Now what'll I do?"

"I have an idea. It's going to require a leap of faith on your part."

"A leap of faith." I gulped. "Okay. Go on."

"Let's leave this place. Right now. Let's jump on a plane and fly home."

"Home?"

"South Orange. Back where it all began. You'll be clear about your future when you see the past for what it really is."

"For what it really is. What's that?"

"Nothing."

"Nothing?"

"Well, almost nothing. The past exists but only as an idea in your head. Nothing more."

I stared blankly at him.

"Don't worry. You'll see. There are some things I want to show you—things you might not recognize at first."

"Okay, but there's something I need to do before we go."

I returned to the scene of the crime—the glass palace in Golden Meadow. The late-afternoon sun danced across the palace's grand façade. The American flag rippled at full mast. I pulled into the roundabout and parked in a visitor's spot in front of Building A. The towering glass doors stood before me, beckoning. I entered.

Art Charrington had left the office for the day, so I visited Jeanine Templeton, our director of human resources, and she walked me through all the formalities. It took less than thirty minutes to complete the paperwork. Before I left the building, however, there was someone else I needed to visit.

"Hello, Alex." I entered the office of Alexander Mountainfort with a relaxed smile and just a bit of a swagger. "I've just come from a visit with Jeanine. As of a few minutes ago, I no longer work here."

"Jeanine who? I'm busy, Williamson. I don't have time for your games."

"Oh, I assure you, this is no game. I just quit."

"Like hell you did. You need to finish what you started. You need to get your ass on a plane to China and close the Doltz deal."

"No, I don't. I'm done."

"Think carefully about what you're doing. Actions have consequences."

"Yes, they do." I turned to go.

"You'll regret this, Williamson!"

I turned back and looked Mountainfort straight in the eye. "No, I don't believe I will."

With that, I marched out of his office and left the building . . .

Free.

This time for good.

CHAPTER SIX

Wednesday, September 5–Thursday, September 6, 2001
South Orange, New Jersey

Approaching Newark International Airport with the sun setting behind its tail, the Boeing 757 spread its massive wings over the runway and landed us safely embosomed within the fading magentas and violets of twilight. Earthbound, the lumbering giant taxied our aching bones to the gate, where we leaped to our swollen feet and commenced performing the highly anticipated ritual of deplaning. Retrieving young Ricky's carry-on from the overhead bin, I received in return a warm smile of gratitude. The boy had slept through the entire flight, and he wasn't yet fully awake. Even so, his azure-blue eyes sparkled with life.

After claiming my checked bag at the carousel, we rented a car and drove under a fresh blanket of darkness to a hotel in West Orange, just minutes from our beloved hometown of

South Orange. A light but satisfying meal in the hotel's restaurant left us pleasantly drowsy. A glass of wine for me and a slice of apple pie à la mode for my son sealed the deal. My son. We didn't bother correcting the waitress. Instead, we thanked her, finished dessert, and retired to our room.

I was dog-tired and longing for sleep yet filled with anticipation. It felt as if I were once again a little boy being put to bed by my parents on Christmas Eve. My ears rang with their promises of a visit from a jolly old elf sporting a long white beard and rosy cheeks. Of rather hefty girth and clad all in red, this benevolent elf was said to be piloting a sleigh drawn by eight flying reindeer and bearing gifts that wouldn't arrive until I was fast asleep. Each year, I listened for the sound of hooves prancing on the rooftop . . . fighting to stay awake yet always succumbing in the end . . .

Tonight, my elf was none other than a ten-year-old boy, who, at the moment, was brushing his teeth. The bathroom door was half-open. The boy's silhouette leaned forward and spat into the sink. On the following day, he would present me with the gift of a guided tour of my hometown, which I hadn't seen in over twenty years. During this tour, he would show me something new . . .

The past for what it really is.

Surrendering at last to my exhaustion and murmuring an incomprehensible "Good night" to young Ricky, I slipped between the sheets of the nearest of the two twin beds, allowed my heavy eyelids to fall, and drifted into a deep and dreamless sleep.

Resolved to cover as much ground as possible, we rose with the sun and began our tour at the campus of Seton Hall University, where my father had taught history. As we strolled through the fifty-eight-acre campus, I experienced a flashback of climbing over a chain-link fence and sneaking onto the football field with my pal Joey. Positioning ourselves on the twenty-yard line, we'd engaged in a contest of kicking a woefully underinflated football through the uprights. We hadn't yet reached halftime, and we were deadlocked at three field goals apiece when an ill-tempered groundskeeper chased us away. Wishing to validate this memory, I kept my eyes open, but the field didn't present itself. I soon guessed the university had dropped football as a varsity sport, torn down the goalposts, and reconfigured the land to accommodate the needs of the soccer and baseball programs.

Leaving the campus behind, we proceeded west at a leisurely pace down South Orange Avenue. The midmorning sun bathed us in warm, ambient light as we sauntered along the southern border of Grove Park. A young mother pushed a carriage down a path that meandered aimlessly through the park's greenery. A squirrel chased its mate up an old telephone pole, perhaps the two mistaking it for a tree trunk. A flock of birds congregated overhead in a mammoth oak. Their chatter rose above the ubiquitous sound of cicadas humming in the background.

Ahead of us, a bakery appeared, followed by the police station. Next, we came upon the bank where I had opened my first savings account with a deposit of ten dollars I'd earned raking leaves for my father. The teller had handed me an emerald passbook, which I'd kept hidden under my pillow. The building itself had changed little over the years, yet with an apparent change in ownership, the bank was doing business under a name I didn't recognize.

On our left, the patina-shaded steeple and sandstone exterior of the church where I was baptized—the First Presbyterian and Trinity Church—came into view. Just past the church and on our right, the copper-domed octagonal clock tower of Village Hall commanded the municipality's modest skyline. A murder of crows loitered on the ledge beneath the roman numeral VI.

Passing Village Hall and crossing Scotland Road, we entered what was unmistakably the heart of South Orange, the central business district. But it bore little resemblance to the picture in my mind of the village of my youth. It seemed smaller now and a bit shabby, I thought, even though most of the storefronts had been remodeled to suit the times.

Many of the local businesses no longer existed. The record store where I'd bought my first 45—Paper Lace's "The Night Chicago Died"—was now an open storefront. A For Lease sign hung in the window. And the space formerly occupied by ShopRite—our family's go-to grocery store throughout my early childhood—was abandoned.

ShopRite held fond memories for me, dating back to the days when I was small enough to sit in the cart and kick my mother in the ribs as she trolled the aisles for nutritious staples. I was partial to Twinkies, Ho Hos, and Ding Dongs. And I wasn't too shy to express my desires out loud. But a stern look and harsh whisper from my mother kept me in line.

After outgrowing the cart, I took to the aisles on my own, racing around the store in search of provisions that would satisfy my hankerings. It wasn't long after becoming thus ambulatory that I discovered and developed a taste for the jumbo-size, deli-style kosher dills kept fermenting in a barrel and sold individually at the delicatessen counter located in the back corner of the store. Just the sight of that old-fashioned wooden barrel—almost as tall as I was—was enough to activate my salivary glands and send me running back to my mother to beg for "just one jumba picka, please, Mama, please!"

Also missing from the storefronts along the avenue was Gruning's, the ever-popular food emporium and soda fountain, famous for its hamburgers, cold drinks, ice cream, and homemade confections. Gruning's had been a South Orange Avenue landmark since 1929 and a personal favorite of mine until we moved away in 1977.

The boy had been right. My past wasn't to be found in these store windows. It existed nowhere other than in my own head.

We spent the rest of the morning exploring this strangely unfamiliar business district, stopping only for a quick lunch at some nondescript chain café across the street from the train station.

After lunch, we took Vose Avenue north to Mead Street, which we followed under the railroad tracks to the Baird Community Center. Flanking the facility were the four diamonds that made up the Little League fields to the north and Cameron Field to the south. According to local legend, Babe Ruth and Lou Gehrig had played in an exhibition game at Cameron back in October of 1929, just a few days before Halloween. Some swore their ghosts returned each year to continue the tradition. I believed in ghosts. Perhaps they were watching us now . . .

Beyond Cameron Field lay the South Orange community pool and its looming high dive.

"Look over there at the fields," said young Ricky. "Do you recognize them?"

I did. The four diamonds were well maintained and hadn't changed much with time . . . at least not yet . . .

"I struck out every at bat in my first year of Little League. They called me the Strikeout King."

"Yes, that's true. In your second year, however, you were an all-star and led your team all the way to the championship game—"

"Before losing to Danny's team in a rout."

"Let's take a stroll to the pool," the boy said, unperturbed and smiling.

"Um, I think I'd rather not." A feeling of trepidation started to burn a hole in my gut.

"Come on, Ricky." He held out a hand to me. "It'll be fine. I promise."

The pool was closed for the season, and the grounds were deserted. All those kids who once filled this same air with roars of exuberance, which echoed across the hot summer days of my youth, were grown up now, with families of their own . . . and jobs . . . and bills to pay . . . And all the boys and girls who'd frequented this pool in the summer of 2001—roaring those same roars of exuberance—were back in school now, learning the basic skills they would need to continue the cycle of life and someday join their parents' generation in the workplace. A corporate America I'd just left behind.

We pressed our faces against the ten-foot-high chain-link fence surrounding the three-pool complex and peered in. A barren wasteland. The decks had been stripped clean of furniture and all other appurtenances. The pools—main, intermediate, and wading—had been drained and covered with graying tarps that once had been some shade of green. Frayed around the edges, the tarps were stretched across the basin of each pool and ready for the impending change of seasons.

Autumn and a flurry of leaves dancing the Lindy across the deck . . . winter and a heavy coat of ice and snow, a time of rest . . . buried beneath the tarps, bittersweet memories of summertime . . .

In my troubled mind, this stark scene quintessentially represented the transitory nature of all worldly things. *Hopeless.* After a moment or two, my eyes were drawn to the far end of the main pool. There stood my old nemesis, the high dive. The towering behemoth glared down at me with utter contempt. I shrank in terror . . .

What the hell are you waiting for? An invitation?

You waitin' for a swift kick in the ass? That can be arranged!

Dive in already!

I'm eight years old. My toes are hanging over the board's edge. A golden sun reflects off the aqua-blue water below . . .

A long procession of droplets paraded down the back of my neck and through the narrow divide separating my shoulder blades.

We don't have all day, kid!

You're holding up the line!

My lips quivered.

What are ya? Chicken?

Chicken? He's Chicken Little!

Go on, Chicken Little! Jump!

My heart thumped madly.

Jump, Chicken Little! Jump, Chicken Little! Jump, Chicken Little!

Attempting to gain control, I clenched my jaw and ground my teeth together in a circular pattern—clockwise and then counterclockwise.

Jump, Chicken Little! Jump, Chicken Little! Jump, Chicken Little!

"Where are your tormentors now, Ricky?"

"They're . . . they're gone. They've all grown up and moved on, I guess."

Following Mead back under the railroad tracks, which thundered under the weight of a passing train, we turned north onto Vose and east on Raymond Avenue for a short jaunt to Scotland Road. After a lengthy wait for an opening in the fierce midafternoon traffic, we crossed Scotland, dodging a truck that seemed to come out of nowhere. Lucky to escape with our lives, we turned north to Turrell Avenue and then headed east. The sidewalk was bare, yet it would be adorned with a fresh blanket of capped acorns and shiny, bright-eyed chestnuts in only a few short weeks.

We were almost home.

Arriving at the intersection of Turrell Avenue and Grove Road, we turned north, and there it was: a redbrick house fronted by yellowing rhododendrons and lined on each side with my father's prized rosebushes. Deprived of their annual sixty-four-gallon dose of fresh manure collected from a nearby farm and transported—much to my mother's dismay—in the trunk of our family's Pontiac LeMans, the roses were no longer thriving. Only a smattering of sickly blooms remained.

The house appeared to be uninhabited. The lawn was ungroomed and overrun with dandelions and crabgrass. The trim of each southern-exposed window was badly in need of a fresh coat of paint. A thin, jagged crack split a second-story pane into two roughly equal parts. All curtains were drawn tight, closing off the home's interior from the outside world's prying eyes.

With a glance, but without a word passing between us, we crept across the driveway, through Daddy's enfeebled rosebushes, and up to the den's French windows. There, partially hidden under the shadow of a nearby oak, we attempted to peer through the opaque curtains, but to no avail. The fortress appeared to be impregnable. Then, just as it seemed our adventure had come to an end, young Ricky took me by the hand and instructed me to close my eyes. I obeyed him without question, and my entire world instantly became as black as night . . . and quiet . . . and still . . . very, very still . . .

At first, I felt nothing. Then, a surge of warm electricity passed through my hand and flooded my body with the most wonderful sense of boundless ease and weightlessness. It felt as if I could fly! Together, we floated upward . . .

In a state of buzzing euphoria, the eighty-six billion neurons in my brain lit up in a spontaneous dance of kaleidoscopic colors across the northern sky of my mind. And still, we floated upward . . . upward . . . surrendering all control to some unknown power. The dance grew more rapid and more brilliant in intensity . . . and still we floated upward . . . upward . . . spinning now as if into the vortex of a wormhole . . .

When the dance reached a crescendo of whirling, polychromatic ecstasy, it was too much. Too much light. Too much color. Too much motion. *Escape!* I needed to escape. I tried to pry my hand loose from the boy's grip, but I was unable. I opened my mouth to scream; no sound came out.

In a sudden rush, the colors receded over a dark horizon, leaving behind a sliver of pulsing neon green that seemed to form a buffer between this world and the next. Coming to rest, young Ricky and I stepped across the buffer and onto a fuzzy and invitingly warm surface.

"You can open your eyes now," said young Ricky.

We were in the house, our feet planted in the den's thick shag carpeting. The curtains were open. It was getting dark outside. Inside, two little boys leaned forward over the back of a well-worn love seat, their noses pressed against the French windows and their eyes focused on Grove Road. The shadows of an autumn evening blanketed the street. The boys trembled with anticipation . . .

A pair of headlights appeared, and a burst of squeals rippled through the room.

"Daddy's home! Daddy's home!"

A powder-blue LeMans pulled into the driveway.

"Daddy's home! Daddy's home!"

Jumping up and down, the two boys watched the LeMans roll past the windows and disappear around the house's southwest corner. Without a moment's delay and with young Ricky and me in hot pursuit, they then scampered into the living room and up to a window from which they tracked the remainder of the car's journey toward the garage. From the living room, they dashed past the front staircase, veered left, and beelined down the hallway. Stifling their squeals, they hid behind the door leading into the back entryway.

As soon as their father set foot inside, the boys let out a fresh trill of squeals and leaped from their hiding place. In feigned surprise, the man's jaw dropped, and his eyes popped wide open. He took a half step back. Throwing themselves at him, they reached for his legs and clung to his thighs and waist. There would be no escape.

"Daddy's home! Daddy's home! Daddy's home!"

Surrendering to the boys' assault, the man put down his briefcase, took a knee, and held them close.

"It's my father!" I said. "He looks so young."

"Hello, men!"

"Hello, Daddy," I whispered.

"It's so great to see you!" He smiled at my mother, his eyes twinkling. "I can't tell you how great it is to see you."

After dinner, the family gathered in the living room. Daddy built a fire that soon hissed and crackled and filled the room's every corner with a warm amber glow. Shadows frolicked on the walls like fairies at play. A deliciously woodsy scent hovered, an invisible cloud sprinkling pixie dust here and there. All cares melted away.

Stepping forward, I entered the scene and curled up in my father's lap. His strong arms cradled me in a gentle embrace. Home now. Only a breath away from the hearth. My heartbeat slowed and became quiet. At peace. I closed my eyes and snuggled more deeply into the tranquil sanctuary of my father's love.

I'm safe. Nothing can hurt me—

"Ricky . . . Ricky! You need to come back now. It's time to go."

Young Ricky's voice snapped me out of my reverie. Smiling tenderly at me, he took me by the hand, and we rose to the second floor and into my parents' bedroom.

A young boy was sitting next to his mother on the edge of an unslept-in bed. He stared blankly into her wretched, tearful eyes. She held him at arm's length, her fingernails digging into his shoulders. The room's only light came from an hourglass-shaped lamp perched on the nightstand. Covered with dust and scorch marks, the lamp's shade diffused a pale yellow luminescence into the space between mother and son. I grew light-headed at the sight and found myself swaying from side to side like a fair-weather Jack on rough seas. My stomach whined in protest, and I started to feel queasy.

"I don't think I can . . ."

"Yes, yes, you can," young Ricky assured me, tightening his grip on my hand.

From the shadows, we watched the scene unfold . . .

The boy's mother took a deep breath and released it with a sputter.

"Listen to me, Ricky. Your father died last night. He's not coming home. Not ever."

The skin between the boy's eyebrows wrinkled into a knot of defiance.

"No!"

"Ricky—"

He stood up, breaking their connection. "It's a lie! I don't believe it!"

"Ricky, he's gone."

"No, he's not! I'll prove it to you."

The boy sprinted out of the room and returned less than a minute later with his father's hunting jacket.

"He's alive, Mom. And not far away. I can feel him, and I can smell him."

"Oh, Ricky . . ."

"Here. Smell his jacket."

"Ricky, no, I can't—"

"Yes, you can." He thrust the jacket into her hands. "Here!"

Tentatively, she raised the jacket to her face, inhaled deeply, and sighed.

"Ricky . . ."

He nodded and gestured for her to take another sniff. She did so, this time savoring her dear husband's scent until succumbing once again to tears. She buried her face in the jacket and wept. The boy began to stroke her hair.

"See?"

"Oh, Ricky, my dear, sweet boy . . ."

"I told you. He's not gone. He's still with us."

I stepped forward into the light.

"You were more right than you could have possibly known," young Ricky whispered.

Mother and son collapsed into each other's arms.

Giving my hand a gentle squeeze, young Ricky pulled me back into the shadows, and together we rose through the ceiling, out of the house, and into a brilliant, star-drenched sky. Once clear of the asphalt-shingled rooftop and brick chimney, he transported us across the street and safely to rest at the elementary school's side entrance on Turrell Avenue. It was the same entrance I'd used every morning so many years ago when I was in the second grade.

The stars faded into a cold and gray winter's morning. The risen sun was concealed behind a thick and impenetrable veil of clouds that stretched across the sky from one horizon to the other. Patches of crusty snow dappled the grounds. A thin layer of ice covered shrubs that formed a crystalline barrier around the building. Two boys had arrived early, both waiting impatiently for the bell to ring and doors to open so they could escape the frosty air that nipped mercilessly at their extremities. Beyond the doors, another day of learning the fundamentals of reading, writing, and arithmetic awaited them.

A skinny little runt. That was how the smaller of the two could best be described. His hair was disheveled. His expression downcast. He had profoundly sad eyes that had once been azure blue. Something about this morning had turned them from their natural color to the same dull gray that prevailed above and all around him.

The other was built like a tank. He had dark, inscrutable eyes and long brown hair, parted down the middle, brushed back from his cannonball-shaped face, and feathered on the sides. Clad in Pro-Keds, his oversize feet shuffled nervously on the concrete. Left and right . . . left and right . . .

Neither boy spoke. The skinny one gazed downward with eyes glued to the sidewalk. The muscular one focused his on the front door of a house across the street, as if expecting it to swing open at any moment. It didn't.

Finally, the muscular boy decided to take a stab at breaking the awkward silence.

"I heard about your dad, Ricky. That really sucks, man."

The skinny boy's body stiffened, as if run through by a harpoon. The sidewalk held his gaze. It was impossible to look away. A breath of air, and his shoulders slackened. His hands found the front pockets of his corduroys and disappeared inside.

"Yep."

That one word—barely a croak—was all he could manage. Anything more would have opened a floodgate of emotion, and that was unthinkable. He couldn't let himself cry. Not in front of anyone, especially not a classmate with a reputation for being tough. *Really* tough. He couldn't let this boy—Greg was his name—know what he was feeling inside. Whatever the cost, he had to hide his despair, his feelings of weakness and utter worthlessness. If only he could vanish . . .

A longer and even more awkward silence followed. Greg, pretending to remove a stray eyelash, wiped away a tear. And another. Ricky was too preoccupied with the sidewalk—lost in his own world—to notice. So, there they stood—only a few feet from each other, yet miles apart—until finally more kids arrived and began assembling in front of the entrance. A chorus of chitter-chatter arose, surrounded them, and swallowed the silence.

The school bell rang. The two boys blended into the herd and disappeared inside. The doors slammed shut.

"That boy's name was Greg," I said. "I always thought he was just a mean-spirited bully, but he cared. He really cared. Didn't he?"

"It wasn't just Greg. There was a whole community of people who cared."

"There was?"

"Yes, there was. In fact, without exception, every single person within these walls was feeling your pain that morning. Maybe they didn't know quite how to express it, but they did care. The students, teachers, staff, administrative personnel, and Principal McFadden—all of them—were grieving for your loss. And it wasn't just the school. Your neighbors and all your parents' friends cared for you throughout the ordeal, supporting your family during the days, weeks, months, and even years following your father's death. They visited your home with homemade cookies, cakes, and pies. They prepared meals and helped with the housework. They brought your mother flowers. They kept her company when you were at school. The history department at the university collected money and started a fund that helped put you through college."

"I never knew."

"Merchants in town donated their goods and services. The police department assigned a squad car to check in on your family from time to time. Even the mayor and his wife stopped by your house to offer their condolences. Ricky, the entire village was behind you."

"I thought I was alone."

"You were never alone, Ricky."

Emerging from Daddy's rosebushes with nary a scratch, we lumbered away from the redbrick house, weary from our travels. Something fluttered in my peripheral vision. My heart leaped. Glancing back, I half expected to see a little boy waving goodbye but saw only the setting sun's reflection radiating from the den's

French windows in sparkling hues of amber and gold. Evening was almost upon us. It was time to move on.

Across the road, a gas streetlamp hissed and flickered to life. Passing the lamp and the school, we proceeded along Grove Road under a vast network of branches casting a multitude of overlapping and crisscrossing shadows at our feet. Lining the boulevard, a convoy of streetlamps and towering oaks escorted us in the direction of Grove Park.

Coming full circle and completing our grand tour of the village, we entered the park from the north. Too tired to celebrate, we surrendered to gravity and collapsed on a plot of lush, fragrant grass. Burrowing ourselves into nature's warmhearted embrace, we watched the sun set over trees that stood like sentries around the park's perimeter. Protected thusly, we knew ourselves safe from any marauding forces that might threaten to disturb our well-earned moment of repose.

"There's somewhere we need to go," young Ricky said in a solemn whisper.

"Where? We've seen just about everything there is to see. It's getting late. We should—"

"Don't worry about the time. Just relax. Relax, close your eyes, and breathe . . ."

I closed my eyes, and young Ricky took my hand in his. The now-familiar surge of warm electricity passed into my body. I gasped in delight. We'd just begun our ascent into the dancing lights when I must have lost consciousness because the next thing I knew, we were standing at the intersection of Maine State Route 4 and the dirt road leading into Camp Abenaki Valley.

It was nighttime. The moon was full. Before us, the Tunnel of Doom loomed large. Like a black hole, the tunnel's gaping mouth captured the moon's brilliant beams and swallowed them whole. Still holding hands, we marched in. Under the dense canopy of tangled branches and overgrown foliage, it was too dark to see, yet together we managed to find our way. There were no visits from Burning Sky, and as for Spencer Black . . . well, Spencer Black was long gone . . .

Emerging from the tunnel, we arrived at the camp's main gate. A chain was extended across the road. A wooden sign dangled from the chain. It read: "Closed for the Season. But Know This: Abenaki Valley Honor Continues Year-Round!"

Ducking under the chain, we entered the camp's welcome area and approached the administrative building that once housed the offices of Mr. Gordon and his high-spirited assistant, Miss Howard. The building's screen door had come loose and was slapping open and closed in the breeze. The hinges responded to each slap with a groan. Young Ricky lowered a shoulder and muscled the door into its weather-warped frame. The latch clicked, and we continued our trek.

Passing the athletic fields and the riflery and archery ranges, we made our way to the mess hall and climbed the stairs leading to its elevated deck. The railing beckoned to us. From there, drenched in luminous moonlight, we were treated to a panoramic bird's-eye view of the camp commons. I immediately recognized everything: Lewis Lodge, Parson's Pond, Parson's Abode, Cabin Row, the wide-open and gently sloping field where boys would play Frisbee or lie lazily in the sun listening to their transistor radios before dinner. But the camp seemed foreign, like someone else's memory, a tale told and retold yet never assimilated as my own.

I tried to conjure up ghosts from the Camp Abenaki Valley of the summer of 1976—perhaps a foursome of campers taking a stroll to the lodge for a game of foosball, or a group of boys sauntering to soccer practice with their cleats slung carelessly over their shoulders, or another group sprinting down to the pond . . . *the pond* . . . for an after-dinner swim—but they refused to appear. It seemed they belonged to a world to which I no longer had access. Like the camp itself, their tale was a foreign one. Unfortunately, the same couldn't be said of the ghosts that lingered along the water's edge of Parson's Pond . . .

Straight downhill and just beyond the tree line, the pond's glassy surface reflected a grand ensemble of dancing moonbeams that, while brilliant, were incapable of concealing the horrifying memories that lay just below. Spencer Black was long gone—intellectually, I understood this to be an indisputable fact. Still, I could see his acne-scarred face, his cold and lifeless eyes . . . smell his terrible breath . . . feel the pain and humiliation of his brutal assault . . .

My bile began to rise . . .

"There's the pond," I said. "That's where it happened. They pretended to be my friends, and then they betrayed me. They attacked me and stole my innocence and left me alone to die. In one night, they destroyed who I was and changed the course of my entire life. I'll never forget."

"You don't have to forget, but if you want to move forward, you'll need to take responsibility—"

"Responsibility? Are you serious? *Me?* Take responsibility? I don't understand you. I don't understand you at all—"

"Responsibility for your life regardless of the actions of others and regardless of unfortunate or even tragic circumstances.

Look around you, Ricky. Look all around you. Behold the woods, the trees. Invite them in . . . *and listen . . .*

"There's great wisdom within each tree—its branches, its trunk, its roots . . . A tree knows how to live its life with responsibility. In the spring, it buds and produces leaves. In autumn, its leaves turn brown, fall, and decompose into the soil. The tree is left standing naked. Yet within the tree, there's pure acceptance—no shame, no fear, no complaining, no blaming, and no suffering. When the wind blows, the tree bends and bows. There's no resistance. None. When lightning strikes, the tree submits to its fate and burns to the ground. When spring returns, a seed takes root and sprouts. Once again, the tree flourishes and is welcomed back into the forest by its brothers and sisters."

"That's a nice story, but I don't like the idea of submitting to fate. I want to be in control of my destiny."

"That's just your ego talking. There's no wisdom in that. But take heart, Ricky. Unlike the tree, you have the power of choice, which is very different from the illusion of control. You have the power to choose whether to live the rest of your life as a slave to the memory of that night at the pond—in other words, as a helpless victim—or to live your life from this day forward as a man of courage who survived the most heinous of crimes. That choice belongs to you, not Spencer Black or anybody else."

Pondering his words, which reverberated in my ears like a bell calling me home, I faithfully followed my young teacher down the stairs, away from the mess hall, and toward Cabin Row. We walked in silence, passing one stilted, single-story cabin after another. Behind the cabins, a grove of red maples swayed in the breeze.

My cabin—the one painted blue—appeared in the moonlight. I stopped. A sound had come from inside. I was sure of it. Tilting my head toward the cabin's door, I became very still. It was music! A simple three-chord progression. My counselor, Wayne, was strumming his beloved guitar. Underneath the music, voices of the ghosts of my cabinmates—Miles, Willy, Keith, Salad Bowl, and the others—reached out to me, whispering . . . whispering . . . whispering . . . I strained to listen and perhaps decipher the intended meaning of their message, if there was one. But just then, a sudden gust whisked the voices away . . .

Leaving Cabin Row behind, we set out for Parson's Peak, which had been—so very many years ago—the venue for our weekly Sunday evening campfires. As we followed the moonlight along the uphill and winding path, the chirps and chitters of the woods merged into a glorious medley of singing crickets, tree frogs, and a host of other creatures, including an owl that performed quite capably as soloist. The breeze gained strength and, like an ensemble of flutes, whistled through the interconnected web of leafy branches above us.

At Parson's Peak, we climbed to the top of the amphitheater, whose aging benches showed marked signs of wear and tear from years of exposure to the elements. Finding a section that seemed capable of supporting our weight, we first checked for splinters and then sat. A ferocious wind blew across the exposed peak and smacked us head on. A shiver shot up and down my spine. I braced for another blast of cold air. Then suddenly, with one final gasp, the wind came to an abrupt stop.

All was quiet. Above us, stars blanketed the heavens. Below us, a man appeared. Well groomed and clean shaven, he wore small-framed spectacles with lenses that formed perfect geometric circles. In his large and powerful arms, he cradled a guitar, which he began to play with loving care. When he opened his mouth to sing, his voice rose and drifted over Parson's Pond . . .

Behind the man, the fire pit was barren and cold, but the flames of an ancient blaze came to life and warmed me from within. Listening intently to the man's rendition of Don McLean's "Vincent," I wrapped an arm around young Ricky's shoulders and held him close.

Thank you . . . thank you, my love . . . thank you for my life . . .

When the man was finished, he adjusted his tiny spectacles and—*poof!*—his body instantly became a cloud of ashes that hovered for a moment before descending into the pit. Wiping a tear from my eye, I looked up. Beyond the far edge of the peak lay Abenaki Valley in all its natural splendor. In the very heart of the valley, the glassy waters of Parson's Pond appeared as a bright reflection of the moon, safely ensconced within a bowl that had been carved into the earth eons ago.

A single loon floated across the center of the pond and cried out into the night . . . Moments later, he was joined by another . . . and once again all was quiet . . .

Friday, September 7, 2001
New York City

The following morning, we climbed aboard a commuter train bound for New York. The night before, young Ricky had suggested a trip into the city to revisit some more memories. I had no objections. In fact, I was looking forward to reliving some of the happier moments of my childhood, exploring the streets and neighborhoods of the Big Apple with Mom, Dad, and Danny.

Settling into a window seat, I pressed my nose against the glass and gazed out at the platform. A fierce animal with a thick mane glared at me. Defying anyone to disagree, a poster read: "*The Lion King*: Broadway's Award-Winning Best Musical!" The train lurched forward. The station receded. Suddenly, I was overcome by a presentiment that I was being drawn not into a city of blithesome childhood memories but perforce directly into the lion's den.

Scanning the compartment, I studied each passenger in turn. A pair of eyes darted about nervously. A rigid body shifted awkwardly in its seat. A woman clad in stiff business attire checked and rechecked her wristwatch. A young man standing in the aisle loosened his tie and unfastened the top button of his shirt. His temple shone with a thin glaze of perspiration. I wasn't alone in feeling anxiety. An intangible sense of unease had pervaded the entire train. It was as if we were being propelled inexorably toward a common fate that would change our lives forever . . .

Thirty minutes later, young Ricky and I emerged from Penn Station and onto the streets of Midtown Manhattan. It wasn't yet nine o'clock. The air was thick with an energy that portended death. A heavy, methodical beat commenced.

Da-doom, da-doom, da-doom . . .

I knew that sound. It was an ancient one. It inhabited my dreams and the dreams of my ancestors. It resided in our DNA. A primitive tribe of bloodthirsty savages had begun pounding on their drums of war.

Da-doom, da-doom, da-doom . . .

Overhead, the sky was hazy, yet the clouds appeared to be surrendering to a rather insistent September sun. Behind us, a wave of agitated commuters rolled out of Penn Station, swallowed us, and carried our bodies off toward Fifth Avenue.

Da-doom, da-doom, da-doom . . .

At Fifth Avenue, we turned north and passed the Empire State Building. The dreadful beating of drums faded behind us. We were safe . . . for now . . .

Hiking at a good clip, we made it all the way to Seventy-Ninth Street, where we cut across Central Park along the Transverse Road. Leaving the park, we turned south on Central Park West and arrived at our first destination of the day, the American Museum of Natural History, home to cherished boyhood memories and birthplace to a dream of someday becoming a paleontologist. Eventually, this ambition became lost in my pursuit of more practical endeavors. Yet my fascination with strange, prehistoric life-forms never waned. Bursting through the doors and sprinting inside, we spent a couple of hours gawking at dinosaurs and other creatures long extinct from the face of a planet now ruled by an even more curious and much more dangerous species known as *Homo sapiens.*

We resumed our journey south on Central Park West under a brilliant sun that had burned away all traces of the morning's haze. At Columbus Circle, we joined Broadway and continued from there to Times Square. Soon, we grew tired of walking and took the subway to Lower Manhattan.

At half past noon, the subway dumped us into the heart of the financial district. The tribal drums of war returned, closer and much louder than before. The beat was all around us, caroming off sidewalks, striking windows, and rocking buildings that sprang from the concrete like massive stalagmites reaching into an impossibly blue sky.

Da-doom, da-doom, da-doom . . .

Hypnotized by the drums' seductive rhythm, we followed their primal beat through streets flooded by a sea of suits. An undertow gobbled us up, and when we resurfaced, a pair of towers appeared. At their base, a sprawling plaza entreated us forward. The beat increased in volume and tempo.

Da-doom, da-doom, da-doom . . .

Waves of working professionals poured out of the Twin Towers and onto World Trade Center Plaza. Some were on their way to lunch. Others, perhaps divining the end of the world, hurried home to add a few precious hours to a weekend of clinging to their families and loved ones. For almost three thousand of these souls, it would be their last weekend on earth . . .

Da-doom, da-doom, da-doom . . .

Still following the hypnotic beat, we drifted into the middle of the plaza and gazed upward. Rising together in tandem like a pair of ancient monoliths, the towers disappeared into heaven and left us below with our mouths hanging open. Humbled by the sheer size and majesty of the structures, I felt no more significant than a single grain of sand on a beach stretching from the New Jersey shore to the southern tip of Key West.

All at once, it dawned on me how lost, how utterly lost, in self-absorption I'd become. I was so preoccupied with my own suffering that I was unable to relate to others as human beings worthy of attention and unconditional love. Something unimaginable was going to happen in that plaza. Innocent people were going to lose their lives, and families were going to be ripped apart forever.

Yet I persisted in holding on to the past, blaming others for my circumstances, and living my fearful little life as a helpless victim.

That choice belongs to you, not Spencer Black or anybody else.

Surrounded by those ill-fated men and women, I realized I'd spent my entire life feeling sorry for myself, without so much as a thought for the welfare of others. My so-called concern for the child laborers in China was much more about self-righteous indignation—*How good it felt to make myself right and Mountainfort wrong!*—than true empathy for the suffering of fellow human beings. What was my suffering compared to the suffering of those unconscionably abused children, who yearned for nothing more than to be restored into the loving arms of their families? What was my suffering compared to the suffering that would befall thousands on Tuesday, September 11?

Returning my gaze to earth, I noticed we'd wandered over to the edge of a large circular fountain. An enormous bronze sphere rose from its center. The drumming seemed to be emanating from inside.

Da-doom, da-doom, da-doom . . .

Without stopping to think, I leaned forward, plunged my hands into the water, and grasped the fountain's base. The drumming stopped. The flow of humanity reversed itself, and the masses retreated into the towers like animals sensing an impending tsunami and instinctively heading for higher ground.

Except for a few stragglers, the plaza was empty now . . . and quiet . . . very quiet . . .

Who am I? What am I? What am I really?

An answer came from the fountain.

Nothing, absolutely nothing . . . but love . . . pure, sparkling love flowing generously into this beautiful world of forms . . .

From the plaza, we made our way to the northern end of Battery Park. Untouched by the development of Battery Park City, an old pier protruded into the harbor. We scampered out to the edge. Wavelets lapped at the mooring poles. Across the bay lay Ellis Island and the Statue of Liberty. I knew this place. It was the very same spot from which we'd watched the parade of tall ships on July 4, 1976. *All those years ago.* On that historic day, the piers had been overrun by droves of euphoric Americans celebrating our nation's bicentennial. Now, except for a few tourists and a flock of squawking seagulls, they were deserted.

Behind us and a few blocks to the north, the Twin Towers loomed in the foreground of an immaculate sky.

"I don't know how I know this," I said, "but something horrible is going to happen. Beyond horrible. Beyond words. Thousands of people are going to die. There must be something I can do."

"There's not."

"But—"

"It's not up to you to save them."

"Then what the hell are we doing here?"

"Be patient, Ricky, and you'll see."

"When? When will I see?"

"Not for a while, perhaps, but you will see. In the end, every-thing will become clear. For now, close your eyes."

I did.

"Now open them."

The pier is jam-packed with revelers. People of all ages, shapes, sizes, and colors are channeling their eyes into the harbor and toward the Statue of Liberty. Gone from the scene is young Ricky, who's been replaced by Mom and Danny, along with our close family friends, the Andersons and Walkers. In all, our little coterie consists of twelve souls huddled together in the middle of a boisterous mass of flag-waving, patriotic humanity. With bated breath, we wait for the tall ships to sail into view.

It's a hazy, overcast afternoon that does nothing to dampen the spirits of thousands of bicentennial celebrants lining the shores of the Hudson. Above us, the Goodyear Blimp circles the harbor, humming a happy tune. All around us, portable hibachi grills charge the air with the mouthwatering aroma of hot dogs and hamburgers. My stomach growls. The first tall ship approaches, its ivory sails fluttering in the breeze—

A sharp pain shoots through my solar plexus. Reaching for my gut with both hands, I double over and fall to my knees. My chest heaves. My breath comes in short, raspy spurts. Bewildered, I raise my head and find myself gaping into the scornful eyes of a boy, no more than eight years of age. His face is copper-toned; his hair, a jet-black mop. With a chuckle, he flashes me a wicked smile.

"You want another one?"

It's Jihad! From Camp Abenaki Valley! He's the one who slugged me in the face and took my place in line to impress his older brothers . . . Jihad . . . my half brother . . . What's he doing here? And why the hell did he just sucker-punch me in the stomach? Does he know we had the same biological father? Hassan . . . Hassan al-Wahhabi . . . died in 1976 . . . before I even knew—

My train of thought is interrupted by a deafening roar. I glance up. A twin-engine jet airliner—

Kaboom!

The force of the blast throws me forward and facedown onto the dock. In pain, but not seriously injured, I fight my way to my knees and bend my eyes toward the World Trade Center. A massive cloud of black smoke envelops the North Tower. In slow motion, the cloud burgeons toward heaven and blots out the sky. A conflagration consumes the upper portion of the building with the ferocity of a giant roman candle. Ash spews into the atmosphere and across the Lower Manhattan skyline. Large chunks of falling debris bombard the plaza and surrounding city streets.

I can hear nothing but an incessant, high-pitched ringing in my ears. Noxious fumes invade my nasal passages and saturate my sinuses. My head grows heavy with the stench of jet fuel. The acrid taste of terror oozes into my mouth. A bubbling stream of hot bile rises into my throat. A cough sends a thick gob of mucus onto the dock.

The ghostly figure of a man glides in front of me and blocks my view of the unfolding apocalypse. He's wearing a turban. I swallow hard and peer into his cold, dark eyes.

It's the man with a black beard and coppery skin . . . the man who's been haunting my dreams . . . the man who appeared in the rearview mirror of my car . . .

He grins fiendishly at me and cackles. "You want another one?"

"Jihad! You're Jihad, aren't you?"

Without another word, this grown-up version of Jihad vanishes into thin air.

The sound of an approaching airplane buzzes the harbor. Coming from the south, this second plane paints a shadow across the docks and passes directly overhead. Although it's at least a thousand feet in the air, the tremendous roar of its engines overwhelms me, and I duck in a ridiculous attempt at self-preservation.

Kaboom!

The South Tower bursts into a mass of flames, pours more clouds of smoke and ash into the sky, and rains debris onto the city. Waves batter the shoreline. The pier shifts and rocks under my feet. Yet I remain utterly transfixed.

In a sudden flash of brilliant emerald green, the smoke clears, and the immaculate September sky returns.

Once again, young Ricky was standing next to me on that same pier just north of Battery Park. It was just us. The seagulls had taken flight and were chasing the late-afternoon sun across the Hudson River toward New Jersey. The tourists had moved on and were boarding a ferry to Liberty Island. And the towers . . . the towers had been restored to their previous state of magnificence and undeniable grace. They were perfect, intact in every respect . . . yet still looming, looming, looming . . .

I shared nothing of my experience with young Ricky. Instead, I turned inward and fell into a gulf of profound introspection. Asking no questions, he respected my need to ruminate and process all I'd seen, heard, smelled, tasted, felt . . . But he never left my side. The darling little boy never left my side. Together, we walked to the train in silence.

Back in our hotel room, young Ricky flung himself onto one of the twin beds and fixed his eyes on the ceiling. I collapsed on the other bed. Together, we stared upward, as if into the constellations. Finally emerging from my thoughts, I asked him what he had in mind for the following day.

"Do you remember a family vacation late in the summer of 1972?" he said. "You would've been six, almost seven at the time."

"Yes. Yes, I do remember! It was right before school started. I was going into the first grade that fall. Danny was going into kindergarten. Our father took us to visit Washington, DC, for a couple of days, and then on an excursion into the Blue Ridge Mountains. I remember it like it was yesterday. Danny and I had such a great time that we begged and pleaded with him to take us back someday. Yet someday never came."

"That's right. It never did."

After a lengthy silence, I added, "He was a history professor with a passion for American government and politics. He felt Danny and I should be well acquainted with our country's history and the heroic sacrifices made by the forefathers. He insisted on instilling in us a strong sense of national pride. But he was no zealot. In fact, he was quite the opposite. He wanted us to learn to think for ourselves, to question our leaders and hold them accountable. He had high hopes for us. In Danny, he saw an athletic prodigy in the making. In me, he perceived something very different—something I myself have never been able to see . . . until perhaps just recently.

"I think, just maybe, he would've liked me to get involved in politics. To be of service. To be the voice of the disenfranchised. To represent the disillusioned, the discouraged. To offer hope to those with no hope. In retrospect, I can see taking us to Washington was his way of steering me in that direction."

"Would you like to see Washington again, Ricky?"

"Yes, I think I would."

"It's settled, then. In the morning, we're bound for our nation's capital."

Saturday, September 8, 2001
Washington, DC

Rising with a bloodred sun that was peeking inquisitively through the gossamer-thin curtains of our room, we packed our things, took breakfast to go, and settled our bill at the front desk. Our rented Mustang was waiting faithfully for us in the hotel parking lot. The top was down. We leaped in.

It was a new day. A new beginning. The images of what I'd seen in New York had evaporated from memory like nocturnal phantoms in the first light of dawn. My heart was full. My mind was clear. The hedge separating the lot from the street rustled in the wind. The open road lay beyond.

By noon, we were in Washington. Without breaking for lunch, I parked the Mustang, and we entered the National Mall at Twelfth Street. Tourists speckled the grounds. Noticeably absent were children, who must have returned to school that week. Turning west onto a gravel walkway, we strolled under the leafy branches of American elms not yet showing even a hint of their autumn colors. By and by, we drew near the Washington Monument, which rose from the earth like the needle of a giant sundial. Its midday shadow was relatively short, yet it was long enough to indicate we were heading in the right direction.

Crossing Seventeenth Street, we ambled along the Reflecting Pool toward the Lincoln Memorial. Young Ricky dipped a hand in the water and splashed himself. His face glistened in the sun. A duck chased another across an image of the great temple, leaving behind a gentle ripple. The image was inverted, steps resting atop the colonnade, and enormous Grecian columns melting into the sky below.

Upon our arrival at the memorial's base, we climbed the steps, passed through the columns, and entered the central hall. Seated there in fiery contemplation, our sixteenth president paused for just long enough to regard us with a glance of utter indifference before returning to his thoughts. Respecting the solemnity of this sacred venue, I took no umbrage but simply stood gawking at the imposing white-marble representation of the one man who'd meant more to the preservation of our nation than any other. An epitaph to this effect was engraved on the wall above his head.

IN THIS TEMPLE
AS IN THE HEARTS OF THE PEOPLE
FOR WHOM HE SAVED THE UNION
THE MEMORY OF ABRAHAM LINCOLN
IS ENSHRINED FOREVER

After about twenty minutes of uninterrupted silence and some fiery contemplation of my own, I began to feel over-whelmed by the magnitude of the experience and quickly exited the shrine.

On the southern-facing side of the structure, I found a quiet spot between two columns and closed my eyes. The sun shone pink on the inside of my lids. Its rays warmed my face. A pleasant breeze washed over me. Refreshed, I opened my eyes and found myself gazing across the Potomac River toward the Pentagon. A little farther to the north lay Arlington National Cemetery, home of the Tomb of the Unknown Soldier and final resting place of JFK.

Da-doom, da-doom, da-doom . . .

Suddenly, I felt sick to my stomach. My head spun. My vision blurred. I reached toward a column for support and retched.

Da-doom, da-doom, da-doom . . .

Finding me on my knees and quite incapacitated, young Ricky took me by the hand and helped me to my feet. Staggering, I followed him down the steps and away from the Lincoln Memorial. We crossed a street and then another. Muffled by the traffic's buzz, the Potomac seemed to be calling to us in a low, gurgling whisper. Soon, we were making our way along the riverbank in the direction of the FDR and Jefferson Memorials.

"The other side of the river," I groaned between waves of nausea. "Something's going to happen on the other side of the river. I heard the roar of another airplane—"

"Yes, Ricky, I know. Another airplane."

"—followed by an explosion . . . followed by the voices of hundreds of people crying out all at once. Please, please don't tell me there's nothing I can do."

Young Ricky squeezed my hand yet offered no reply. We both knew there was nothing I could do to prevent the 9/11 attacks.

Although my experience at the Lincoln Memorial had cast a shadow across the day, we continued our tour, which eventually led us back to the mall and east toward Capitol Hill.

As we neared the Capitol with its unmistakable neoclassical architecture and formidable cast-iron dome, I became increasingly conscious of a strange feeling. It was as if someone were sneaking up behind me, pinching my earlobe, and giving it a firm tug. I stopped and took a peek. Nothing. No one was there. Still, it felt like we were being watched, followed, stalked. Was this my imagination? No. My forebodings would soon be confirmed by two separate encounters with a man I believed to be Jihad.

The first encounter occurred at the bottom of the Capitol's west steps. Just as I was about to begin my ascent, I once again felt that tugging sensation at my earlobe. Whirling around, I found myself staring point-blank into a pair of dark, villainous eyes sizing me up with no less than murderous intent. Jihad! He'd followed us to Washington.

"Hello, Ricky."

Reaching out to me from across the years, his voice was an angry swarm of hornets flying into my ears and injecting their deadly venom into my brain. Feeling faint, I broke into a cold sweat. My knees turned to jelly. I began to stumble . . .

I've got to hold on . . . no matter what . . .

Fighting the effects of the venom, I battled to remain upright and keep my wits about me.

"Wh-what the hell do you want from me?"

Responding with only a smirk, he fled into a crowd of tourists and disappeared.

"Hey! Someone stop that man! He's . . . he's a terrorist!"

A terrorist? Is Jihad somehow involved in the plot to attack the World Trade Center and the Pentagon? Is that why he keeps appearing?

A few startled faces stared hard at me, as if trying to assess my credibility. No one took action. Perhaps they thought I was the threat to national security. In any event, it was too late. Jihad was gone.

The second encounter occurred after we'd completed our tour of the National Mall. Crossing Constitution Avenue and cutting across the grassy Ellipse, we navigated our way around the eastern border of the White House grounds to Pennsylvania Avenue. From there, we stood in silence, surveying the front lawn and northern façade of the elegantly porticoed mansion that was, at the time, home to George W. Bush, our forty-third president.

"Martin Luther King had it right."

Young Ricky maintained a fixed gaze on the front of the building. His face bore an expression of firm determination and absolute conviction.

"Nonviolence through love and forgiveness," he continued, "is the only solution to the world's problems. If I were president, that would be the central theme of my presidency."

I thought his solution to the world's problems was simpleminded and naïve, but not wishing to contradict the boy, at least not directly, I smiled and slipped my hands into my front pockets.

"If I were president—"

"Hello again, Ricky," said Jihad, "or should I say, President Williamson?"

The venomous hornets returned. With no less than a Herculean effort, I shut them out.

"Terrorist!" I pointed a trembling finger at Jihad's face.

With a contemptuous grunt, he was off and running once again. This time, however, young Ricky took the initiative and pursued the man down Pennsylvania Avenue, his chicken legs flapping in a wild blur behind him. Pausing for only a moment to admire his alacrity and blinding speed, I joined him in the chase. Weaving through pedestrians and heedless of traffic, we followed Jihad for four city blocks and then down an alleyway.

A dead end! We've got him now . . .

We arrived huffing and puffing at a graffiti-covered stone wall. The air reeked of grease, rancid meat, and other kitchen refuse. A large garbage bin stood next to a dented sheet-metal door. Except for a couple of milk cartons and a few scraps of rotting debris, the bin was empty. The door was marked "Deliveries." I gave the handle a yank. It was locked. Jihad was gone.

Impossible! We were right on his tail!

Choking on the alley's stench and struggling to recover my breath, I managed to speak. "That man . . . He was in New York.

I know him. I'm sure of it. He's . . . he's—"

"Jihad."

"Jihad. Yes. That man is the boy from Camp Abenaki Valley. The one who punched me in the face when I was waiting in line to sign up for activities."

"Yes. And he's your—"

"Half brother."

"Yes."

"My half brother. A couple of years ago, I found him on the internet. I was searching for my biological father, and I discovered he had four sons. The youngest one was Jihad. What was he doing in New York? And why is he here in Washington? Was I right before? Is he a terrorist?"

"I can't say, Ricky. You'll have to figure that out for yourself."

It would be a long time before I encountered my half brother again.

Sunday, September 9–Monday, September 10, 2001
Blue Ridge Mountains

After a morning of sober contemplation at the Holocaust Museum, we spent the afternoon ducking in and out of various Smithsonian venues. Each told a story that wove lessons learned from the past with possibilities of what might lie in the future. Our tour concluded at the National Archives, where, with a lawyer's eye, I reviewed our nation's most precious documents, including originals of the Declaration of Independence, the Constitution, the Bill of Rights, and the Emancipation Proclamation. Maybe there was hope after all . . .

We left Washington by six and drove west through Virginia, following the day's last light toward the Blue Ridge Mountains. By the time we arrived in Front Royal, the sun had bowed its head behind a silhouette of peaks, leaving us in the hands of a cool yet cozy twilight that embraced us like an old friend. In no particular hurry, we bypassed Main Street and discovered a neighborhood nestled in the outskirts of town, a tiny slice of heaven accessible only by crossing a bridge made of nothing but moss and stone. Below the weatherworn structure, a creek produced a murmur that lingered in my ears for some minutes. Passing an old, vine-covered colonial, we were then treated to the savory aroma of a Sunday evening pot roast. One home after another emanated a similar scent—fleeting—that quickly blossomed and withered in the night air. Insensible to any possibility of a threat to the security of hearth and home, those within would soon be preparing for bed and the beginning of another workweek.

Returning to Main Street, we cruised through Front Royal's lightly populated downtown area, turned south onto Skyline Drive, and entered Shenandoah National Park. Some twenty mileposts later, we arrived at an inn, which bore no other name than Inn. I parked the car in the unpaved lot, and we carried our bags across the threshold. Inside, it smelled of lavender and cedar shavings. A single floor lamp suffused the lobby with a soft amber glow.

I know this place. I've been here before.

Whether by unconscious design, supernatural intervention, or some other impalpable means, we'd chosen the same inn our family had visited twenty-nine years earlier. And perhaps even more remarkable, as evidenced by the welcome sign in the lobby, the establishment was owned and operated by the same couple, Thomas and Marjorie Peabody.

Originally from Richmond, Thomas and Marjorie had been married in the spring of 1972. They were honeymooning at the inn and decided to stay for good when the owner, an elderly woman hankering for retirement, offered to sell it to them. Our family had been among the Peabodys' first guests that summer.

A service bell sat on the front desk. I gave it a tap. The handsome couple emerged from the shadows like a pair of amiable ghosts, joined at the hip. They had aged, of course, yet I recognized them immediately by their warm Virginian hospitality, guileless nature, and eyes that shone with incandescent kindness.

Mr. Peabody handed me a guest registry and asked us to sign. After jotting down my name, I passed the book to young Ricky, who signed as "Richard Atticus Williamson Jr." The son I never had.

"How long will you be staying with us?"

Before I had a chance to consider the question, young Ricky answered on our behalf.

"Just this one evening," he said, settling the matter with a winning smile.

Acknowledging young Ricky's smile with one of his own, Mr. Peabody accepted return of the signed registry and handed me a key. He was about to show us to our room when I took the opportunity to mention I had visited once before.

"I was six. We were on a family vacation. It was the summer of 1972—"

Mrs. Peabody let out a whoop of delighted surprise and scurried out of sight.

"Well, I'll be doggoned," said Mr. Peabody.

A few moments later, she returned with the registry from that year.

Opening the book's frayed cover, I paged forward to the August entries. The signatures of my mother and father sprang from the yellowing parchment. Below them appeared childish scrawls that had once belonged to Danny and me. Tears of nostalgia and profound longing came to my eyes.

My father held this book in his hands. He signed his name on this page. He was right here in this room. We all were! I can almost see his face, hear his voice, feel his reassuring hand on my shoulder . . . He's so close . . . and yet so far away . . .

Although it was well past dinnertime, our hosts threw together an impromptu meal of French bread, cheese, fresh fruit, and wine in honor of their "special guests." Inviting them to join us at the dining table, we listened to their personal story, which they told with great enthusiasm, squeezing each other by the hand, finishing each other's sentences, and giggling like schoolchildren. They'd met at a Richmond café where Marjorie was working as a waitress. Thomas was trying to summon the courage to ask her out when she spilled a bowl of steaming-hot chili in his lap. They were married within two years.

They rarely left the inn, taking only an occasional vacation, and they planned to remain as long as they were able. They had two grown daughters, both with families of their own, who often came to visit.

"The mountain air is like a drug," said Mr. Peabody. "Once you've taken a breath, you can't get enough. And those grandchildren of ours, they don't ever wanna go home. Anyways, we've never seen any reason to return to the city."

"What about you boys?" Mrs. Peabody leaned forward in her chair. "What brings you to these parts?"

I told them we were from South Orange, New Jersey, that we were on a pilgrimage of sorts, in search of answers. In a way, we were following a trail of bread crumbs left behind by my father. We then shared with them our impressions of our travels to New York and Washington, leaving out, of course, all references to Jihad and the impending 9/11 attacks.

All in all, I had a lovely time dining with our hosts, except . . . except for a nagging feeling that kept prodding me like a stick in the side . . .

Somehow, I knew this would be my last supper with young Ricky.

After a slice of the best apple pie I'd ever tasted, which did wonders to ease my troubled mind, the couple led us to our room. Gathering us in their arms like family, they bid us good night. The door swung shut, and my face hit the pillow. Immediately, I fell into a dreamless sleep.

On the following morning, young Ricky and I entered the park at a trailhead near the inn and set out on a hike, retracing the steps our family had taken twenty-nine years before. It was a glorious day. The sun shone bright. Evergreens laced the mountain air with their invigoratingly fresh fragrance. An unseen brook babbled like a child reciting a nursery rhyme. Ambling along the trail, we enjoyed each other's company as never before—chatting about nothing in particular, telling silly jokes, and laughing in spite of ourselves.

Soon, we walked in silence, simply listening to the sounds of nature, at long last away from civilization and the cares of man.

Stopping to rest and without breaking our tacit agreement to be silent, I delved deeply into young Ricky's twinkling azure-blue eyes. He had fulfilled my need for a son these past two weeks. And he'd been my teacher. Could it be I'd been his teacher as well? That I had satisfied his need for a father?

Morning became afternoon. As we climbed to higher elevations, the sun's rays gained strength and assaulted the mountain with unrelenting ferocity. All living things ran for cover. Only the boy and I remained exposed. The air turned into a gelatinous substance barely suitable for human consumption. Panting, I struggled to keep pace. Perspiration trickled into my ears and streamed down the back of my neck. My legs became heavy. My feet ached. Yet young Ricky didn't seem to tire. He forged on as if on a mission.

It was late in the day, and I was ready to collapse when we came across a wide gorge that cut a V-shaped notch into the mountainside. Its glazed walls fell precipitously downward. At the gorge's highest point, a rocky ledge stood watch over a waterfall. Beyond, a breathtaking vista presented itself. Carved deep into the earth, a lush valley stretched from north to south as far as the eye could see. A lone hawk entered the picture and soared over a river that snaked aimlessly across the rolling terrain. To the west, a mountain range stood as a barrier to whatever might lie on the other side.

Young Ricky stepped onto the ledge. The waterfall released a spray of mist into the air. Catching the light just right, the mist spawned a rainbow that formed a multicolored aura around the boy's head. A gust of wind, and the colors vanished.

"Maybe you shouldn't stand quite so close to the edge," I said apprehensively.

"This is it, Ricky." He turned to face me. "It's time for us to go our separate ways . . . for now . . ."

The boy took a step backward. The sound of the waterfall surged thunderously from the gorge's gaping mouth.

"No! Don't go." My voice rose to an urgent shriek. "I need you!"

"Goodbye, Ricky. When you dream, dream with your heart and dream big. Always dream big . . ."

He took another step.

"I love you! I know that now. I'm not ashamed to say it. I love you more than my own life. Please . . . don't leave me here. Let me come with you."

He smiled at me through eyes brimming with tears.

"You're here for a reason, Ricky. You're going to do something important. You're going to make a real difference in people's lives. I need to go back now so you can fulfill your destiny . . . so you can fulfill *our* destiny. Remember this, my love—I am you. If you love me, that means you love yourself. Never let go of that. And know I'll always be with you . . ."

With one final step, he disappeared over the cliff.

I dashed to the edge, peered down, and saw nothing but a swirling maelstrom.

"Oh my God. I've lost him. What'll I do now? I'm all alone . . . again . . ."

My heart pounded out a familiar rhythm in my chest.

A-lone, a-lone, a-lone . . .

A blast of arctic air shot across the valley. Charcoal clouds eclipsed the bright September sun. The sky darkened into an ominous shroud of purple. The heavens opened and pelted the mountainside with a pitiless rain. Within moments, the rain became an all-out deluge, mixed indiscriminately with marble-size hail.

Frozen on the cliff's edge, I stared helplessly into a cascade of raging water crashing against the jagged rocks below.

It must be a hundred-foot drop.

Growing dizzy, I wavered to and fro. The ledge had become dangerously slick, and suddenly, I lost my balance. Arms flapping wildly, I managed to grab a nearby shrub and regain my footing.

What the hell just happened? Where am I? How did I get here? And, and . . . wasn't I with someone?

No answers came. Later, my memories would return. For now, I couldn't even recall my own name.

Cold rain and hail battered my body. Red welts broke out on my arms and legs. One cautious step at a time, I retreated from the cliff. On safe ground, I covered my head, turned, and ran as fast as I could. Slipping and sliding and tumbling down the mountainside, I received some nasty bumps and bruises. Yet I persevered.

After what seemed like an eternity, I came across a grove of eastern white pines—known to the Iroquois as a sacred symbol of peace—and took refuge at the base of a tree nestled safely within. Suspended over my head like a giant umbrella, an expansive network of needled branches provided protection from the storm and relief from its merciless barrage of hailstones.

From this safe haven, I watched the storm's neon currents pulsing across the purple sky.

Spectacular. More than spectacular. Beautiful.

All my fears melted into a deep well of peace. My heart opened to everything around me—the trees, the soil, the plants, the sticks and stones. I felt a special connection to the chipmunks, squirrels, rabbits, foxes, and all of nature's other little critters, who, like me, had scurried into the grove for shelter. We were brothers and sisters. The valley, the mountain, the dark clouds above, and the sky itself formed a rich tapestry, of which each was an essential part.

I felt light, joyful, boundless, free . . .

My insides quivered and quaked with an unfamiliar sensation—a vibration that started as no more than a faint giggle before rising into a crescendo of emotion that matched the storm in both intensity and volume. And there I sat under the tree of peace, laughing with all my heart and soul, tears and raindrops merging into a river that flowed down my cheeks until the storm passed, leaving me in a quiet state of grace.

CHAPTER SEVEN

Monday, August 9, 1976
A Cabin Painted Blue

ARLY IN THE MORNING on the second Monday of August 1976, in a cabin painted blue, a ten-year-old boy named Ricky woke with bright eyes, a big smile, and an open heart. Without moving at first—just savoring the moment like a drop of honey dangling from the tip of his tongue—he lay in bed and felt his body coming to life with a surge of raw energy emanating from deep within. Filling his lungs to capacity, he released a long sigh and allowed every ounce of his seventy-pound frame to surrender to gravity as it sank into the spring-supported mattress. Yielding, the springs produced the day's first few notes of music—a prelude to a lighthearted melody that would play in the boy's head throughout the day.

On this morning, unlike any other during his three weeks at Camp Abenaki Valley, Ricky felt rejuvenated. Relaxed from head to toe! He was as well rested as if he'd spent the night in his own bed under the watchful eye of his beloved nightlight. The colonial American lighthouse had served as an unwavering beacon and loyal friend throughout his childhood years. Soon, they would be reunited.

His smile stretched from ear to ear.

Am I awake? Is this real?

No more or less real than any other experience of reality. After all, isn't reality simply a dream of our own making? When we're awake, we have the power to choose what dream we dream. When we're sleeping, we're at the mercy of whatever seeds have been planted in our subconscious minds. Either way, it's a dream.

Okay . . . so does that mean last night was a dream?

What do you think?

Realizing he was engaged in a Socratic dialogue with his father, Ricky giggled. Then, absent-mindedly reaching into the pocket of the blue jeans he'd slept in, he ran his fingers along the contours of a curious object. The heart-shaped stone! It was still there. And it was real. Its texture, solidity, and mass proved it was real.

"Thank you, Daddy," he whispered. "Thank you for opening my eyes to the power of choice. From this day forward, I choose to be happy."

Ricky then closed his eyes, and his thoughts drifted to the previous night . . .

He was at the intersection of the dirt road leading out of camp and Maine State Route 4. A bright moon flooded the sky and bathed him in a shower of warm light. His shadow extended across the highway's shiny veneer. His head—outlined in silhouette—was plagued with worry and doubt. Yet he stood there with a full heart, listening to the stillness of the night . . .

An errant Canadian wind flew into the hollow of his ear.

Have faith.

The part of him that yearned for security and a familiar routine wanted to ignore the wind's advice and go back to the cabin. Instead, he chose to move forward.

For the first time in his life, Ricky Williamson made a choice. A powerful choice. Beyond reason and beyond all thoughts of right and wrong, he chose to cross the threshold and begin a journey into the unknown. Ultimately, his journey would lead him twenty-five years into the future, where he would come face-to-face with a man in desperate need of his help.

When the adventure was over, he returned to the summer of 1976. Once again, he found himself at the end of the dirt road, his feet planted firmly in the grainy dust. The same brightly lit moon cast his shadow across the highway. The same errant Canadian wind blew in, providing no advice this time, only relief from the summer heat. He'd come full circle. And something magical had happened. He was no longer afraid but rather filled with love. And free. Free from old beliefs of shame, worthlessness, and self-loathing. Free from the prison of his own mind.

Unencumbered by the past and its demons, Ricky was now free to create a better future. An inspired future. One that would make a difference in the lives of others.

Feeling light as a feather and with the Canadian wind at his back, Ricky knew he could soar to his cabin now—with an open heart—and face the world he'd left behind. He turned toward the Tunnel of Doom. With its thick canopy of tangled branches and overgrown foliage fending off the moonlight, the tunnel was as dark and seemingly perilous as before. This time, however, he had no fear. The ghost of Burning Sky was no longer a threat. Spencer Black was no longer a threat. Through a simple shift in perception of reality, no evil spirit, no living person, including Spencer Black or any other boy at camp, would ever harm Ricky again.

He peered into the tunnel's mouth and took a step . . . and then another . . . and another . . . Darkness engulfed him. He hesitated, breathed deeply, and continued. Soon, he was sprinting down the dirt road toward camp, his body light and his spirit free . . .

Ricky opened his eyes. A single ray of light squeezed through a crack in the shutter of the front window closest to his bed. Another ray slipped through. A third, a fourth, a fifth . . . He lost count. Converging, the rays blossomed into a ball of golden luminescence that released a buttery glow into the room. The boy in the bunk below him, Salad Bowl, stirred but didn't wake. He was missing a miracle. The dawning of a new day . . .

"Thank you," said Ricky. "Thank you for this day. And thank you for whatever it might bring."

Turning his attention to the ceiling, he examined a series of unevenly spaced two-by-fours that made up the rafters. The cabin's inhabitants stored everything there, from archery bows to fishing tackle to water skis. Dust motes congregated and swirled in the light. From the shadowy intersection of two beams directly over Ricky's head, an intricate pattern began to emerge, seemingly random at first . . .

"A web," he mused. "How wonderful!"

The boy became so engrossed that everything else faded into the wings. Each silk strand caught the light in a different way, revealing infinite shades in the spectrum from white to gray. And each played an essential role in supporting the interconnected whole. The overall design reminded him of an old banyan tree that once stood by the gulf-side swimming pool where he'd almost drowned at the age of four. A message had been hidden in the tree's aerial roots, but Ricky had been unable to decipher it. It seemed this delicate yet lethal net—hovering not two arm's lengths away—contained the same message.

Relaxing his gaze, Ricky allowed the pattern to come into focus in very much the same way a picture hidden within a stereogram might magically appear in 3-D.

And there it was! Like the banyan tree's roots, the strands came together to form the internationally recognized symbol for peace. Designed in 1958 by British artist Gerald Holtom, the iconic image was a simple circle with one vertical line down the middle and two lines radiating from the center at descending forty-five-degree angles. How was this possible? Was the creator of this marvel Mr. Holtom's protégé? Possibly. It's more likely, though, that our budding artist simply drew upon the same universal wellspring of creativity to which we all have access.

The morning light pulsed with increasing intensity, and the web twinkled like a Christmas tree before dematerializing in a brilliant flash. The phenomenon left behind no evidence of its existence. No hint of its origin. No clue as to its destination. Nothing. Just dust motes settling into the recently vacated space at the intersection of the two beams.

Amazing!

Ricky closed his eyes again and listened to a chorus of not-yet-conscious campers crooning to a steady beat. Their vocals came together in perfect unison. Taking center stage, Wayne, the cabin's senior counselor, snored in a low vibrato.

From the deck of the mess hall, the Governor's Bell joined the chorus.

Dooong . . . Dooong . . . Dooong . . .

The bell reverberated throughout camp and the nearby countryside, formally welcoming a new day. *What a lovely sound!* Hearing the bell used to fill Ricky with anxiety and dread. Not anymore. On this beautiful morning, it was sweet music resonating harmoniously in his ears.

The bell interrupted Wayne's solo, which was immediately replaced by a raspy growl.

"That goddamned bell!" Wayne sat straight up. "Okay, everybody, get the hell out of bed. We're not gonna be the last ones to breakfast this morning. Understood?"

Wayne's edict was met by a new chorus—a chorus of groans. Slowly, the boys began to emerge from their torpor.

Unable to contain his enthusiasm, Ricky leaped from his bunk and landed on the floor with all the skill and grace of a tai chi master. And, like a true master of the tradition, he made not a sound. Standing there, perched at the bedside, he allowed the hardwood floor to caress the bottoms of his feet.

Am I taller? I think I grew taller last night!

From this newly acquired perspective, he marched proudly toward the bathroom, greeting his bunkmate, Salad Bowl, with a cheerful "Good morning!" Salad Bowl shot Ricky a look of absolute incredulity. Without missing a beat, Ricky flashed him a smile and continued on his way.

Salad Bowl exchanged a glance with Rex, who'd just crawled out of bed.

"What's gotten into him?" said Salad Bowl.

Responding with a raised eyebrow and a mischievous grin, Rex held two fingers to his lips and inhaled a long stream of air, as if smoking a joint.

Before reaching the bathroom, Ricky stopped. Miles was at the edge of his bunk, working the sleep out of his eyes. Ricky sat down and put an arm around Miles's shoulders.

"Good morning, Miles. Did you sleep well?"

Miles peered at Ricky warily. "Yeah, I guess."

"Good!"

Ricky stood and took a step toward the bathroom. A floorboard creaked. He paused, then turned back.

"Listen, Miles, I still have your *Archie* comic book. I'd like to return it to you. And I've got some baseball cards you might like. They came in a care package last week from home. I know you're a big Mets fan. I've got Tom Seaver, Jerry Koosman, Jon Matlack, Dave Kingman, and Joe Torre. They're yours if you want them."

Miles scanned the room to see if the other boys were listening.

"Aren't you afraid of what people will think," he said, "if . . . if they see you talking with me?"

"No, I'm not afraid," said Ricky. "Not anymore. What d'ya say, Miles? Would you like to be my friend?"

Miles regarded Ricky for a long moment. Then, absorbing the unqualified sincerity of Ricky's luminous smile, he let down his guard.

"Sure!" he said with a bright smile of his own.

At breakfast, Ricky sat with his cabinmates, including Miles, drinking bug juice, telling jokes, and sharing stories. Although puzzled by his transformation, they asked no questions. Rather, they accepted him for who he'd become, for who he'd always been deep down inside. They enjoyed his company. His enthusiasm. It was highly contagious. Soon, the entire table roared with laughter. He'd had no idea how much work it was to be sad and depressed, how easy it was to relax and have fun.

I'm going to share this secret with the whole world!

Camp Director Gordon ambled over to Ricky's table.

"Good morning, boys!"

They responded with a lively round of overlapping greetings.

"Good morning, Mr. Gordon!" "Good morning!" "How are you this morning, sir?" "Morning, Mr. G!" "Good morning . . ."

"There's only two weeks left of camp this summer. You boys planning on making the best of it?"

"Yes, sir!" "You bet!" "Absolutely, Mr. Gordon!" "Without a doubt!"

Ricky turned to face Mr. Gordon. There'd been a heaviness, a deep sadness in this little boy, even before the night of the dance. Mr. Gordon had tried to get to the bottom of what had happened that night, but the boy had refused to cooperate. In any event, he was lighter now. Illuminated from within, his azure-blue eyes shone like those of an angel. Mr. Gordon could feel Ricky's joy, his love.

"Mr. Gordon, I've decided I'd like to learn how to swim after all. Is your offer still open?"

"Why, yes, Ricky. Absolutely. We can begin today, if you like. Are you free fifth period?"

"Yes, I am."

"I'll see you at the pond."

"Great!" Ricky gave Mr. Gordon a wink. "Thank you, Mike."

Mr. Gordon returned the wink.

Turning back to his meal, Ricky glanced over at the next table and caught sight of Spencer Black. Sandwiched between his two gigantic henchmen, Spencer was slouching over a tray, his long, greasy hair spilling into a pile of scrambled eggs. Their eyes met.

A flash of anger shot up and down Ricky's spine as the memory of the dance and what had happened at the pond came rushing into consciousness. Unable to break free from Spencer's cold, dark stare, Ricky felt the hickory branch's sharp sting spread across his shoulders as keenly as on the night of the attack. It was all he could do to stop from crying out. He felt the first few drops of blood ooze out of his open wounds and drip down his back. Spencer's voice rang in his ears . . .

Lie still and take your medicine, you worthless little shit.

Diving deep and drawing upon all his internal resources, Ricky took a full breath and let it go. He let it all go—the pain, humiliation, anger, and the overwhelming desire for revenge, which had been thinly disguised, as it always is, as a call for justice. Even the ringing in Ricky's ears faded as Spencer's words retreated into the past, never to return.

Then, in a sacred moment of grace, on that glorious New England morning in August of 1976, Richard Atticus Williamson found the power to forgive. Forgive the unforgivable. With his heart open wide and his spirit soaring, he took another breath, released it, and filled Camp Abenaki Valley's mess hall with pure, unconditional love.

A tray clattered to the floor. Everyone stopped and grew perfectly still. The sun filtered through the east-facing windows and cast long, sinuous shadows that cut across a lumpy landscape of oatmeal and a puddle of spilled milk. Soft amber hues added a timeless, dreamlike quality to the scene.

With each breath, another wave of Ricky's inexhaustible supply of love rolled through the cavernous dining room. And there was only silence—a pristine silence, unadulterated by so much as a whisper or even a thought. This silence lasted for only a few seconds, but in those precious few seconds, the world shifted . . . shifted ever so slightly . . .

Everyone felt the shift. Without understanding what was happening, each boy in the room was transformed in a way that would change his life forever. In turn, there'd be a ripple effect, and countless other lives would be touched in profound and far-reaching ways.

Many boys went home that summer and reconciled with their parents or mended troubled relationships with siblings. Others recommitted themselves to their educations and went on to graduate from high school with honors and achieve academic excellence in college and postgraduate studies. Among the 154 campers, 12 served as valedictorians of their high school classes. There were 31 National Merit Scholars, 27 members of Phi Beta Kappa, and 6 Rhodes Scholars. One boy thrived in public service and sailed above the political fray to become president of the United States. He was later lauded for leading the country out of one of the darkest, most divisive chapters in its history.

A handful of boys shocked their parents by coming home and asking for piano lessons. A few grew up to pursue artistic endeavors. One boy followed his passion for music and flourished into a world-famous opera singer.

Many of the campers chose to devote themselves to alleviating suffering and improving the lives of people across the globe. One boy studied medicine and spent his career working tirelessly for Médecins Sans Frontières (Doctors Without Borders). He even helped establish its USA affiliate in 1990. Another boy attended Harvard Medical School, became a prominent oncologist, and dedicated his life to cancer research. Another ran a Peace Corps program designed to provide clean, safe drinking water to villages throughout Africa. One boy started out as a volunteer before rising to the level of executive director for the Hunger Project, an organization whose mission is to end world hunger and poverty by empowering people to lead lives of self-reliance.

Miles graduated summa cum laude from the Georgetown University Law Center and came to be known as one of the most highly esteemed human rights lawyers in all the world. Ultimately, his career led him to serve on the international executive committee of Amnesty International. When he was nominated for the prestigious Robert F. Kennedy Human Rights Award, a reporter from the *New York Times* asked what drove him to commit his life so completely to the advancement of human rights. He answered both simply and humbly.

"It's an honor and a privilege to serve." Miles paused and thought for a moment before continuing, "My life is a blessing for which I am eternally grateful. I am extraordinarily blessed and thankful for the opportunity to make a difference in the lives of human beings in need."

Willy realized his dream of becoming an advocate for a cause near and dear to his heart. Settling in Washington, DC, he worked as a federal lobbyist for the Deaf and Hard of Hearing Alliance. Willy's brother, Sam, attended the US Air Force Academy and achieved his dream of becoming a fighter pilot. He spent the bulk of his career with the air force, flying F-15s. Later, Sam distinguished himself as the world's first deaf astronaut. A revered member of the NASA team, he flew space shuttle missions until the program was terminated in 2011. In all, he logged over two hundred days in space, most of them on board the International Space Station. In retirement, he advised NASA regarding a manned mission to Mars, as well as the possibility of permanently colonizing the red planet.

Numerous boys opted for careers in education, some as administrators, others as teachers at the elementary, secondary, and post-secondary levels. A few earned their livings as tenured professors in the Ivy League. Henry Hatfield, who'd been Spencer's right-hand man until that fateful night at the pond, became an elementary school teacher and devoted his entire life to working with children with physical, mental, and emotional disabilities. Perhaps this was his way of making amends.

Most of the boys chose to live simple lives in service of others through volunteerism and a myriad of community-enhancing projects. Each contribution—no matter how small—made a difference. A real difference. Collectively, they made the world a better place.

Ricky's love touched every boy present. But four were missing. Jihad and his three older brothers weren't in the mess hall that morning. They'd been sent for the previous day, due to a death in the family. Their father had been gunned down in front of the family's Midtown Manhattan brownstone late Saturday night. Leaving most of their things behind, the boys left immediately for New York. Most campers, including Ricky, were unaware of their departure.

Surrounded by a warm glow, Ricky held Spencer's stare.

I've been on an amazing journey, Spencer, and I have you to thank for it. Without you, I never would have crossed the threshold. Thank you, thank you, thank you . . .

As for the rape, I'm not angry. Not anymore. I see now something must have happened to you. Something dreadful happened, and you lost track of the fundamental truth that we're all connected, that love is what binds us together. I don't blame you. It's not your fault. You didn't know what you were doing. I love you, Spencer. I love you like a brother, and I forgive you with all my heart.

Gazing into Spencer's eyes, Ricky saw that Spencer was terrified. Terrified that Ricky would report him. Ricky had no such intention. Rather, he cast his penetrating gaze more and more deeply into those frightened eyes . . . until finally he could see into the soul of that sad and lonely sixteen-year-old boy . . . and feel his pain . . .

It was late. Spencer didn't know exactly how late. It must have been after midnight, though. Daddy wasn't home, and Spencer had been tossing and turning for at least two hours. His sheets were moist and cold with dread. Halloween was coming. It wasn't, however, a ghost or goblin or ghoul he feared. It was something else . . . His bedroom was dark. The clock's face was invisible. Yet he could hear the second hand advancing . . .

Tick, tick, tick . . .

Six months earlier, on April 3, 1968, Spencer's sister, Suzie, turned thirteen. The party gathered in the dining room of the Black family's modest two-story home in Maynard, Massachusetts. Spring had sprung early. The trees on the boulevard bloomed red and white and pink.

Suzie wore earrings, a touch of her mother's makeup, patent leather shoes, a chiffon party dress, and a bra. She was no longer a little girl. The boys at school had started to notice. She could feel their eyes on her. Even her father noticed the change. The previous week, when she came down to breakfast in her new dress, he called her a "knockout," then cautioned her against becoming a "whore."

She was all grown up now, she told Spencer. Not too old for cake and ice cream, though. Her closest friends—an adolescent coterie of four whispering, giggling girls—sat on either side of her at the head of the table. Spencer was permitted to stay. At eight, he was a pest, but Suzie's friends thought he was cute. For their sakes, she tolerated his presence. Well . . . not just for their sakes. Truth be told, she loved her little brother Spennie.

Suzie and Spencer had a brother named Frankie, who would have been eleven, but Frankie died three years earlier.

"You're a good kid, Spennie," Frankie said just before his death. "When you're old enough—next spring—I'll take you fishing at the pond."

The pond was straight out of a Mark Twain novel or Norman Rockwell illustration, complete with reeds, cattails, lily pads, dragonflies, and bullfrogs. In the summer, local kids would skip stones, swim, and fish. In the winter, they'd go ice-skating.

Next spring never came for Frankie.

Spencer was told Frankie's death had been a terrible accident. Prone to dizzy spells, he'd tumbled down the basement stairs, rolling head over heels until he hit the concrete floor. His neck snapped, and he died instantly.

Spencer wasn't so sure. His brother had been athletic—tall and slim with long, sinewy muscles in his arms and legs. And surefooted. He took karate lessons, and he was the best basketball player in the neighborhood.

And the best swimmer.

Careful not to be seen, Spencer would often follow Frankie and his pals to the pond, hide in the bushes, and watch the older boys at play. On one occasion—on a dare—Frankie leaped from a rock, executed a perfect backflip, and plunged into the water. A full minute passed. Spencer wanted to go in after his brother, but he knew Frankie would be angry if he did. So, he remained still.

Finally, Frankie reappeared.

Spencer breathed a sigh of relief.

"Piece of cake!" Frankie exclaimed, holding up a newt by the tail.

Suzie grinned, and with just one breath, she blew out all thirteen candles. The cake was white with lemon filling, coconut cream frosting, and a swirl of pastel flowers on top. The ice cream was vanilla. Spencer had two pieces of cake and three scoops of ice cream, slathered in chocolate sauce. Suzie never stopped smiling.

That was six months ago. Suzie didn't seem to smile much anymore.

Tick, tick, tick . . .

With each tick of the clock, Spencer felt more dread. The dark closed in on him. He shivered. His thumb found its way into his mouth. Daddy was late every night now. When he got home, it was best to be asleep. Sound asleep. Of course, Spencer couldn't sleep, not when he knew what was coming . . . so he curled himself into a little ball, buried his head in the pillow, and pretended . . .

It was always very nearly the same.

The front door would burst open and slam shut. Pictures on the wall would shake. One night, a framed black-and-white of Suzie, Frankie, and Spencer dropped to the floor and shattered. The next morning, tiny glass shards speckled the entryway. The first-floor bathroom mirror was cracked and smeared with blood.

Each night, the stairs would moan under the weight of Walter Black's drunken footfalls. Arriving at the landing, he would always stop to catch his breath. Always.

Maybe he'll fall this time. Like Frankie.

He never did.

Instead, he would stagger into the hallway and pass Spencer's room, swearing incoherently, or belching, or both. Then, he would pause, as if trying to make up his mind about something. The pause would last forever, or so it seemed to Spencer.

Please, Daddy, just go to bed.

Each night, Walter Black would collect himself, ease the door open, and slip into his daughter Suzie's room.

Spencer didn't know what was happening in there. He did know one thing, though. He knew Daddy didn't belong in Suzie's bedroom late at night. Afterward, he thought he could hear her crying. What could he do? He wanted to go to her . . . yet didn't know what to say . . .

Spencer loved his sister. Adored her. He also hated her. Hated her weakness. It infuriated him. Why couldn't she be strong and tell Daddy to leave?

Tick, tick, tick . . .

This night promised to be a bad one. Daddy had lost his job—a job he'd held for over fifteen years—and Spencer had heard his parents shouting that morning. The argument had ended in a slammed door, the car screeching out of the driveway, and Mommy in tears. Daddy would be drunk when he got home and even more ill-tempered than usual.

Sucking his thumb, Spencer curled more tightly into fetal position.

Tick, tick, tick—

The front door exploded open, and a blast of cold air invaded the house. Walter Black clambered up the stairs and into the hallway. Without stopping this time to catch his breath and without pausing at Suzie's door, he barged in and knocked over a lamp. It crashed to the floor. The bulb shattered.

Suzie screamed.

Walter's monstrous silhouette swayed side to side in the hazy glow of a castle-shaped nightlight. His hair was a tangled mess. His beard was ragged and infested with bits of popcorn, peanut shells, and other such debris. A thick neck protruded from a rumpled shirt. Long arms dangled apelike from rounded shoulders, extending almost to the floorboards at Walter's feet. His body exuded a foul odor that comes only from drinking whiskey and beer into the wee hours of the morning.

Wheezing, he lurched toward Suzie's bed.

She screamed again.

"Li'l gurl, you keep quiet now," he sputtered.

Spencer sprang from bed, burst into Suzie's room, and found Daddy on top of his sister, tearing at her nightclothes.

"Stop it, Daddy!" Spencer cried.

Walter turned on his son. "Go back to bed, Spencer."

Spencer stood his ground. "No."

Mommy appeared at the door. "Just do what your father says, Spencer. Please!"

"Both of you," said Walter, "get the fuck out!"

"No, Daddy," said Spencer.

Walter came at Spencer and walloped him across the jaw. Spencer's head struck the floor, and he blacked out.

When Spencer regained consciousness, he was lying in a hospital bed. His mother was lying on a slab at the morgue, awaiting an autopsy. His father had been taken into custody and charged with her murder. Catatonic and unable to speak, his sister had been sent to the state mental institution in Waltham. As soon as he recovered from his physical injuries, Spencer would be sent to live with an aunt in Upstate New York.

Ricky's heart swelled with compassion. Tears flooded his eyes and rolled down his cheeks. He got up from his place at the table. The mess hall remained silent and still. Other than Ricky, no one moved. They were still under his spell.

Ricky made his way over to Spencer's table. Spencer peeked up at him through strings of his long, greasy hair. Ricky extended his hands. Trembling like a newborn fawn, Spencer rose from his seat. The boys fell into each other's arms, weeping.

All they'd ever wanted was to feel safe and secure and loved. Yet, as young children, they'd both experienced horrible loss and devastating trauma. They'd lived with fear for most of their lives. Neither one of them had felt he belonged. But they did belong. They belonged to each other. They were connected. They would always be connected.

Spencer could now see the truth. Like Ricky, he had within him the power of choice. He could choose to live as a survivor, a person of great courage and integrity, regardless of the past. He was ready to move forward.

The weight of the world lifted from his shoulders and took flight. His spine lengthened and became straight. For the first time in years, he stood upright. His slouch would never return. He felt light, open, free . . . It was time to heal his mind, to mend his broken heart. He made a decision. To walk a new path. A path of recovery . . .

. . . he didn't know how to do that, but he knew where to go
. . . back home . . . there was a meeting . . . just off Main Street
. . . in the basement of a church . . .

LOVE

Saturday, August 28, 1976
A Redbrick House

THE SUMMER OF 1976 WAS COMING to a rapid close. On Monday morning, Ricky Williamson would emerge from the redbrick house, cross the street, march through the front doors of Marshall Elementary, and begin the fifth grade. He wondered if the other kids would recognize him. He was taller, more confident, and happier than he'd ever been. His heart fluttered in anticipation. But Monday would come soon enough. In the meantime, he wanted to make the most of this glorious, sun-soaked Saturday afternoon in his beloved hometown of South Orange.

Ricky bounded up the stairs, tapped at the half-open door, and peeked in. Danny was at the foot of his bed, sitting cross-legged on the floor. The morning's paper lay spread out before him.

"What are you doing, Danny?"

297

"Nothin'. Just oiling my glove."

Ricky stepped in. With an old rag, his younger brother was working linseed oil into the palm of his baseball glove. A knot of determination crinkled his brow.

"You were right, Danny. I did see you in the mess hall that one time."

"Huh?"

"On our first day of camp, I saw you in the mess hall having breakfast with your new friends. I pretended not to see you. It was a stupid thing to do. I'm sorry."

Danny paused and looked up from his glove.

"Oh, that," he said with a shrug. "That's okay. One of those guys explained to me later it's not cool for big brothers to sit with their little brothers."

Returning his attention to the job at hand, he continued working the oil into the glove's rich, full-grain leather.

Ricky smiled tenderly at his brother. "Danny . . ."

"Yeah?"

"I love you."

"You're weird."

"I know. Let's go play."

"Okay!"

Ravenous from an afternoon of romping through the neighborhood and all over town with their friends, the Williamson boys returned to the redbrick house for dinner.

"We're home, Mom!" said Ricky.

"Yeah, and we're hungry!" added Danny.

The screen door slapped shut behind them.

"I'm in the living room, boys."

They found their mother in her favorite chair, gazing into the backyard.

She turned to them and smiled. "Look at you two. You've both gotten so big. I remember when you were barely tall enough to see out this window."

She paused and placed a hand on the sill.

"Back then, you had this nightly ritual. Remember? At five thirty, the two of you would meet in the den. Your father was coming home from work, and you wanted to be ready. You'd start out with your noses pressed against the French windows, and you'd wait there, trembling with excitement and fogging up the glass with your breath. When the Pontiac finally pulled into the driveway, you squealed like two little piggies. But you didn't move. Neither one of you. Your eyes stayed fixed on that car. Then, when it disappeared around the bend, you raced into the living room, bellied up to this window, and watched—breathless—until your father had parked."

All three of them stared at the garage as if expecting the ghost of David Williamson to emerge.

"That's right," said Ricky. "And then, we'd hide behind the door in the back hallway and jump all over him when he came inside. Each time, we thought it was gonna be the biggest surprise ever. But he knew. He knew exactly what we were up to. Didn't he?"

"Of course he did. In fact, he would've been surprised—and disappointed—if you weren't there waiting to ambush him. He loved you boys so much. Now go wash up for dinner. It'll be ready soon."

Danny bolted upstairs.

Ricky lingered. "Mom?"

"Yes, dear?"

"I'm sorry," he said, "for the way I've behaved these past couple of years, especially right before we left for camp. I said some awful things."

"Honey, you don't have to—"

"I do. You see, I had this idea in my head you loved Danny more than me."

"My God, Ricky! Where would you get an idea like that from?"

"It was a belief I was holding on to. A belief there was something terribly wrong with me, that I was defective and therefore unlovable. But something happened at camp this summer—a miracle—that opened my eyes and allowed me to see the truth."

"What is the truth, Ricky?"

"I'm lovable. We're all lovable. No matter what might have happened in the past. No matter what our beliefs. I was only unlovable because I believed I was unlovable. When I realized I could choose to let go of this belief, I saw the truth."

When illusion is removed, only truth remains . . .

. . . we are love . . .

"My darling, what was it? What on earth happened up there that made you so wise?"

"Let's just say I went on a journey this summer. An amazing journey."

Ricky transcended his grief, his pain, his anger to live a life of inner peace, abundance, generosity, and love. It was a life devoted to public service. It was a life that inspired him to great achievements. It was a life of which his father would have been proud. It was not a life free of challenges, difficult choices, and loss . . . as we shall see . . .

END OF SECOND BOOK
IN THE
HERO'S PATH SERIES

ACKNOWLEDGMENTS

I'D LIKE TO BEGIN BY THANKING each of those beautiful souls who've encouraged and supported my journey toward publication of the Hero's Path series. Two down, and one to go. We've got this!

First of all, there's Lori Kampa for her eternal optimism and enduring patience. I understand it can be challenging to live with someone whose words flow most easily from a pen, and sometimes not at all. Yet your belief in us never wavers. Every day, you inspire me to take another leap of faith. Thank you, my love!

Next, there's the rest of my clan: Mike Ristau, Laura Ristau, David Ristau, Claire Ristau, Rip Burgwald, Larry Koll, and my mother, Susan Koll. I'm still searching for a way to express how much I love each of you. Perhaps one day I'll succeed in this endeavor.

Independent voices are necessary for the advancement of a freethinking, democratic society. Indeed, our very survival may depend on these voices being heard. Thank you to Hanna

Kjeldbjerg, Alicia Ester, Lily Coyle, Becca Hart, Dan Pitts, and the editorial team at Beaver's Pond Press for offering writers like me an opportunity to tell stories that dare to fill hearts with hope and minds with dreams of possibility.

Thanks to the Independent Book Publishers Association (IBPA) for furnishing a wealth of resources that empowers us, as "indie authors," to promote and market our work, to Mark Jung and his dedicated team at Itasca Books for their critical role in sustaining the independent book movement, and to all the librarians, booksellers, and readers who took a chance on *A Hero Dreams*.

I'd like to offer a special note of thanks to Margaret Duarte and all my friends at the Visionary Fiction Alliance. The VFA is a small, but growing, insurgency committed to deepening global consciousness, one story at a time. As a member, I'm proud to join the VFA on the forefront of a spiritual revolution—one that will ultimately nurture, in all of us, a gentler, kinder, and more inclusive way of being.

I'm truly grateful for my friendship with fellow author Kate Towle, with whom I share a vision for a world that will one day embrace the simple truth that each of us is an essential part of an interconnected, interdependent whole. A vision of peace. Also sharing this vision is Laurie Beth Fitz, whom I thank for inviting me and other like-minded artists as guests on her thought-provoking *Connections Radio Show*.

My writing journey continues to draw me—time and time again—to South Orange and a small cluster of bedroom communities just west of the Hudson, and I'd be remiss in failing to acknowledge Vicky and Rich McGlynn for making me feel at home every time I visit. And a very special thank you to

Tilly-Jo Emerson for her friendship and boundless generosity. Your kindness, Til'-Jo, is a reminder that there is still a place for me in a world that gave rise to my earliest childhood memories, including those that served as the spark for my journey on the Hero's Path.

Finally, thank you to my father, David Lorenz Ristau. Daddy, you left us many years too soon, yet you're still with me in every way that matters. Your spirit continues to serve as my guiding light. I love you.

ALSO AVAILABLE

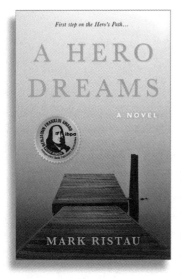

First Book in the Hero's Path Series:
A Hero Dreams

Devastated by his father's sudden death, eight-year-old Ricky begins to see things—a ghostly silhouette in his bedroom window, a gruesome train accident involving four local teenagers, a terrorist attack that won't occur for another twenty-five years. After a traumatic incident at a New England summer camp, the visions become more frequent, more vivid, and more disturbing. A mysterious voice assures him everything will be okay if he crosses the "threshold." But just what is the threshold? And what lies beyond?

"In the pages of *A Hero Dreams*, novelist and consummate storyteller Mark Ristau takes his readers on an epic journey along the furthermost frontiers of human consciousness and into a miraculous realm where anything is possible."

–Midwest Book Review

**YOU'VE JUST BEEN CALLED TO BREAK FREE
FROM THE SHACKLES OF YOUR PAST AND BEGIN ANEW.
BUT FIRST, YOU'LL NEED TO FACE YOUR GREATEST FEAR . . .
ARE YOU WILLING TO TAKE THE FIRST STEP?**

Order *A Hero Dreams* at www.MarkRistau.com

BEAVER'S POND
PRESS